The woman in the bathtub winked at Jeremiah

It was an advertising gimmick, he realized. To promote the opening of a bath boutique. She must be Fancy O'Brien, the owner. Unconsciously, he moved closer to the store window.

She plucked a sponge from the soapy water. One leg emerged from the bubbles, stretching in a rainfall of bathwater until her polished toenails pointed to the ceiling.

Someone in the crowd behind him wolf-whistled, and Jeremiah had a sudden, surprising insight. Although he had no business feeling proprietary about her, the crude whistle had promoted a surge of pure male jealousy. And he hadn't even spoken to her yet.

He smiled. Apparently, life in Webster Station had just become more interesting...

FANCY-FREE

BY

CARRIE ALEXANDER

MILLS & BOON

*MILLS & BOON and the Rose Device are trademarks of the publisher.
TEMPTATION is a trademark of Harlequin Enterprises II B.V., used
under licence.
First published in Great Britain 1995
by Harlequin Mills & Boon Limited, Eton House, 18-24 Paradise Road,
Richmond, Surrey TW9 1SR*

© Carrie Antilla 1995

ISBN 0 263 79317 6

21 - 9512

*Printed in Great Britain by
BPC Paperbacks Ltd*

1

"IT'S OBSCENE. Utterly obscene!"

Jeremiah Quick dropped the previous month's circulation report and rose to greet his unannounced visitor. Perhaps it was time to rethink the open-door policy he'd established as the new publisher of the *Webster Station Chronicle*. Hester Hightower had just barged into his office with one too many five-alarm warnings of insidious obscenity.

"What is it this time, Mrs. Hightower?" he asked, steeling himself to withstand one of her typical tirades.

"Filth," the middle-aged woman spat. "Pure filth."

Jeremiah thought back to the *Chronicle*'s last front-page photo—an innocuous depiction of the Azalea Festival Queen candidates, all gleaming white teeth and helmet hair. Nothing to set Hester off, unlike an earlier shot of Mayor Mitzi Janeway in a cut-to-the-navel gown at the community awards banquet. Hester considered cleavage, especially published cleavage, highly offensive.

"Is Rubens running rampant in the public library again?" he asked suspiciously. Hester had once attempted to censor the local library's collection of art books. Her group, the Ladies' Society for Decency, had also found Raphael, Titian and Tintoretto a bit too "fleshy" for their delicate sensibilities.

"How I wish this scandal was contained within the pages of a book!" Hester declared dramatically as she plopped her hefty canvas bag on Jeremiah's desk. She withdrew an industrial-size can of pepper spray, a pair of tube socks, a clipboard and compact binoculars before retrieving her cellular phone. "Mr. Quick, as editor of the *Chronicle*, you simply must aid us in chasing this scourge from the streets." She pressed out a number, her bulging brown eyes glaring at him through the thick lenses of her clunky glasses. When he stared back, stoically refusing to crumble, she put the phone to her ear. "Fritzi? Grab the picket signs we stored in your pool house and get to the corner of Main and Dogwood. ASAP! We've got a nude woman on the loose!"

"A nude woman?" echoed Jeremiah, his newspaperman's senses perking up. Providing Hester wasn't referring to the Calvin Klein ads in the fashion magazines at Mitch's, she could be on to something. There wasn't enough action in this town to warrant ignoring even the merest hint of a story.

Hester put her hand over the mouthpiece. "Yes, indeed. A nude woman, Mr. Quick," she said triumphantly, and returned to her call. "I'll phone Maybelle. You get in touch with the others," she commanded Fritzi Janeway, the society's vice president. "We've got work to do!"

"Now, Hester," Jeremiah said soothingly, "why don't you hold off on the pickets until you're calm enough to evaluate the situation rationally. Have a seat and tell me all about it."

"Hester Hightower shall not be found sitting while blatant nudity rips asunder the very fabric of this community's moral standards!"

"Of course not." He tapped one finger against the brass base of his desk lamp. "What's the story on this . . . nude woman?"

"It's positively indecent. And she's displaying herself on Main Street, no less."

"A *live* nude woman?" he asked carefully, hoping to define Hester's outrage before assigning a reporter to cover something like the society's "covering" of the mermaid fountain in the park.

"Winking and giggling and posing," she sputtered. "It's disgusting!"

"Are we talking nude as in no items of clothing covering the crucial body parts?"

"Naked as the day she was born." Hester settled her crossed arms beneath her formidable bust in a what-are-you-going-to-do-about-it stance.

Jeremiah hesitated. Hester had cried wolf before. "And would this allegedly nude woman still be there?"

Her nose twitched as if she was smelling an offensive odor. "The Jezebel is enjoying it. She's cavorting!"

Jeremiah snagged his jacket off the back of the chair. Even the admittedly remote possibility of a naked woman cavorting on Webster Station's Main Street was finally enough to propel him out to the newsroom. He motioned to his best reporter. "Alice Ann. Let's go."

Alice Ann Keating looked up from the blinking cursor awaiting her review of the Webster Station Players' production of *Arsenic and Old Lace*. "What's up, boss?" she said around the pen clenched between her teeth, grabbing a notebook off the lopsided files stacked beside her terminal.

"There's a nude woman on Main Street!" Hester announced triumphantly.

An abrupt unnatural silence descended on the newsroom until broken by Jeremiah's secretary, meek Willa Clark. She raised her hand—forgetting she was no longer in Journalism 101—and asked tentatively, "Did you say a . . . nude woman?"

Every man in the room—which amounted to three beside Jeremiah—rose as one and made for the door. Leo Bean, the craggy sixty-year-old who made up the entire sports department, led the charge. Trailing him was Hamish Hightower, Jeremiah's circulation manager and the fiftyish bachelor brother of Hester's late husband, Horace. Beauregard Quick put a little giddy-up into his characteristic amble and caught the door from Ham. He was Jeremiah's younger brother, a burned-out photojournalist who'd taken to hanging around the *Chronicle* during his extended vacation. He and Jeremiah shared a strong family resemblance.

Jeremiah went in the opposite direction, down a narrow hallway to the darkroom where his photographer was usually sequestered. He rapped smartly on the door and barked, "Pringle, get out here."

After a long moment, the door creaked open and Pringle's unlikely form loomed from the darkness. At six-five, the photographer was put together like an emaciated albino Frankenstein's monster. His face was long and homely, and lank strands of almost colorless hair hung in his pale eyes. He pushed them back with a bony index finger, blinking like a groundhog after a long winter.

"Naked woman on Main," Jeremiah said shortly.

A shadow of a smile passed over Pringle's pale face. He caressed the camera hanging against his concave chest.

"See if you can get something printable," Jeremiah added, still wondering if this could be true. Hester had been known to employ a certain exaggeration in her quest for publicity.

Pringle glided away in a swirl of chemical smells. Jeremiah followed. The newsroom had emptied of everyone but Willa and Hester. The female staffers had also left, drawn by curiosity if not voyeurism.

"Watch the phones," Jeremiah told Willa as he moved swiftly toward the exit. Hester joined him, strutting jauntily.

Willa drooped. "Sure."

Jeremiah considered her wilting-daisy posture and made a hasty detour into his office, returning to drop a sheaf of papers on the immaculate surface of Willa's desk. "Why don't you go over Mitzi's Azalea Festival copy while I'm gone?" he suggested. "She's still refusing to get near a computer, so use Leo's terminal once you've deciphered her handwriting. And cut the frilly gossipy excess, please."

"Oh, yes, sir!" Willa had been praying for such a chance. "I'll do my best, Mr. Quick. If you're sure?"

He grinned at her eager naiveté. "Have a go at it, Willa."

Outside, Pringle was already halfway down the block, loping to catch up to Alice Ann, who was buttoning her cardigan as she strode purposefully toward the crowd at the other end of Main Street.

At least by Webster Station standards, it was a crowd. Twenty-five or thirty chattering people had gathered around a newly refurbished storefront at the corner of Main and Dogwood. Bright pennants fluttered and balloons bobbed in the spring breeze, adding to the sideshow atmosphere.

"Voyeurs," sneered Hester as she elbowed her way through them. "You see—" she gestured at the shop's window display "—nude. Totally nude. It's shocking!"

Jeremiah could only stare in amazed silence. For once Hester Hightower was correct. There *was* a nude woman on Main Street. Or, to be more precise, in a *bathtub* in a *window* on Main Street.

"It's the most appalling display this town has ever seen!" Hester declared.

If he'd been able to speak, Jeremiah would've disagreed. Appalling? No. Startling? Yes. Enticing? Most definitely.

"Lordy, Lordy, Lordy..." Ham muttered, breathing heavily through his open mouth, his face pinker than usual.

"That gal sure does snap my suspenders," Leo said while Beau approached the window and braced his arms on the freshly painted white frame.

On the other side of the window, the woman in the bathtub tossed her head in laughter. She lifted a sudsy hand and blew a kiss. Tiny bubbles floated through the air. "Yeah, baby," Beau purred, his breath steaming up the glass.

An outraged Hester was huffing and puffing furiously. Someone clapped her on the back, and she expelled a lungful of air with a whoosh. "Perverts," she bellowed. "Voyeurs! Heathens! Wastrels!"

The crowd didn't seem to mind the insults spraying like buckshot from Hester's indiscriminate mouth. They were accustomed to the Widow Hightower's histrionics. As a relative newcomer to Webster Station and conscious of his editorial responsibility, Jeremiah felt compelled to listen. Besides, she'd caught his elbow in a wicked grip and was yanking his arm out of its socket.

"This lewd prurient display caters to the lowest instincts of the male gender. As one of this town's most respected citizens, Jeremiah, you must make it a point to decry such filth."

"How would I do that?" he asked mildly, his gaze straying back to the astonishing, delectable and, yes, perhaps prurient window display.

"By writing an editorial condemning such obscenity of course. Expose that shameless woman to the scorn of public opinion!"

"I'd say she already has all the exposure she needs," Jeremiah observed dryly.

Hester gasped. "Mr. Quick, this is not a humorous situation!"

He sighed. "Mrs. Hightower. Hester. Isn't it possible you're overreacting?" He glanced back at the window. "There's no harm being done."

"No harm? No harm!" Hester grabbed ten-year-old Billy Hooper by the scruff of the neck, yanking him away from his prime position at the front of the crowd. "What do you think is happening to this young man's innocence? Such a trauma will blight the rest of his childhood."

Jeremiah looked at the squirming boy. Billy appeared to be traumatized more by the experience of being clasped to Hester's heaving bosom than by the sight of the woman in the bathtub. "Nowadays kids this age see more at the beach—"

Hester flung her arms out dramatically. Billy made a hasty escape, hopping onto his bike and pedaling off down Dogwood Avenue. Probably to sell tickets to his fifth-grade buddies, Jeremiah reflected.

"Now is the time for all good citizens to rise up and protest the decay of this country's family values," Hester was sermonizing. "If you and the *Chronicle* won't come to our aid, the Ladies' Society for Decency will be forced to wage our campaign on the streets of this town. On the very street corner sullied by this Jezebel's disregard for decent public standards!"

"This public seems to be enjoying the show."

"My reinforcements!" Hester crowed, ignoring Jeremiah, as a rusty station wagon drove up to the curb with a blast of its horn. She stalked off to marshal her more compliant forces, but not without one more overwrought pronouncement. "We shall make our righteous indignation known!"

"I've known Hester's righteous indignation too often for it to do my righteous indigestion any good," confessed the man who'd been cowering behind Eudora Vincent since

Hester's arrival. Albert "Mitch" Mitchell, the owner of the drugstore down the street, rubbed his well-padded midsection regretfully. "Much as I hate to miss the rest of the show, I better get on back behind the counter. Hester might spot me and send in Maybelle or Fritzi to scoop up all my *Vogue* and *Bazaar* magazines for revenge."

As the targets of Hester's past and present umbrage, he and Jeremiah shared a moment of silent commiseration before the crowd shuffled around to make way for the druggist's departure. Pringle insinuated himself into the narrow slot between two housewife types and the brick wall, angling his camera for a shot that included both the crowd and the woman in the window.

"Isn't she going to get pruney soon?" one of the housewives asked.

"How long's she been in there?" her companion countered, giggling bashfully. "And how will she get out of that tub without showing her you-know-whats?"

Good question, Jeremiah thought. He planned to stay to see it answered.

"Well, now," said one of the old men who spent many an hour on a bench beneath Ice Cream U Scream's pink-and-white awning across the street. "I reckon it's going on a good twenty minutes."

"Did you see her get in?" Ham asked avidly.

The old-timer shook his head with obvious frustration. "She slipped in when my head was turned."

Leo guffawed. "Twelve years settin' on that bench and Elmer's head is turned for the most exciting event in Main Street history."

Elmer joined in the good-natured laughter. "I aim to stay rooted to this spot so I don't miss not'ing else. She's bound to get cold sooner or later." His milky eyes swiveled back to the window display hopefully.

Alice Ann scribbled in her notebook. "May I quote you?"

"Heck, yeah." Elmer grinned, revealing bare gums. Pringle lifted his camera and Elmer nodded at the woman in the bathtub. "How 'bout taking a picture of me and her for my scrapbook?"

Jeremiah didn't know if the woman in the window could hear what was said, but as Elmer moved into position she sat up straighter, shiny wet arms crossed over her chest, and smiled prettily for the camera.

"Wanton exhibitionism," shouted one of the Ladies for Decency as they unloaded Fritzi's station wagon. "You should be ashamed!"

The woman in the window stuck out her tongue saucily.

Who is she? Jeremiah wondered, eyeing her dubiously as he struggled to contain an automatic male response to the provocative display. Clearly she enjoyed being the center of attention. She was bold and unabashed, yet there was also a sweetness to her smile that prevented him from labeling her brassy. Jeremiah sensed she was a free spirit. Truth was, he envied her that.

He tipped his head back to read the sign newly installed beneath the tall narrow second-story windows: HAUTE WATER.

A Grand Opening banner had been strung across the fanlight above the shop door. The rainbow colors of the flapping pennants and clusters of balloons brought the turn-of-the-century redbrick building gaudily into the modern day.

Alice Ann stepped over to her boss's side. "It's an advertising gimmick." Disappointment shaded her tone. She'd been hoping Mayor Janeway was finally making good on her Lady Godiva threat. *That* would've been a story.

"But what an advertising gimmick." Jeremiah's gaze was unerringly drawn back to the dark-haired woman in the window. She certainly appeared to be nude, just as Hester had claimed. But with all those bubbles, who could really be sure? "What do you know about this place? Haute Water?"

"It's a bathroom boutique. Today's the grand opening."

"I can see that. What about—" He cut himself off, not sure how to phrase the question. But he had to know who she was.

"Name's Fancy O'Brien," Alice Ann supplied as if she'd read his mind. "She owns the joint."

"Francy O'Brien," he said musingly. She'd settled back in the bathtub, up to her bared shoulders in bubbles, and was picking up a sponge.

"Nope," Alice Ann said. "It's Fancy. No *r*. Baby talk for Francine is what she told me. I interviewed her for last Wednesday's business section. Don't you read your own paper, boss?"

Jeremiah moved two steps closer to the window without realizing it. He had read Alice Ann's blurb about Haute Water. But after a full day of number-crunching with his accountant and subscription list, the details hadn't registered anymore than those of the softball league's spaghetti feed and the latest town council tax tussle. Maybe if he'd known that Haute Water's owner would soon be taking a bath on Main Street he would've paid more attention to the particulars.

Because Fancy O'Brien's particulars were mighty fine.

She squeezed the sponge. Water sluiced down her forearms, thinning out the mounds of bubbles that were all that protected her modesty—if a woman taking a very public bath could be said to have any.

Behind the two multipaned corner windows that gave an imaginative viewer the sense of being a Peeping Tom, the spacious display area had been done up like a Victorian lady's lavish powder room. Flowered wallpaper covered the back walls. Set to one side was an elegant pedestal sink with brass fixtures, and beside it a stack of striped hatboxes. Hanging from a row of brass hooks were a man's dressing gown and something long, frilly and beribboned. A stiffly boned corset had been tossed on a royal blue velvet chaise longue next to a pair of sheer stockings, arranged as though they'd just been peeled from Fancy's smooth white legs. A dressing table with a ruffled skirt and an ornate mirror had been positioned on the Dogwood Avenue side, its surface cluttered with crystal flacons, porcelain pots and an engraved gold vanity set. A strand of pearls spilled from an open jewelry box beside a jug of fresh lilacs.

All very nice, but to Jeremiah's way of thinking, a mere backdrop to Fancy and her bathtub.

The tub was one of those boatlike antique reproductions, yards of spotless cream porcelain with sinuously curved sides and edges and ball-and-claw feet. It was filled to the brim with what had to be rapidly cooling water and a heap of definitely disintegrating bubbles.

Fancy seemed quite unconcerned. She was admiring her reflection in a hand mirror, merrily dancing eyes flirting with her rapt audience.

Jeremiah thought her a fey creature. She had the sort of skin a man ached to touch to discover if it was as tender and smooth as it looked. Her face glowed, its complexion as dewily perfect as rose petals. A length of knotted lace held her hair in a tousled pile atop her head. Swirling tendrils had escaped to frame her face, some of them dampened and sticking to her skin in pixie curls and arabesques. A drop of moisture slid down her short straight nose, and her tongue flicked out to catch it in an unstudied impulse that set Jeremiah's blood racing.

Fancy cocked her head, turning slightly to meet Jeremiah's gaze. Her grin was bewitching, a slight uplifting of her lips that formed a tiny dimple in one creamy rounded cheek. Her gray-blue eyes held his until he put one hand up to the window, long fingers tensed as if they might pass through the glass and reach in to scoop away the bubbles, plunging beneath the surface to find the warm wet curves of her naked body.

Fancy winked.

Jeremiah gulped, realizing he was pressed up against the window like a lonely man at a peep show. A rather unseemly position for the publisher of the local newspaper. He backed away, shoving his hand into the pocket of his gray flannel trousers. Fancy's delighted chuckle was audible even through the window that separated them.

Sliding lower, she again plucked the sponge out of the water. One leg emerged from the bubbles, stretching in a rainfall of bathwater until her polished toenails pointed to the ceiling. It was a pose Jeremiah might have seen in *Playboy* but doubted women assumed in real life. He closed his eyes thankfully. Real life had just got a whole lot more interesting.

"Ooh, baby," Beau crooned.

Someone at the back of the crowd gave a wolf whistle. Jeremiah's eyelids flashed open with a sudden surprising insight. Although he'd no business feeling proprietary about Ms. Fancy O'Brien, Beau's comment and the crude whistle had prompted a surge of pure male jealousy. Amazing. Before he'd even spoken to her, this woman was arousing much more than a merely physical response. He found that especially provocative.

She drew the sponge down her leg with an excruciatingly slow stroke, then repeated the maneuver on her other leg. When she leaned forward to reach her dainty ankle, Jeremiah saw a good three-quarters of her back. No bikini strap in evidence. So she was truly nude, he thought, and released a breath he hadn't been aware of holding.

Settling back into the tub with a shimmy, Fancy tossed the sponge aside. The people gathered around the window followed each move as she grinned impishly, slipped one hand into a loofah mitt, added a dab of gel and began to lightly scrub her arms and shoulders.

"Lemme do your back!" someone called.

"Lemme do your front!" came a raucous reply from the other side of the crowd.

Jeremiah responded instinctively. The bubbles had evaporated enough to reveal the top swells of Fancy's breasts. They bobbed slightly with her movements, making small ripples in the water. He even thought he'd spotted a pert pink nipple winking through the remaining bubbles—and wasn't eager for anyone else to do the same. Spinning around to face the crowd, he used his body to block their view.

"Okay, folks, I think we've all seen—"

"Hussy!"

"Tramp!"

"Harlot!"

The crowd turned toward the screeched epithets. Seven or eight women, half the membership roster of the Ladies' Society for Decency, had formed a picket line along the curb. Hefting homemade placards to their shoulders, they began to march back and forth, sanctimony in their hearts and insults on their lips.

Hester pointed at the window display. "We shall not support moral turpitude!" she shouted thunderously, a clarion call that could probably be heard all the way to the town limits. Hester had no need of a megaphone; she'd once studied voice with a coach who'd pronounced her projection astonishing.

The ladies started a chant: "No nudity! No nudity! No nudity!"

Except for Pringle, crouching beside the corner mailbox to get an angle on Hester's flaring nostrils, the rest of the crowd turned back to the window, muttering in dismissal. "It's just Hester," said one of the housewives. "Ignore her," said someone else.

"Hey, lookit!" Elmer exclaimed. "She's gonna get out." An older woman had entered the display through a narrow side door. She was trimly turned out in a Victorian lady's-maid costume, with a starched apron and laced ankle boots. A pert white cap sat atop her short salt-and-pepper hair. She stood beside the bathtub, shaking out the dressing gown she'd taken from the hook, holding it up between the tub and the window with widespread arms.

"Goldarnit," groaned Elmer.

Behind the curtaining paisley robe, Fancy rose from the bath. She stepped onto a patterned carpet, bare ankles and feet peeping out beneath the hem. For an instant Jeremiah saw the curvy silhouette of her body against the thin silk, but then she was wrapping it around herself, tying the ruby sash around her slender waist. He wondered if his hands would span it as easily.

A deep sigh, half frustration, half appreciation, rose from the males in the crowd. They applauded. Fancy curtsied gracefully and made her exit.

"No nudity! No nudity! No nudity!" chanted the picketers.

"That's that," Alice Ann said, snapping shut her notebook. "Not much of a story, after all."

"On the contrary," Jeremiah murmured, considering the window display. It was charming in itself, but without

Fancy, the last of the fizzled bubble bath looked cold and unappealing. "I'm sure our subscribers will enjoy reading all about it. Why don't you get a quote from Hester or one of the others?" He wasn't crazy about featuring the society's censorious efforts. On the other hand, they made news and that was his business. "Then interview Ms. O'Brien about her motives."

"Free publicity, what else?" Alice Ann scoffed.

"That," Jeremiah said wryly, "she's got. In spades."

His reporter, who aspired to write stories of a more global nature, squared her shoulders for the task ahead. Someday the petty squabbles of Webster Station would be far behind Alice Ann Keating. Until then, she had rent to pay. "Right, boss," she said, and strode off to confront the picket line.

The sidewalk in front of Haute Water was clearing. Elmer and the other seniors returned to their bench, muttering about a round-the-clock plan to keep a watchful eye out. Most of the *Chronicle* staffers headed back to the newsroom, but Mitzi Janeway, both mayor and gossip columnist, was the first in Haute Water's door. Soon a group of women jammed the shop entrance, jabbering about the loofah, thick towels and bath crystals they'd spotted in the window.

Jeremiah stayed on the sidewalk, thinking. Hester had called him a respected businessman. It was true he'd become something of a community leader since his move to Webster Station. As such, he was practically *required* to introduce himself to Fancy O'Brien, officially welcoming her and Haute Water to Main Street. It would be the proper thing to do.

Civic responsibility had its benefits, he decided, smiling as he pushed open the shop's glass door.

Just then a squadron of boys on bikes wheeled up to the window. "Oh, man," moaned Billy Hooper. "We missed it!"

FANCY KNEW she must look a fright. Her hair was damp, sticking to the nape of her neck in wet strings, and what was dry was about to flop onto her face. She'd stepped into the paisley robe without toweling off; now its thin fabric was uncomfortably plastered to her goose bumpy skin. Her feet were bare and getting quite chilly.

She really should go to the dressing room and make herself warm, dry and decent, but this was a moment to be savored despite her dishabille.

Haute Water was a success! A smashing, crashing, humdinger of a success!

The shop was crowded with customers. Brett Randolph, her new part-time clerk, was ringing up a steady round of sales on the cash register. Fancy's mother, Stella, circulated in her maid's costume, handing out freebies as she chatted to the friendly folks of Webster Station.

Even better, Fancy figured she was about to get a load of free publicity. She'd hit the jackpot when the picketers had arrived—how lucky that Pringle and Alice Ann had been on the spot to record the resulting fracas. Haute Water was practically guaranteed the front page.

She set her hands on her hips and made a quick survey of the shop. The interior was bright and airy, perfumed with pot pourri, scented candles and soaps. At the front of the store, a glass-topped, U-shaped sales counter was filled with the pricier items: crystal atomizers, some of them antique, clustered like a collection of cut jewels before rows of designer perfumes; cloisonné, silver and gold vanity sets; tiny curio boxes in enamel, porcelain, copper; several expensive jewelry and music boxes she'd picked up at estate sales. Bleached pine shelves lined the walls, stocked with bath products and fanciful containers heaped with pumice stones, shaped soaps and nail brushes. Big wicker baskets on the floor held loofahs, natural sea sponges and long-handled body brushes.

Fancy moved toward the rear, where her small office and the dressing area formed a barrier between the shop and the large back room that displayed the bathroom fixtures she hoped would be her real money-maker. This section was meant to look like a boudoir, with rose-wreathed wallpaper and heavy velvet draperies that could be pulled for greater privacy. Cushioned chairs invited customers to sit alongside an armoire filled with a treasure trove of vintage and reproduction peignoirs, chemises and nightgowns. Towels had been tucked away on convenient shelves and stacked on a wire maid's cart.

The bell over the front door chimed to announce another visitor. Fancy was about to disappear into the dressing room when the sight of the newest arrival stopped her.

It was Mr. Tall-Dark-and-Handsome, the man she'd noticed at the front of the crowd during her bath. He'd looked sexily rumpled in gray slacks and a white dress shirt with rolled-up sleeves and a loosened tie, one finger casually hooking a suit jacket over his shoulder. He had the lean ranginess of a man of action; the gleam in his eye told her he liked the action to be of the enjoyable sort. She'd watched him watch her, the awareness between them an almost tangible thing. It had been a delicious sensation.

But now there was no window between them. Fancy shivered as his gaze slowly swept the interior of Haute Water. He stood head and shoulders above the mainly female crowd, exuding an aura of control and command. She might have assumed he was Webster Station's mayor if she hadn't already been on the receiving end of Mitzi Janeway's garrulous version of a conversation.

Still, he had to be someone important. He'd watched her performance with a speculative, almost foreboding con-

centration. He'd tried to shoo the crowd away when—
Prickles of apprehension raced over Fancy's skin. He could
very well be the town *sheriff*. He might even be here to arrest her!

Her first instinct was to confront him. She even stepped
forward before common sense prevailed. It would be prudent to change into a garment less flimsy than a wet silk
dressing gown before charging off to take on the sheriff. She
turned to leave, but it was too late. He'd already picked her
out of the crowd. He was coming her way!

At the same moment, Mitzi Janeway's cloud of improb-
ably yellow hair popped up from behind the sales counter
on the other side of the room. She waved her arms wildly.
"Yoo-hoo, Fancy!" she warbled.

Bent on avoiding both of them, Fancy hurried toward the
dressing room. She was only two steps away when a hand
touched her shoulder. "Pardon me—"

She whirled to confront him, eyes narrowing suspiciously. "I won't go peacefully!"

The man she'd assumed to be the sheriff raised his hand
and backed off a step. "You're Fancy O'Brien?"

Identifying the suspect? she wondered. "That's me," she
warily acknowledged. "I don't have ID on me at the moment."

"Obviously." Lips quirked in amusement, he allowed his
gaze to meander down her dressing gown, lingering a little
too long over the curves revealed by the clinging silk.

Fancy's bare toes curled nervously. An officer of the law
shouldn't be so blatantly admiring, no matter how forcefully their mutual attraction had affected him. It just wasn't
politically correct.

"Fortunately I don't require any," he added.

"You mean—" she blinked in consternation "—you're
going to arrest me. Just like that?"

"Arrest you?"

"At the very least you have to read me my rights!"

The sheriff shook his head, looking disconcerted. "You've been watching too much TV."

"You can't mean that in Webster Station you arrest people without reading them their rights? I've seen movies like this. Redneck sheriffs running roughshod over the Constitution, throwing innocent people in jail on trumped-up charges—"

"Aw shucks, ma'am, that only happens in Alabama."

"You think this is funny?" Suddenly her mouth snapped shut. He wasn't wearing a uniform. Shouldn't he be wearing a uniform, like Andy Griffith?

"I'm not here to arrest you."

"You're not?" Fancy reached up to push back her untidy hair. She'd better watch her words. This might be a ploy to trick her into saying something incriminating. They probably had plainclothes cops even in a small town like Webster Station.

"But I'll be happy to frisk you," the sheriff added with a teasing grin. His eyes were a sharp hazel, and Fancy was suddenly much too aware of how the robe's thin wet silk was clinging to her breasts, delineating her budded nipples.

"I haven't broken any laws," she protested. "I don't think."

"Only the one about creating a public disturbance."

Fancy snorted. "What *I* did was a public disturbance? What about the women out there?" She gestured toward the front of the shop and her hair flopped into her eyes. "Look at them. Blocking my door. Shouting and chanting. I ought to swear out a complaint!" Overcharged, she stopped to pant, wisps of hair floating about her face like dandelion fluff in the breeze.

The sheriff didn't seem particularly impressed. The picketers had lost much of their zeal now that the crowd was gone, although they continued to march along the short length of sidewalk in front of Haute Water. Not a single customer inside the store was paying them any mind.

"You wouldn't want me to run roughshod over the Ladies' Society for Decency's right to free speech, would you?" he asked. "They're not disturbing business."

"Of course not. You're probably one of those redneck sheriffs who presses charges against every outsider you can get your hands on, deliberately ignoring the real trouble-makers because they were once Aunt Bea's neighbor or Opie's baby-sitter." Fancy extended her arms, wrists turned up. "Go ahead. Arrest me. Lock me up. But I can guarantee you'll be hearing from the Civil Liberties Union!"

Before he could slap on the handcuffs, the gray-haired lady's maid arrived. "Fancy! What's going on here?"

"This man is here to arrest me, Mom."

Stella O'Brien scowled. "What are the charges? Where are you taking her? How much is bail?" She patted Fancy's shoulder. "Don't worry, dear, I'll spring you even if I have to empty the till."

"There's been a misunderstanding," the sheriff said. "I'm not arresting anyone."

Stella shook her finger in his face. "You'd better not."

"But you said I'd created a public disturbance," Fancy reminded him. Getting arrested would've been good for several weeks, maybe months, of free publicity.

"You were. I like public disturbances."

"What?" Fancy frowned quizzically. "Why would a sheriff . . . ?"

"Allow me to introduce myself. I'm Jeremiah Quick, publisher of the *Webster Station Chronicle*. You could say that public disturbances are my stock-in-trade."

"Aha," Stella said, nodding. "I'm Fancy's mother."

"Mrs. O'Brien. Your daughter jumped to some pretty zany conclusions and assumed I was here to arrest her. It seems she's a ready martyr to the cause of public nudity."

"My Francine can be a tad impulsive."

"It's not as if they could see anything," Fancy interjected.

"I told you there'd be trouble over this stunt!" Stella heaved a put-upon sigh. "It's just like the time you and the men's swim team decided to play bikini ball in the college president's backyard. Her husband looked out the window and was so appalled by all the jiggling parts he called campus security. I had to drive over to—"

"Mom, please, let's not get into ancient history. I've put all that behind me."

"Or the time you wanted to win an Alaskan cruise in a radio-station contest. You jumped into a vat of lime Jell-O wearing an extremely skimpy mermaid costume and a scuba mask."

Fancy smiled wanly. Stella didn't seem to know the meaning of the word *discretion*. No wonder her daughter was having such a difficult time learning it, let alone living it. "I doubt Mr. Quick wants to hear all about the follies of my youth."

"Sounds like an interesting story to me," he countered.

"That Jell-O stunt happened three years ago," Stella cheerfully continued. "I'd hardly call twenty-seven still a youth."

Fancy's eyes rolled. "Thanks for revealing my age, Mom. Maybe you should go tell *all* my customers that I'm about to turn thirty!"

"Don't be touchy, Fan. Thirty is nothing. Wait till you're staring into the maw of seventy or eighty. Then you can complain, for all the good it'll do you."

It was Fancy's turn to sigh. Stella, who'd never told her daughter to act her age, obviously didn't understand. Fancy had always figured the teens and twenties were prime time for fun and foolishness. She'd had every right to frolic for all she was worth. But thirty was different. Thirty represented the beginning of responsible adulthood. It was a decade of decorum. Thirty-year-olds settled down to marry accountants with horn-rimmed glasses or were themselves accountants with horn-rimmed glasses. They wore sensible shoes and discussed putting Mother in a retirement home. They voted regularly and never for Howard Stern. They made babies, not public disturbances.

And in approximately two months, on the twenty-eighth of June, Fancy O'Brien would become one of them. A thirty-year-old.

Of course her birthday was a momentous dreaded occasion!

Apparently unaware of her daughter's turmoil, Stella brandished her basket of tiny bath sachets. "Time to peddle my wares. Nice to meet you, Mr. Quick. Don't be fooled by Fancy's exhibitionistic tendencies. Underneath she's a levelheaded young lady." She started to wander off, then turned back to add, "I do believe it began when she was just a child. She used to bolt from her evening bath to parade around the house in her birthday suit, belting out 'The Star-Spangled Banner.'"

Fancy moaned in mortification. "I was only five." She winced up at Jeremiah. "You won't print any of this, will you? Frankly I'd rather go to jail."

He smothered his laughter. "Strictly off the record. But you'd better hope Mitzi Janeway and Hester Hightower don't hear of your escapades."

Fancy already knew about Mitzi. She was the nosy gossip columnist/mayor who lived in the Janeway mansion with her twin sister, Fritzi. Fortunately, or perhaps unfortunately, Mitzi had just cornered Stella behind the velvet draperies. It didn't bear dwelling on. "Hester Hightower?" Fancy prompted.

Jeremiah pointed outside. "She's the loud stocky one in her midfifties." Which described half the membership, so he elaborated. "The undisputed leader of the Ladies' Society for Decency."

"My picketers."

"I wouldn't worry about them. Last month they were campaigning against Calvin Klein ads. Tried to get Mitch Mitchell down the street arrested as a distributor of pornography."

"Mitch? You're kidding. He's such a mild harmless guy." Fancy watched the ladies march past her door, thinking less about free publicity and more about the hassle they might cause. "What are they chanting? I can't make it out."

"'No Nudity' is their standard rallying cry."

Her hand strayed to the sash around her waist, checking the knot. "What nudity? I was covered with bubbles."

"The merest hint of public nudity is enough of a threat for Hester Hightower." Jeremiah's glance went to her hand, now clutching the lapels. "A bit too late for modesty now, Ms. O'Brien," he said with a playful lilt, although his eyes were more serious. And hot enough to sizzle.

Fancy grabbed one of the towels stacked on the wire cart and pressed it to her chest. "You can call me Fancy," she said, ready to poke fun at herself to relieve the situation, especially with Jeremiah staring at her like that. "After all, you've watched me take a bath."

She fumbled with the towel, letting it unfold down her torso. Jeremiah's unavoidable male magnetism had made her vividly aware of all the bare skin beneath her dressing gown. She felt a hundred times more on display than she had during her performance. Up to this moment she'd never been the shy type.

"So has half the town, Fancy."

Not quite, but she wasn't in any position to argue. "Anything to please my customers," she tossed off with a light laugh, realizing that half of them were keeping one eye on the merchandise and the other on her encounter with Jeremiah Quick. "Speaking of whom," she added formally, "I should be attending to them. If you'll excuse me, Mr. Quick?"

Again he stopped her with a hand on her shoulder. It was a touch warm and firm and gentle and exciting all at once, a touch that sent shivers scurrying down to her pink-polished toenails.

"Call me Jeremiah."

Fancy meant to dart only a quick glance up at his face; instead, her attention was thoroughly engaged by what she saw. His hair was thick, short at the sides and back, wavy on top, dark, dark brown but for a smattering of silver at the temples. His features had a chiseled Roman look, tending slightly toward boniness, as did his tall lean body. She'd thought his eyes were hazel, but up close they were as golden brown as sweet thick honey. The same full sweetness dripped from his rich Southern-accented voice. She could have easily become mesmerized and had to force herself to blink.

"Excuse me, please, Jeremiah?" she whispered huskily.

His fingertips grazed her shoulder in a near-caress as he slowly removed his hand. "Something tells me I'd excuse you anything, Fancy O'Brien," he murmured for her ears alone.

She was torn between an urge to rush to the safety of the dressing room and a desire to tuck herself up under Jeremiah's chin. He would definitely warm her up. She was hesitating, twisting the towel in her hands, when the swinging door of the dressing room bopped her on the backside.

"Whoops, sorry about that, Fancy," said the shapely young woman who'd emerged. "Are you ready for me to go on?"

It took a second for Fancy to adjust to the intrusion. "Jessica, do you know Mr. Quick?"

"Sure. How are you, Mr. Quick?" Jessica's brow furrowed. "Will my photo be in the *Chronicle* again?" she asked him. "I don't know what all Daddy will think . . ."

Jeremiah looked from Jessica to Fancy and back again. Jessica was wearing a white dimity duster. Fancy could see the moment he realized that Jessica Dandy, fresh from her reign as Miss Azalea, was about to take a bath. "Oh, no," he muttered. "Not you, too, Jessica."

"Don't be a fuddy-duddy," Fancy quickly replied. She put her arm around the statuesque blonde's waist. "Jessica wants to be a model. This job will give her experience so she won't land in Manhattan a raw amateur."

Jessica nodded eagerly. "Fancy's paying me, Mr. Quick. That makes me a professional."

"Go on, Jessica," Fancy urged before Jeremiah could comment further. "Stella was going to draw you a nice hot bath with lots of bubbles."

"Gee, I hope so. My boyfriend and the rest of the cheerleading squad promised to stop by. I just hope Aunt Hester doesn't make too much of a fuss." Jessica flashed them a beauty-queen smile and trotted to the front of the store, the duster floating open to reveal her strapless swimsuit.

Jeremiah breathed a sigh of relief. "So you weren't nude, either?" he asked Fancy. "What a tease you are."

"We-e-ell . . ." She debated the advisability of telling him the truth. "Let's just say that *Jessica* will wear a suit. I wouldn't want Hester Hightower accusing me of corrupting a minor."

Jeremiah remembered the sight of her very bare back. "Do you mean . . . ?"

Fancy's gray-blue eyes sparked with mischief as she nudged open the swinging door. Turning a respectable thirty was the last thing on her mind as her agile fingers undid the sash. Ducking into the dressing room, she whipped open the paisley robe and, for just a millisecond, flashed Jeremiah Quick.

His jaw dropped in shock.

Webster Station Chronicle
Talk of the Town by Mitzi Janeway

SOME LIKE IT HAUTE

A haute time was had by all at the splashy grand opening of Webster Station's newest business. If you were unlucky enough to miss the fun, darlings, at least you've got Mitzi to tell you all about it! Haute Water is the name of a new bathroom boutique, owned and operated by the charming Fancy O'Brien. Fancy, 29 and a Cancer, came to Our Town via Washington, D.C., where she'd previously worked as a legislative assistant in Senator Victor Smack's office. (Insert your own joke here concerning the relationship between politics and bathroom fixtures!!) Fancy says that since Senator Smack took a bath on the last election (drat that partisan investigation!), she was pointed in the right direction.

Fancy Takes a Bath, Too

Anyhoo, all eyes were drawn to the corner of Main and Dogwood when Miss Fancy appeared live and in person amid the simply cunning Victorian bath display in the window. Let me tell you, they were a-crawlin' out of the woodwork when she proceeded to—would Mitzi lie to you?—*take a bath!!* Of course, a heap o' bubbles screened the lovely Fancy's unmentionables, but all the men stayed on—just in case something bobbed to the surface! And yes, fellas, Fancy is single. (So start your engines!)

Natch, where there's nudity there's Hester Hightower and the Ladies' Society for Decency, who set up a picket in record time. Not that their folderol stopped anyone from enjoying the show—or the subsequent performance by model-to-be Jessica Dandy. I wonder what Auntie Hester had to say about that?!

Betty Jo Dandy, who's ignored what big sis Hester has had to say since she was old enough to spell hyperbole, was on hand to snap pix of her daughter's first professional assignment.

See you on the cover of *Vogue*, Jess!!

The Sweet Smell of Success

Needless to say, Haute Water's grand opening was a glorious success. The shop was crowded all day long, and each customer was presented with a cute muslin bag of bath sachets. Fancy's instructions were to swish it in bathwater, in case y'all were wondering why Miss Mitzi smells like lavender, rosemary and thyme. (Yummy!)

Helping out in the store was Stella O'Brien, not only Fancy's chief investor but her mother, as well. Stella, a Capricorn (I never reveal the age of a woman over thirty—even if she's Catherine Deneuve!), and Fancy have moved into a darling little cottage on Cherry Street. Don't you adore seeing a mother and daughter so close? By the by, Stella also revealed that she's divorced. Just a tidbit for you older fellas (even though you're a mite slower to rev up your engines!).

Oh, dearie me, I'm out of space for today's column. And weren't y'all just dying to hear about how Fancy *flashed* my esteemed publisher and made him turn fire-engine red?!!

2

FLASHED BY FANCY O'BRIEN.

A foolish grin had been glued to Jeremiah's face for the past forty-eight hours. Neither could he erase Fancy's image from his mind: sassy, sexy, short and trim, but curvy where it counted. Her skin (all that skin!) as rich and smooth as cream, looking so soft and caressable the need to touch it could have brought a grown man to his knees. Her personality: capricious, flirtatious, momentarily almost bashful, then decidedly, boldly, provocative.

For ten minutes he'd been distractedly studying the same circulation report Hester had found him reading on Saturday; today he saw nothing but gibberish. He set it aside and focused on Mitzi's latest column with no more success. Fancy O'Brien truly had him bamboozled.

Jeremiah rose from behind the old oak desk that had been part of the package deal when he'd purchased the newspaper the year before. He walked around it and yanked open the office door. Willa Clark, ever ready to please, looked up expectantly, pale eyelashes fluttering.

"Yes, Mr. Quick?" Her voice was wispy, with a rising inflection that turned every sentence into a question.

He laid several papers before her. "Willa, you did such a good job of editing Mitzi's Azalea Festival article, I'm putting you in charge of "Talk of the Town." Whip it into shape for the next edition. If you have questions, see Alice Ann, not me."

Even though he continued to be a type-A hands-on sort of publisher despite all efforts to the contrary, "Talk of the Town" was one responsibility Jeremiah was glad to relinquish. He'd learned quickly enough that most Webster Stationers would rather count Mitzi's exclamation points than read half a page on U.S. foreign policy. Although he accommodated their taste for gossip, he'd rather not deal with it himself. Especially after Sunday's column.

"I'll do my best, sir," Willa said almost gravely.

"Maybe you'll earn a promotion."

"Gosh." Willa sighed breathlessly, slender fingers paging through the pink sheets filled with Mitzi's swoopy swirly handwriting.

Pringle opened his eyes and untwined his elongated limbs from the twin swivel chairs he'd been napping on. "Hold on, J.Q. I've got the proof sheets from Saturday's shoot."

"Why didn't you say so?" Jeremiah asked with some impatience, illogical as it was. "Let's take a look."

They went over to the streetside window, holding the proof sheets up beneath an arc of peeling stick-on letters that read ELCINORHC NOITATS RETSBEW. Jeremiah studied the rows of tiny square photos. He saw Fancy with a dollop of bubbles on the end of her nose. Fancy blowing Beau a kiss. A smoldering Fancy peeking over one shoulder with a come-hither look. Hester stomping along the curb as if her drawers had been starched. Billy Hooper pressing his nose against the window. Fancy soaping a leg. There were also similar poses of Jessica Dandy, but he gave those only a cursory inspection.

"Great shots, Pringle." He tapped one of the sheets. "I want this one for the front page." The photographer had caught Fancy laughing with delight, one shapely leg cocked and streaming with sudsy bathwater. Superimposed over her image were the distorted reflections of the ogling, goggling, giggling onlookers.

Jeremiah was too absorbed by the proofs to notice his brother's arrival. "I'd go for the sexy one myself," Beau said, snatching away one of the sheets. He perused it with an efficient professional eye, whistling softly under his breath. "Did I say the sexy *one*? Make that the sexy dozen."

Jeremiah reappropriated the photos. "Hands off, Beau."

Beau grinned, dangling his motorcycle helmet by its chin strap as he made a futile grab at the second sheet. "Are we speaking of the photos or the lady?" he asked with the debonair confidence of one rarely denied.

The question made Jeremiah pause. He looked at row upon row of Fancy's sexily playful image. Then he looked at his brother, tousled and dusty from yet another hour of roaring around the countryside revving up the interest of the local lasses. It wasn't a difficult decision. "Both," he said firmly, using his big-brother-knows-best voice.

"Aw, that's no fun," Beau protested. He winked at Willa, who was gaping at him from behind her desk. Blushing furiously, she ducked behind her in-tray. "I saw Fancy first," he pointed out.

Jeremiah had no intention of allowing a mere ninety seconds decide his future. "Weren't you saying just yesterday that you've collected more phone numbers than MCI?" Beau had been camping out on his brother's couch for three weeks now, waxing poetic about the virtues of Virginia debutantes in sundresses versus the head-to-toe shrouding of Saudi Arabia's cloistered females. Jeremiah was frankly amazed that his playboy brother had held out long enough to complete the assignment in the Mideast that had led to this vacation. "Stick to your little black book," he advised Beau sternly, "and stay away from Fancy."

"Interested, Jer?"

At Beau's question, every eyebrow in the room lifted, every ear cocked. Jeremiah wasn't pleased. He'd hoped to retain his authority over the newsroom despite Mitzi's unseemly revelation. Better not to answer than to reveal himself as the besotted swain he'd become, he decided, turning to Pringle with a no-nonsense expression. "We should also include a shot of the protesters. Alice Ann expects to have her write-up finished by noon."

Pringle saluted, bony knuckles knocking against the bill of his frayed Orioles cap. "Right-o, J.Q. The prints will be on your desk this afternoon." Eager to sink his hands into a pan of fixative, he loped off toward the darkroom.

"Pringle?" Jeremiah called after the photographer, striving to sound offhand. "Why don't you print up some of the others as long as you're at it? Just in case I need them . . ." For his own personal collection. That shot of Fancy's bare shoulders and an inch or two of cleavage had him burning up inside. "Will somebody please open a window? It's damn hot in here for late April."

Beau laughed knowingly. Alice Ann stared intently at the file she'd opened across her keyboard, and Pringle ducked his chin into the collar of his plaid flannel shirt to muffle a snicker.

Only Willa jumped to do Jeremiah's bidding. "Right away, Mr. Quick!" she said. It wasn't until she reached the window that she realized it was already open.

"SO WHAT DID YOU THINK of him, Mom?"

"Him who, dear?"

"Jeremiah Quick, of course. The publisher of the *Chronicle*." Fancy stepped back to survey the window display. One of her three mannequins had been employed as a stand-in, or, more correctly, a sit-in. She'd unscrewed Niña at the

waist and set her upper half in the tub among a pile of pseu-
dobubble bath.

"Sheriff Quick?" Grinning, Stella held up a sheet of bubble paper, the sort used as packing material. "You'd better
add another layer of this to the tub or he'll be back to arrest
you. No doubt Hester Hightower files complaints against
even inanimate boobs."

"Takes one to know one," Fancy muttered, cutting
crookedly around the bubbles to achieve a frothy effect.

"I hope you're referring to Hester and not me," Stella said
placidly.

Fancy exchanged a wave with the passing Betty Jo Dandy,
then tucked the bubble paper around Niña's fiberglass
breasts. "Mitzi Janeway was in asking questions for her
column, and she told me he's forty-three."

Stella fluffed the mannequin's brunette wig. "Who?"

"Moth-*er!* Jeremiah Quick of course." Fancy pressed her
cheek to the window and looked down Main Street to the
big brick building that housed the newspaper. "He's forty-
three."

"Really? A very young forty-three, I'd say."

"He does have some gray hair."

Stella tsked her dismissal. "A barely discernible sprin-
kling of silver at the temples does not a middle-aged man
make." She pushed back her own decidedly gray bangs.
"Jeremiah's still a young whippersnapper."

Fancy kneeled beside the tub and thrust her arms into the
bubbles up to her elbows, trying to fluff them into a sudsy
look.

"More your generation, Fancy," Stella added pointedly
as she tied a lacy bow and loosened several strands of the
wig so that they curled around Niña's perfect ear.

"He's only six years younger than you, Mom. Plenty of
women date younger guys. In fact, six years isn't even

enough to be called an age difference." Stella didn't need a poky, staid, Barcalounger kind of guy—Fancy could see that now. In their admittedly short acquaintance, Jeremiah Quick had certainly seemed intriguing, vital and...*young*.

"Really, Fan, don't tell me we're back to your unending mission to find your old mom a man!" Stella grimaced. "Well, I suppose it's a moot point. I don't see Mr. Quick beating down the door to ask an O'Brien woman out." But if he did, she was quite sure which one it would be.

Fancy tilted her head as if she was more interested in evaluating the window display than Jeremiah. "You do find him handsome, don't you, Mom? And charming?"

Stella gathered up the scissors, a foam wig stand and the remainder of the bubble paper. "You tell me."

Fancy followed her back into the shop. "Of course you do. What woman—a woman of a certain age, that is— wouldn't? He's tall and in great shape. He's got those fabulous tiger's eyes and that mesmerizing Southern accent. Dangerous, that voice. As smooth as expensive brandy and then—whammo!—you're drunk just listening to it."

Stella arched one steel gray eyebrow. "Is that so?"

"Mmm." Fancy leaned her elbows on the glass countertop, her chin in her hands. "Don't you adore his lean, hungry look? It's so ... so ... " She sighed dreamily.

"I'll give you that, dear. He's an attractive man."

Fancy snapped out of her trance. So, her mother *was* interested. Fancy began rearranging the cut-crystal perfume bottles, mulling over the possibility of giving Cupid a shove in the right direction. Although her mother claimed to prefer her life as it was, Fancy had detected a certain longing in her eyes—for a mate, she was sure. Gardening, cooking and reading travel guides were nice hobbies but not very fulfilling. Stella needed excitement, stimulation, adventure. She needed romance!

"Maybe I should amble down the street to get us some lunch," Fancy said ultracasually. It was close to noon and business had slacked off. This was a perfect opportunity for reconnaissance. A dinner invitation might be the way to go.

"Run along, Fancy." Stella steered her daughter away from the cash register. "I see a couple of career gals heading this way to blow their lunch money on bubble bath. Take a half hour if you like, but remember to pick me up something good."

Yeah, Fancy thought. Like Jeremiah Quick.

WEBSTER STATION, Virginia, population 4,492, was nestled among the picturesque foothills of the Blue Ridge Mountains. Its convenient yet rural location meant that it was far enough away from the city to avoid bedroom-community status but near enough to benefit from a healthy tourist trade. The townspeople were justifiably proud of their smattering of historical sites and architecturally significant buildings—chief among them the railway station that had given the town its name and the once glorious now rather shabby Janeway mansion. Building codes had ensured that even the more recent structures—which meant post-Civil War to the locals—didn't clash with their more historic neighbors. Redbrick was in abundance, usually set off by graceful white columns, porticoes and pediments. The residential areas were tidy and lush with flowers and shrubs— the town as a whole was mad for gardening.

So, as Fancy strolled along Main Street, the air was perfumed with a varied bouquet of springtime blossoms. The downtown merchants had adopted a tradition of setting out decorative wreaths and flower-filled window boxes. As she stopped to sniff and exclaim over the various displays, Fancy was greeted with cheerful hellos and friendly waves.

Her rather splashy debut had made her something of a local celebrity.

At the convergence of the town's four main thoroughfares was a manicured green, centered by a white lattice gazebo and the obligatory Civil War cannon. To Fancy's surprise she saw Jeremiah Quick sitting on the gazebo steps.

He'd been watching her approach and now he stood, waving her over to join him. Her jaunty step faltered slightly as she tried to assimilate the bolt of pure pleasure that had zapped through her at the sight of him. She blinked in surprise, but her usual vivacity quickly returned and she strode briskly toward him, head high and arms swinging.

"Jeremiah!" she called gaily. "Just the man I was looking for!"

He thumped his chest with his fist. "Oh, Fancy! I'm mortally wounded you didn't recognize me."

Fancy realized that the man she'd thought was Jeremiah was actually his brother, Beau, who'd stopped by the shop yesterday to introduce himself. Sinking disappointment replaced her tingling anticipation. A very curious reaction, she thought. Beau was just as nice and certainly as good-looking as his brother. Closer to her own age, too. "Sorry, Beau. You two do look a lot alike."

He angled his head to one side. "Tell me I'm an acceptable substitute and I'll recover."

"Well, of course you . . . you're . . ." she floundered, not quite sure what to say. At that fortuitous moment Jeremiah crossed the green from the *Chronicle* side of the square.

"Hello, there," he said, addressing Fancy with obvious pleasure. She looked as fresh and clean as springtime, the peach of her dress echoing the touch of color that sprang to her cheeks. "I hope I'm not interrupting."

"No such luck," Beau said, the corners of his mouth turning down in what most women might have considered an adorable little-boy pout. "Apparently it's you Fancy's looking for."

Jeremiah dropped his hand on his brother's shoulder, giving him a look Fancy didn't quite catch. "So take off, Beauregard," he said.

Beau shrugged. "Big brothers," he muttered, then reached for Fancy's hand and gave it a kiss before shooting a smirk at his impatient brother and finally strolling off toward the café.

"You wanted to see me?" Jeremiah asked Fancy once they were alone.

His presence was enough to erase any lingering thoughts of Beau. Fancy took a deep breath and, as was her habit, made a figurative feet-first plunge. "I wanted to invite you for dinner," she explained, unaccustomed heat suffusing her face and throat. "Sort of a welcome-to-Webster-Station dinner."

"You've got that reversed." Jeremiah smiled down at her pinkening face. "It's the townspeople who should be welcoming you."

Her fingers fluttered in dismissal. "Let me count the ways. Eudora Vincent brought us a coffee cake and stayed to consume half of it. Mama Mitchell sent over a casserole. There are two dozen of Aubergine Rizzo's gingersnaps in my cookie jar. We have five invitations to dinner and several offers to attend barbecues and picnics. The Swertlows asked us over for cocktails and the Bellinghams for tea. Reverend Cripps expects us in church next Sunday. The country club sent a membership application. We've been invited to join the Webster Station Players and the Downtown Merchants Association. There was the Spring Fling at the Loblolly Club yesterday and next weekend the DAR's Discover Your Ancestors seminar..." She wasn't finished but had to stop to take a breath.

"I remember what it was like when I moved here," Jeremiah said. After thirteen months, he still hadn't caught up on all the invitations.

"So. We've been thoroughly welcomed by the citizens of Webster Station."

He raised his eyebrows. "With the notable exception of Hester Hightower."

Fancy's lips curved ruefully. "No, I don't expect to be asked to join the Ladies' Society for Decency any time soon."

"I doubt a woman who played bikini ball in a college president's yard regrets the snub."

She pressed one palm to her cheek, feeling again the rush of heat that signaled her embarrassment. "I do wish you'd forget you heard that. Stella O'Brien has a big mouth. I'll have to tell her to zip it." She was confounded by her reaction. The infamous bikini-ball incident had been covered by the college newspaper—she'd been photographed in a zebra-stripe bikini being marched off by two uniformed campus security officers—and the exposure hadn't bothered her one whit. Why should Jeremiah's teasing grin upset her equilibrium? Was it because she'd decided such silly stunts were not worthy of the soon-to-be mature and sedate Fancy O'Brien? Or was there an even more disturbing reason?

It couldn't be because he was so attractively eligible. She'd once, for all of a heady three weeks, dated the most sought-after unmarried congressman in D.C. and hadn't reacted so. While her head might have been momentarily turned by the flattering attentions of the eligible politician and his attendant paparazzi, he'd never made her feel anything like this.

And *this* was ridiculous. Let Stella suffer the nervous stomach and out-of-control hormones. Fancy had other more sedate plans—just as soon as she turned thirty.

Jeremiah solicitously asked, "Would you like to sit down?" probably because he was afraid she was going to keel over at his feet.

If you only knew, she thought, assenting with a ladylike nod. Stepping over a border of pansies and impatiens, they perched on the edge of the gazebo. While she gathered her scattered aplomb, Fancy pretended a great interest in the soaring white steeple of Reverend Cripps's church, a dignified wood-frame building fronting the square from the corner of Azalea Avenue and Captain Janeway Drive. She drew a deep breath, somehow finding the nerve to complete her mission. "So what do you say to dinner?" she asked. "Stella's really looking forward to seeing you again."

"Stella?" Jeremiah loosened the knot in his tie. "Sure, I'd like to talk with Stella."

"She thinks you're quite handsome and charming," Fancy blurted. "Yep, those were her exact words. Handsome and charming."

Jeremiah rubbed his chin in an overstated show of deliberation. "Funny, when Stella was shaking her finger at me, I'd have thought that'd be the last description to come to mind. I'll have to thank her for the compliment."

Fancy winced. Why did even well-meant little white lies have to weave a sticky web? "Oh, there's no need of that," she murmured.

Jeremiah's expression was unbelievably guileless. "You'll find I'm a very conscientious sort. For instance, I'll be sure to return your kind dinner invitation forthwith. Just following the proper social form, of course."

Fancy, staring at the tips of her ivory pumps, didn't see the glint in his eyes. She'd been well and truly boxed into a corner by a man as quick as his name. She, however, was adept at squirming out of predicaments. If he actually insisted on a dinner date, she'd think of a way to get out of it and redirect his attention to Stella. She would. Absolutely. "Is tomorrow okay for you?" she asked briskly. Time was of the essence, for reasons she wouldn't examine too closely. "Seven-thirty?"

"We're on deadline at the paper every Tuesday and Saturday. Any chance we could make it for Wednesday evening, instead? If that would fit Stella's calendar, naturally."

Fancy waved at the curly-haired round-cheeked woman going into Maybelle's Café. Aubergine Rizzo was the postmaster's extremely enthusiastic young wife. "Wednesday would be perfect. It'll give me a good excuse to refuse when Aubergine asks me to be her baking-day taste-tester."

"Ah, yes," he said in complete understanding. "Aubergine really knows how to put the snap in a gingersnap."

"Aren't they awful?" she whispered.

"Yeah. Sort of like old hockey pucks."

Fancy giggled. "Bart Rizzo must be a man of great intestinal fortitude."

"And a cast-iron gut. I should warn you about the PTA bake sales. A group of us draw straws beforehand and the winner—or loser, depending how you look at it—buys Aubergine's contribution."

"Wouldn't it be easier to tell her the truth? Gently?"

"Who could do it? Aubergine takes such pride in her housewifely skills. And she's so thrilled when her baking is purchased in the sale's first five minutes."

Fancy crossed her legs, shoulders swaying close enough to brush Jeremiah's. She jerked away from what surely was only a friendly contact, again confused by his effect on her. "Count me in," she said in a rush. "After all, the PTA is a good cause."

Absorbed in watching her leg swing back and forth, Jeremiah didn't notice her lack of composure. His eyes followed the movement of the pump dangling off her enticing toes. Fancy sat up and arranged herself more primly. "I don't suppose I'd actually have to eat the stuff, would I?"

His smile was conspiratorial. "Can you keep a secret?"

"Sure," she answered, a trifle breathless at his intimate tone.

"There's a shoe box of rawhidelike shortbread buried in my backyard. I live in fear that it'll mutate into something unspeakable come the next full moon."

"Gosh. I'd hate—the town would hate to lose you to a cookie mutant."

"If I should disappear in the dead of night, tell Billy Hooper he can enter the monster in the science fair."

Chuckling at their nonsense, Fancy got to her feet. The breeze caught at her hair, blowing the dark strands into a nimbus around her face. "You seem to be so at home here. But Mitzi told me you moved to Webster Station only a year ago." Mitzi had also gladly informed her of his high-powered career in Atlanta, his upscale ex-wife and his three darling children. Apparently all fuel for previous "Talk of the Town" columns.

"Checking up on me?" he asked, his grin slightly lopsided and infinitely charming.

"You know Mitzi. One can't get her to shut up."

"Even if one actually tries."

Fancy's eyes narrowed. Jeremiah couldn't possibly know how she'd primed the pump with a few discreet questions, then practically memorized the deluge of info that had poured forth from Mitzi's indiscreet mouth. "One does one's best," she said sweetly as she turned to leave. She'd secured Jeremiah as Stella's dinner date; lingering any longer might not be wise.

His voice stopped her. "As long as we're here, how about lunch? Have you tried the food at Maybelle's yet?"

Fancy's brow furrowed as she smoothed the pleats of her dress. "I don't think I'm particularly welcome at Maybelle's."

"Why not?" he asked in surprise. While Maybelle Clark was not Webster Station's warmest person, she was usually scrupulously cordial.

"I stopped there this morning for coffee," Fancy explained with a sigh. She'd never before thought of any of her escapades as indecent. "Maybelle is one of Hester's disciples. She didn't refuse to serve me, but there was a distinct chill in the air."

Jeremiah considered her troubled eyes. "You know, Maybelle burned my cheeseburger after I hired her daughter to be my secretary. She'd expected Willa to devote her life to the café. But she got over it. Why don't you give her a second chance? She serves a mean onion ring."

And a mean coffee. "I don't know..."

"Better yet, why don't we eat in the park? You must see the famous mermaid fountain, though I can't promise lime Jell-O."

The midday sun shone in Fancy's eyes as she squinted up at him. "You have the memory of an elephant, Mr. Quick. I might do well to reconsider that dinner invitation."

"Stella would be so disappointed," he glibly protested.

Just like that, Fancy found herself being escorted across the street to the café. Inside, Maybelle Clark, a thin, whipcord-tough woman who stood five-ten in her orthopedic shoes, was at the grill, deftly flipping burgers. Beau lounged in one of the booths, pretty much ignoring Willa, who sat across from him huddled over a strawberry milk shake while he made eyes at a pretty blonde at the counter.

As Fancy and Jeremiah left the café, lunch in hand, Aubergine Rizzo bounced over. Fancy was grateful she could make honest regrets when Aubergine asked her to collaborate on a new no-cal cookie recipe. "Sounds scrumptious," she amazed herself by saying. "Maybe next time." This cavalier attitude might have had something to do with the fact that Jeremiah had taken her hand, making it difficult for her to think straight.

The Fuzzy Frewer Memorial Park was a gladelike Eden tucked into a double lot on North Azalea. As they followed the circuitous crushed-gravel pathway to the fountain, Jeremiah explained that Fuzzy Frewer had been a local behemoth who'd played football with the Green Bay Packers in the seventies. In the eighties his main claim to fame had been the time he drank a case of beer in one afternoon and got stuck in the narrow doorway of his run-down trailer's bathroom. It had taken the fire department four hours to free him.

Fuzzy's trailer had been parked beside the immaculate grounds and clubhouse of the Garden Club. Because of a loophole in the zoning laws, the galled club members had been forced to stand by and watch Fuzzy turn the lot into white trash heaven. After he'd suffered a fatal heart attack, it was discovered that Fuzzy's will had deeded the lot to the Garden Club on two conditions: the club must name the park after him and also erect a mermaid statue/fountain in honor of his common-law wife, Dottie, a peroxide blonde who'd once performed as a mermaid in a Miami water show. Dottie had reportedly vanished during the four hours Fuzzy was stuck in the doorway, leaving town to become either a Las Vegas showgirl or a master carpenter—or so the garbled fable went. No one in Webster Station had heard from Dottie since, but Fuzzy had loved her to the end.

"Supposedly the statue was sculpted to Dottie's exact measurements," Jeremiah concluded. "Fuzzy's will was very precise about the specifications."

Fancy bit into a hot dog liberally piled with condiments and contemplated the buxom bronze mermaid. The depiction was rather lascivious. The curvy mermaid emerged from a spout of water, face rapturous, chest outthrust, arms flung wide. Thin streams of water sprayed from the seashells in her hands. Fancy decided Dottie Frewer was a woman she'd like to meet.

"...so the Society for Decency sent out a press release on the event," Jeremiah was saying. "Hester herself climbed up into the fountain—wearing a raincoat and galoshes—and painted old Dottie a bikini top."

Fancy licked a glob of mustard from her pinkie. Traces of purple paint were still visible in the creases and curves of the mermaid's prominent chest. Fancy's eyes widened. Apparently old Dottie was aroused. Permanently. It was a wonder that Hester hadn't wielded a chisel, as well as a paintbrush. "That must've been something to see."

"Pringle is especially proud of a close-up of Hester, nose to verdigris nipple, with the mermaid."

Fancy choked on a bite of bun. "Maybe I'm lucky Haute Water was only picketed," she said, reaching for her soda.

Jeremiah passed her a paper napkin and the cardboard dish of onion rings. "The very next day Mayor Mitzi was up there scraping off the paint."

"Bet *she* didn't wear galoshes." Fancy daintily selected a huge onion ring.

"She wore a very well-constructed bikini. And discovered pretty fast that it's next to impossible to scrape paint, suck in your gut and strike poses at the same time."

"You gotta love a town that would elect Mitzi mayor," Fancy said with a chortle, then added in a whisper, "Speak of the devil. Don't look now, but who do you think is lurking behind that hedge?" She grabbed Jeremiah's tie when he started to look. "No, no, don't move. I want to see what she'll do."

"What in blue blazes is that woman up to?" he demanded beneath his breath. They were sitting at the fountain's base. With Fancy so close beside him, putting his arm around her seemed the natural thing to do.

"Shh," she hissed. "She's disappeared."

A boxwood hedge quivered. Jeremiah turned his head, following the movement. "There's a red polyester derriere sticking out from behind that hemlock."

Fancy peered over his shoulder. "What does she think she's going to see?"

Although the question had been innocent, as soon as the words were out of her mouth Fancy became powerfully aware of their compromising position. She was half turned toward Jeremiah, her hand resting on his chest. She spread her fingers, testing the warmth of his skin through the thin shirt. A purely feminine anticipation sang in her veins.

Jeremiah was going to kiss her. And she wanted him to.

Fancy's lashes lowered; her breathing grew shallow. Tension pulsed between them. Jeremiah's hand slid upward over the polished cotton of her dress, his fingers seeking the silk of her dark hair. His mouth hovered near hers.

"Oh, Jeremiah . . ." she breathed.

He caught her hand in his, leaned even closer—and plucked off the onion ring that had slipped down onto her wrist.

"Oh! Jeremiah...?" she said in an entirely different tone. Her teeth clicked together as her mouth snapped shut. Dazed, she fingered her coral bracelet and felt a greasy residue. With hands gone numb, she brushed flecks of deep-fried batter from her lap. A kiss? How ridiculous! A kiss was certainly not something a dutiful daughter expects of her mother's dinner date. How impertinent. How...disappointing.

Jeremiah cleared his throat. "About Mitzi."

Of course. A man in Jeremiah's position wouldn't want to be caught kissing by his gossip columnist. She could understand that.

"Her column? 'Talk of the Town'?" he continued.

"Yes?"

"I hope it didn't embarrass you."

"Embarrass me?" Fancy laughed shrilly. "It takes more than a silly bit of gossip to embarrass Francine O'Brien."

"See, Mitzi is more or less uncontrollable. Heaven knows, I've tried. I didn't actually read her last column until it was printed. Still, one of my editors should've eliminated that last line about how you—"

"I *can* be a tad impulsive."

"—flashed me."

Fancy pasted a flippant smile on her face. "It's not as if you saw any—everything."

Jeremiah dumped the remains of their lunch into a paper sack. "Yeah, but for a moment there . . ."

Fancy concentrated on Dottie the Mermaid's ecstatic visage. At least someone was having fun. "As usual I have no excuse for my behavior."

"We don't see many thongs in Webster Station," he said with a more's-the-pity expression. "It being that flesh color was what really threw me."

"It was beige."

"With pink polka dots. You can see why I thought—"

"An optical illusion." Fancy was determined to interrupt until the subject was exhausted.

"And the way it molded itself to your—"

"Adhesive."

"What do you call that sort of top?"

A big mistake, she thought. One she'd never make again. She was definitely finished acting before thinking, leaping before looking. By the time she turned thirty, she would be a responsible, reliable, extremely dull adult. It would probably be advisable if she used the two months till then for practice. Being dull couldn't be as easy as it appeared.

"Totally strapless," she said in answer to Jeremiah's question while carefully avoiding his eyes. Something about them made her want to trash all her resolutions and fall into his arms. Not good, she told herself, fidgeting under his intense scrutiny. Not smart. But, oh, so tempting!

Apparently he saw—or had previously seen—something he liked. "Ahh," he murmured, the deeply satisfied tone of his voice vibrating against Fancy's edgy nerves.

He looked toward the tree that had concealed Mitzi. "I believe my columnist has departed. She's probably racing back to the office to file an update."

"Everyone reads 'Talk of the Town,' hmm? All of this morning's customers commented on it."

"When I tried to tame Mitzi's language most of my subscribers threatened to cancel. You won't always be the star of the front page, Fancy, but I can't make any promises about the gossip column. The most I can do is attempt some damage control."

"It was great publicity for Haute Water."

"Have there been any more problems on the Hester front?" he asked.

"All quiet since the picketing, although who knows what she's cooking up." Fancy's gaze lowered to his forearms, fascinated by the silken down of dark hair below the rolled-up sleeves of his crisp white shirt. She was immensely curious about him, even after inhaling Mitzi's verbal dossier. Jeremiah seemed a man at ease with himself and his life, yet she had to wonder about his past. Why had he divorced and moved to Webster Station?

Given the quality of Mitzi's gossip, she had to admit she might not be fully informed. Going by what she did know, however, it appeared on the surface that Jeremiah was exactly the sort of man she was determined to avoid. He'd left not only his wife but also his children when he'd moved to Webster Station. Mitzi claimed he rarely visited them.

Troubling speculation darkened her eyes. She knew all too well the feelings of anxiety and rejection that tormented children left behind.

She glanced at Jeremiah. He was so calm, so cool; she was so confused. And she kept forgetting that he was to be her mother's dinner companion, not her own!

Leaning back on braced arms, Fancy turned her face up to the sun. She could feel the cool mist of the fountain through the thin cotton of her dress. Okay, she thought, again reminding herself of her upcoming deadline for achieving total maturity. No more footloose and fancy-free stunts, no more flirtations with inappropriate men. It was about time one member of the fractured O'Brien family became sensible about these things. Her parents were hopeless; it would have to be her.

There, that was settled.

Then why was she imagining she could hear Cupid's laughter floating on the spring-sweet breeze?

Webster Station Chronicle
Talk of the Town by Mitzi Janeway

Spring Has Sprung
Don't y'all adore spring? Doesn't it make you want to strip off all your clothes and roll around in the fresh green grass? Now, Fritzi, don't go gettin' your knick-

ers in a knot. (Honestly, folks, would you believe Fritzi and I are twins if our birth certificates didn't swear it's so?) I'm not actually gonna run out and do it! But wouldn't you love to see the yardman's face if I did?!

Mama's Miracle Cure

Spring is busting out all over Webster Station. Even Mama Mitchell overcame her too-numerous-to-list health problems and attended the Spring Fling last Sunday night. She says that Fancy O'Brien worked wonders with a concoction brewed expressly for Mama. Mama absolutely swears it made the swelling in her ankles go down! I figure the proof's in the pudding, 'cause there was Mama, tottering about with just a cane and Mitch—her sweetie of a son—for support. I ought to try that poultice on the bags under my eyes the next time I've danced away the night at the Loblolly. Fancy, you send that recipe right on over to Janeway mansion, you hear?

THE BLIND LEADING THE BLAND

Y'all know your Mitzi J. lives and writes by a see-all and tell-(almost) all policy. But some bigwig, who shall remain nameless (but his initials are J.Q.), has laid down the law.

Well, *law*-di-dah!! As a result this next section is going to be what we in the gossip biz call blind items. Don't worry, folks, you won't need X-ray vision to figure them out!

Item #1: Who was the Miss Tall, Blond and Lovely seen dancing with an older man at the Spring Fling— much to the chagrin of her high school boyfriend? She may be eighteen and legal, but I bet her daddy still thinks this qualifies as robbing the cradle! Hint: Maybe it would be "dandy" if her "beau" works on her portfolio!

Item #2: Her name isn't quite Purple, her husband really knows how to deliver, and apparently they've been doing some home-cookin'! In nine months, give or take, she's gonna make a "special delivery" of her own!!

Item #3: What Mr. Bigwig was seen by yours truly cuddling beneath the mermaid fountain in Fuzzy Frewer Park with an "unplain" newcomer to Webster Station? Hint: They were *not* taking a bath!!

3

AFTER SCANNING the Wednesday-afternoon edition of the *Chronicle*, Fancy gave herself a stern talking-to in the bathtub. The paper was a sodden lump in the wastebasket; she didn't want Stella reading Mitzi's reference to "cuddling." Cuddling? Hah! All Jeremiah had been interested in was an onion ring.

In retrospect Fancy had decided the whole incident had been rather insulting—she *had* practically thrown herself in his arms.

In retaliation she'd begun to list all the reasons they'd never make a match. Jeremiah was much older than she and dating a father figure was too, too Freudian, especially for her. But somehow, after ruthless scrutiny of her psyche, that didn't ring true. The years between them were a gap, but not an excessive one. She had enough self-confidence to consider herself his equal.

Okay, then, what about Stella? She was at that very moment fussing over dinner while singing about a surrey with a fringe on top, a sure sign she was anticipating the arrival of her guest. Could be that Fancy had set things in motion to make Jeremiah her stepfather...

The very idea was enough to make her squirm, imagining herself as a guest on "Geraldo." Topic: Daughters Who Covet Their Mother's Husbands.

"Good grief," she said, sighing heavily enough to blow a path through the bubbles.

Actually, there was only one insurmountable item on her list: Jeremiah's status as a divorced father. According to Mitzi, his children were a long way from Webster Station, both physically and emotionally. What kind of man could so cavalierly dump his family once they were no longer convenient?

Fancy knew very well.

She propped her chin on her hand, a worry line appearing between her brows. Was she projecting her feelings about being abandoned by her own father onto Jeremiah's situation? Was the hurt she'd felt at thirteen still lurking in her almost thirty-year-old heart, ready to sabotage her emotions when they began to turn serious? Something, she admitted, they'd never come close to doing—until now.

Enough introspection for one day, she decided abruptly, slamming the lever that opened the drain. The complications of broken families were not something she liked to dwell on.

Toweling off, she looked into the steamy mirror to conclude her lecture. "Remember your resolution, Francine. As soon as you turn thirty, the very minute, you're going to become sensible and levelheaded. You'll find yourself a nice reliable man who believes marriage vows are forever." She swiped at the mirror's condensation, regarding her reflection dourly. "Someday your children will thank you."

Still frowning, she replaced the cork in the bottle of lavender she'd added to the bathwater. Everything in her history pointed to disaster if she didn't choose a husband very, very carefully. "Look at Dad," she said. "Three wives since Mom, all under the age of thirty. Or even Mom, who nitpicks fiancé after fiancé." She dropped her damp towel. "Clearly, O'Briens love neither wisely nor well."

"Fanceee?" called Stella from the direction of the kitchen. "Who're you talking to in there?"

"Just my heart," she said. "Trying to get it to listen to my head."

"Well, good luck on that!" Stella's voice now came from the other side of the bathroom door. "Try to be done by the time our guests arrive, won't you?"

"Don't you mean our guest? Our singular guest?" Fancy smiled smugly. On the theory that three's a crowd, she'd asked Brett, her shop clerk, to phone later this evening, providing Fancy with an excuse to leave the (potentially) happy couple alone.

"Oh, yes, our guest" was Stella's vague answer as her footsteps faded away.

Fancy scowled at the closed door. When Stella became vague, she was up to something. Fancy began to suspect that her own plans had suddenly veered out of control, as even her best-laid plans were inclined to do.

"Nonsense," she murmured, not confidently. After initial reluctance, Stella had acquiesced to this dinner quite gracefully. Even Mitzi, and thus the townspeople, could be set straight with a few carefully chosen words dropped in the appropriate ear.

As for Jeremiah Quick, Fancy was sure her attraction to him had been a minor aberration. A matter of the heady spring air and . . . proximity.

Maybe a smidgen of animal magnetism.

And a soupçon of chemistry.

A dollop of genuine liking.

And, okay, a teensy-weensy itty-bitty fleck of old-fashioned lust.

Nothing she couldn't handle.

STELLA HAD MOVED FROM *Oklahoma* to *South Pacific* and was adding fresh dill to a pot of simmering soup when Fancy entered the kitchen, shrugging into a peach-and-mauve bathrobe. Fancy took her mother's good mood to mean she'd realized what a major improvement Jeremiah was over Rupert Dailey, her last fiancé. Stella claimed she'd broken her engagement to Rupert because he wore matching argyle socks and sweaters in winter and white vinyl belts and shoes in summer. Jeremiah's style, while rather conservative in Fancy's opinion, would be more to her liking.

"'I'm gonna wash that man right outta my hair,'" Stella sang, the steam from the soup kinking her bangs. Fancy decided not to take the lyrics literally.

She rolled her bottom lip between her teeth. "Have you ever considered coloring your hair, Mom? It'd take ten years off your age."

Stella turned, jamming her fists onto her hips. "Why in the world would I want to look younger?"

Bad idea. "No reason, no reason whatsoever, Mom." Fancy took refuge behind the refrigerator door. "Uh, how's dinner coming along?"

Stella sniffed and flapped her apron.. "I've earned every one of these gray hairs."

So she'd often reminded her harum-scarum daughter. "My salad looks good," Fancy ventured brightly, snitching a slice of cucumber off the top.

Stella brandished the wooden spoon. "Go on with you, Fancy." Dripping soup, she consulted her wristwatch. "Seven twenty-four and you're still in your bathrobe!"

Fancy was peering over the fridge door at the dining alcove. She'd come straight from the shop to lay the table with a Battenburg-lace cloth and three place settings of blue-willow china. Now the small table seemed awfully crowded, not entirely because of the centerpiece Stella had added. Fancy craned her neck. "Why've you—?"

Stella grabbed a handful of mauve terry cloth. "Never mind," she tutted, tugging Fancy in the other direction.

"Wear the pale gray chiffon, dear. You'll look like a dream. My pearls would make an exquisite finishing touch."

"Mom, you're supposed to be the star of this show, not me," Fancy protested as she allowed herself to be steered toward her small bedroom.

"Yes, yes, of course..." Stella's retreating voice was once again suspiciously vague.

Unobtrusive, Fancy decided as she looked into her closet, would be her watchword for the evening. She took out a plain bone-colored knit with bat-wing sleeves. A dull, melt-into-the-woodwork sort of dress. After getting the ball rolling between Jeremiah and Stella, she'd slip unnoticed out of the room to take Brett's call. The plan was perfect in its simplicity. It had almost worked with Rupert Dailey.

She was adjusting a gold chain-link belt around her waist when the doorbell rang. "I've got it," she yelled, hurrying to the front door. She hoped Jeremiah thought to bring flowers. Stella appreciated traditional courtesies.

A fistful of white lilacs, exactly like the ones on the Mitchells' bush next door, was the first thing she saw after opening the door. Mitch Mitchell was the second.

"Mitch!" she said in surprise. He was beaming. Fifteen strands of hair had been meticulously arranged across the top of his bald head—his very shiny and smooth bald head.

Fancy smiled quizzically. "Mitch?" she echoed.

"Mitch!" said Stella, coming up behind her daughter. "So glad you could make it."

Amazingly, his smile broadened. "Mama's gonna heat up the chicken soup Aubergine Rizzo brought over after the Spring Fling. She was feeling poorly, so she told me to take you up on your invitation." The look on his face was that of a poleaxed steer. Mama usually preferred to keep him—at fifty-two the youngest of her six children—at her beck and call.

"And how *is* Mama?" Stella asked solicitously, taking his arm to lead him into the living room. Smoldering in silence, Fancy watched them go.

"She's recovered her spirits," answered Mitch. "Perked right up when I was getting ready to leave. Made me change my tie and cut you some of our lilacs."

"How thoughtful," Stella cooed as the doorbell chimed again. "Fancy, get that, will you?" she called offhandedly.

Fancy obeyed. Jeremiah stood on the doorstep, one hand clasping a bottle of wine.

Fancy pressed her palm to the top of her head, checking if it was still in its proper place. It was; there had to be another explanation for her lobotomized feeling. The laugh lines around Jeremiah's eyes deepened as he grinned. "You're always grinning at me," she said peevishly. "You must find me tremendously amusing."

"I hope you'll take that as a compliment."

A returning sense of humor teased with her pursed lips, threatening to curl them into a smile. Fancy lowered her gaze and noted he was again wearing crisply pleated trousers and a plain white shirt, although this time his patterned tie was neatly knotted and he'd added a tailored navy blue sports coat. Fancy caught the scent of his after-shave, outdoorsy with a hint of citrus. Or maybe the scent was his own. Hadn't she read somewhere that the deciding factor in mutual attraction was a person's smell? There had to be a reason for her reaction to Jeremiah, despite the list of why it shouldn't happen. Pheromones were as good a culprit as any.

"Fanceee," Stella trilled, "shut that door. You're letting in a million bugs."

Fancy peeled her tongue from the roof of her mouth and murmured, "Please come in, Jeremiah."

"I guarantee I'm not a bug," he said with a laugh and offered her the wine.

She grabbed it, nervous fingers caressing the cool glass. "Thank you."

Jeremiah used the tip of his thumb to brush away a strand of hair that had fallen across one of her eyes. Fancy flinched. He tucked the strand behind her ear, letting his fingertips trace its pink curves. "You're welcome," he said, matching her solemnity.

"Mitch Mitchell is here." Her voice was flat, but there were strange little tingles skittering over her skin.

"Oh, really?" Relief and pleasure mingled in Jeremiah's expression. "So we're a foursome."

"Imagine that." Fancy was finally realizing just how neatly her mother had turned the tables. But why with Mitch, of all people? Mitch was a good-natured Milquetoast with even less verve and style than Rupert Dailey! Why *Mitch* when she could've had— "Jeremiah," she breathed. Oh, Lord, what was she going to do with him now?

"Yes?" he asked, and she blushed, afraid he would read her mind. A naughty little devil was sitting on her shoulder, whispering instructions about what she should do with Jeremiah—definitely not things she'd dare repeat. A vision of black satin sheets and smoldering tiger eyes flashed through her wild—and getting wilder—imagination.

Jeremiah saved her from any explanation. "I imagine we'll have a very pleasant evening." *Pleasant* was not the word for what she was imagining! He crooked his arm toward her. "Shall we join Stella and Mitch?"

Carefully placing her hand on his sleeve, she entered the living room as if tiptoeing through broken glass. She would have to negotiate this evening the same way if she was to come out of it with her resolution and her heart intact.

My heart? she thought in alarm. No, no, no. Not her heart. She'd always been willing to risk everything *but* her heart. Not even Jeremiah Quick—intriguing as she found him—would change that.

Stella clasped her hands with satisfaction. "Isn't this cozy? Just the four of us?" Mitch chuckled in agreement.

"A perfect number," said Jeremiah.

The three of them are gloating, Fancy complained inwardly. Outwardly she smiled.

Jeremiah glanced around the room. "It's hard to believe you've been here such a short time. The house looks so comfortable and gracious."

"That's Fancy's talent," Stella said cheerfully. "I do the cooking."

The interior of the O'Briens' cottage was very feminine, decorated in chintz, lace and frills. The walls were painted in broad ice blue and ivory stripes, and the carpeting was the same gray blue as Fancy's eyes. The sofa and armchairs were big overstuffed pieces that the men settled into easily. Lush ferns on a white wicker planter set off the front window, which had been simply adorned with an artfully draped length of lace.

Still holding the wine bottle, Fancy dropped onto the hassock beside Jeremiah's armchair. His legs were stretched out before her, and for a moment she couldn't help but admire the defined muscle in one long lean thigh. She bit her lip and looked up, trying to concentrate as her mother and Mitch chatted on the sofa. Stella patted his knee companionably. Mitch chuckled, lacing his fingers together over his round belly. Stella spoke to Jeremiah. He leaned forward to answer, resting his elbows on his knees. Fancy was aware of his sonorous voice but not his words. The bottle rolled silently out of her limp fingers and onto the rug.

She'd been struck with the clear realization that Stella didn't want Jeremiah.

But I do, Fancy thought. *I do. I do. I do!*

Fancy moaned under her breath, making the others turn her way. She blinked and looked from Stella to Mitch to Jeremiah, who was grinning at her again, his honey-colored eyes alert and amused. Her heart hammered like a tom-tom as they patiently waited for her to speak.

"I made the salad," she offered lamely.

Stella clapped and jumped to her feet, smoothing the skirt of her stylish claret-colored shift. "Yes, how about dinner, fellows?" She motioned Mitch to the table. "We're having roast beef, a real man's meal, but first my special fennel soup."

Jeremiah stood and extended his hand to Fancy. "May I escort you to the table?"

She looked up into his handsome face. His skin was lightly tanned—he obviously didn't spend all his time in a stuffy newsroom—showing his age only by the tracing of lines on his forehead, the crinkling at the corners of his eyes and the deeper slashes made when he smiled. His nose was narrow and high-bridged, his cheekbones and jawline chiseled. It was an intelligent, lively, witty and wicked face. A truly wonderful face.

It seemed to Fancy that she would be saying yes to more than dinner if she placed her hand in his. However, it was not in her temperament to linger for long.

She picked up the wine bottle with one hand, then extended the other. Their fingers touched. Though the contact was light, she felt each one of his fingertips burn hers, a flash point that leapt, sizzling, to ignite a fire somewhere deep inside of her. Her eyes lit up, searching his. Did he feel it, too?

Jeremiah clasped her hand and pulled her to her feet, using a bit more force than necessary so that she was drawn quite close to his broad chest. He brought their interlaced fingers up, pressing a quick kiss on her knuckles just before his other hand came over to blanket hers.

"Come along, then, sweetheart," he murmured, and they went in to dinner.

FANCY SWALLOWED HUMILITY with the anise-flavored soup.

There are times when one's foibles and follies are laid out for examination. This was one of them. Never before had she so clearly seen the reasons behind her campaign to find her mother a husband. Illuminating though it was, the revelation was not especially well-timed.

Stella continued, oblivious. "...so there was thirteen-year-old Fancy, towing home her algebra teacher for an introductory dinner. And this was a girl who'd entered the rebellious phase with a vengeance. She briefly took up smoking—only cigarettes as far as I knew—and truancy and pouting and unremittingly black clothing. Her hair looked like a rat's nest, but I kept telling myself that at least she hadn't shaved it into a Mohawk!"

"I was one of the first punks in Michigan," Fancy said. "I couldn't quite bring myself to shave my head, though."

"One season, John Riggins of the Redskins had a Mohawk," Mitch contributed helpfully.

Stella nodded as if that was relevant. "And Mr. Chester Merriweather became my first fiancé."

"Your first, Stella?" asked Jeremiah. "Exactly how many have you had?"

She giggled girlishly. "Three. Well, four, if we count the one I married."

"You've had four fiancés?" Mitch's eyes bulged. "Four fiancés!"

"It was all Fancy's fault," Stella said without an ounce of compunction. "Richard, my ex, was married the very day Fancy brought home Chester. I'm sure you can see the corollary in that!" Stella laughed gaily as her daughter squirmed. "Richard had eloped with Miss Cherry Blossom, the type of girl who thinks clothes make the woman—or the man, for that matter. Richard had begun to wear Armani at the same time my tolerance was wearing thin. It became obvious our marriage contract was not long for this world." Stella's benevolent gaze sharpened as it zeroed in on Jeremiah. "Do you own any Armani suits?"

He put down his spoon. "Not since I moved to Webster Station."

"Good," said Stella. "I can't abide a fussy man."

Fancy's teeth gritted around her spoon. Why was her mother checking Jeremiah out? Was she interested, after all? She'd better not be!

"I only wear Vernon's Big and Tall," Mitch put in eagerly.

Patting his hand, Stella peered into his empty soup bowl. "You're a man with a hearty appetite," she said approvingly. "How's your appetite, Jeremiah?"

He smiled as he lazily looked toward Fancy. "Ravenous."

The word conjured up all sorts of images—none of them involving food. Finding Jeremiah's gaze as potent as his touch, Fancy gripped her chair to stop herself from sliding out of it and puddling on the floor.

Stella's eyebrows rose. "Then you're sure to enjoy Fancy—her salad, that is. Why don't you fetch it, dear?"

Uncharacteristically silent, Fancy lurched to her feet and collected the soup bowls, then retreated to the kitchen. Even there, she couldn't avoid Jeremiah's gaze. He followed her every movement as she tossed the salad with homemade peppercorn dressing. She twitched her shoulders to shoo away the tiny needles of excitement pricking her skin. A frilly curl of radicchio skittered across the countertop.

"What happened to Chester?" Mitch was asking when Fancy, plus a salad but minus her composure and a few croutons, returned to the table.

Stella began to dish out the salad. "Life was a theorem to Chester. I couldn't live that way. Besides, he tended to leave his slide rule in my bed. You might not consider a slide rule a lethal weapon, but hop into bed with too much oomph, and it'll stab you in the—" At her daughter's glare, Stella stopped to toss a cherry tomato into her mouth. "I guess you get the idea, huh?"

Beads of sweat had popped out on Mitch's brow. Jeremiah shook his head. "I'm beginning to see where Fancy came by her outrageous tendencies, Stella."

"Yes, Mother," Fancy pointedly agreed. "You can be . . . impulsive." She sent Stella a look that pleaded for a return to more conventional dinner conversation. What was wrong with talking about the weather?

Stella blithely ignored her. "Would you like to hear about fiancé number two?" she asked the table at large. "Bolt Devonshire."

"What kinda name is that?" Mitch asked with dismay.

"Bolt was a washed-up male model." Stella's eyes became a little glassy as she remembered their stormy interlude. "That man had pecs to die for."

Dressing spattered Mitch's tie when his fork jiggled. Fancy and Jeremiah exchanged amused glances as Stella dipped her napkin into a water goblet and began to minister to the tie with motherly solicitude. "Fancy arranged a blind date for me and Bolt around the same time Richard was marrying his second little chickie," she said. "Thought I needed a young stud to keep up with the Joneses."

"I had your best interests at heart, Mom. Maybe I was a little confused..." Fancy recalled those days. Her father had divorced his second wife just when she was getting used to having a twenty-four-year-old stepmother. He'd married another young thing, which only worsened the situation because Fancy had been seventeen by then. She'd grown out of her rebellious stage and into her quasi-sophisticated period, calling her parents Stella and Rich. Bolt had been her idea of sauce for the gander, because the goose already had his.

"Bolt was extremely good for the ego," Stella mused. "I might have married him if it hadn't been for that terrible sunburn..." She and Bolt had gone to the Bahamas intending to elope. Her sunburn had postponed the ceremony, and two days later she'd come to her senses.

"Bolt was my idea of a hip stepdad," Fancy remembered. "He knew Cheryl Tiegs and Christie Brinkley. He'd been to Marrakech. He wore Paco Rabanne and a gold chain around his neck."

"Do they still sell that after-shave?" Jeremiah asked. "I'll run out and buy a bottle if that's what it takes to be your ideal man."

Fancy wrinkled her nose. "I should hope my taste has matured since then."

"You gotta tell us about fiancé number three," Mitch urged, finding Stella much more entertaining than watching sitcoms with Mama.

"By then it was the mid-eighties," Stella began.

"Dad, by the way, is a big-time Republican fund-raiser," Fancy inserted. "He was in his glory."

"The only sour note was his wife," said Stella. "Kaitlin had shocked us all by turning into a stockbroker. The money was nice, but she was more concerned with making her first million than catering to Richard."

"Which meant another divorce." Fancy sighed. By that point, she'd gained a college degree and a job at Senator Smack's office. She and her father were finally living in the same city, but beyond a few shared invites to glad-handing lobbyists' cocktail parties, he was too busy for Fancy.

"And soon another marriage for my ex. Heather is still his wife. They have a two-year-old named Brittany and are heavily into family values."

Fancy snorted. "Right."

"Around that time, my dear daughter introduced me to an actuary named Rupert Dailey."

"He was a really nice guy."

"But bo-o-oring," Stella said.

Fancy looked from Jeremiah to Mitch. "After a two-year engagement, Stella ups and decides she can't marry Rupert because he wears matching white belts and shoes and signed an agreement to buy a condo in a Florida retirement village."

"Not only was Rupe boring," Stella said, "he was o-l-d."

"A state Stella is determined to avoid," Fancy said wryly.

Her mother rose as regally as a queen. "Not at all. I intend to get old. I just don't intend to *act* old." She lifted her salad plate, shooting a pointed glance at Fancy. "It's all a state of mind."

Fancy thought of her upcoming thirtieth birthday. She was only just beginning to realize why thirty, while not what anyone could properly call old, represented such momentous upheaval....

Not long after his first taste of D.C. power and glamour, Fancy's father had asked Stella for a divorce. She'd been thirty-two, trained for nothing but housekeeping and child-rearing, but she'd moved herself and Fancy back to Michigan and gone about building them a better life.

Miss Cherry Blossom hadn't even lasted till she was twenty-five. Kaitlin was toast by twenty-eight.

Fancy had to wonder if Heather also had nightmares about her thirtieth birthday.

"Time for the roast beef," Stella announced. She and Fancy went into the kitchen, leaving Jeremiah and Mitch sitting in silence. They looked rather shell-shocked, something to which first-time dinner guests at the O'Briens were prone.

Stella was bending over the open oven door when Fancy sidled up to her. "You never told me about Mr. Merriweather's slide rule before," she whispered. "I'm surprised at you, Mother."

Stella lifted the beef from the roasting pan and set it on a platter. "It was the seventies," she said matter-of-factly. "I was a divorcée and they hadn't invented all these terrible diseases yet." She dumped green beans into a dish.

"But he was my teacher."

"I'd have awarded him a gold star."

"My *algebra* teacher."

"Bosh," Stella said, airily dismissing the subject. "Done to a turn," she said of the golden brown potato *galette*. Deftly turning the pancake onto another blue-willow plate, she garnished it with sprigs of rosemary and thyme. "Let's get back to our guests."

"No more embarrassing stories. Promise me," Fancy pleaded.

"Since when have you worried about being embarrassed?"

Since she'd decided to turn her life around. Since she'd started caring about what Jeremiah Quick thought of her. But Fancy didn't explain any of that as she picked up the vegetables. "Can't we just argue about politics like normal people?"

Stella's eyes gleamed. "Oh, I'd like that!" She sailed off
to the table, the platter of roast beef held high.

Fancy groaned. "Uh, Mom? Wait a minute, Mom. I didn't
mean..."

THEY WERE HALFWAY through the main course and in the
midst of a heated discussion of a recent Supreme Court decision when the doorbell rang. "I'll get it," Stella volun-
teered, throwing down her napkin.

Jeremiah was about to make another point when he was
interrupted by Stella's cry of surprise. He looked toward the
sound of heavy feet stomping through the living room.
Hester Hightower appeared in the dining alcove's open
doorway. Trouble, he thought immediately. Big trouble.

Hester had stopped in her tracks. "Albert Mitchell!"

Seated with his back to her, Mitch froze with a mouth full
of potatoes. Jeremiah watched as a curious blend of apprehension and guilt spread across the druggist's purpling face.
His eyes darted from side to side, as frantic as a trapped
rabbit.

"Albert Mitchell! What in the world are you doing here?"
Mitch's shoulders slumped lower and lower as Hester ha-
rangued him. "Albert, you answer me right this minute.
Right this minute!"

"Mitch is our dinner guest, which is more than I can say
for you, Hester."

Hester whipped around to confront Stella. Her scathing
gaze swept the other woman, the room and the dining table. "I wonder if Mama knows about this," she said to the
back of Mitch's head.

At least on this point, Mitch had a defense. "Mama told
me to come. She even sent flowers." He pointed a stubby
finger at the urn of white lilacs set on a lace-draped side table.

"Mama told you to come?" Hester repeated in disbelief. "Mama would never send you over to have dinner with the—the O'Brien hussies!"

Jeremiah stood up abruptly, nearly toppling his chair. "Enough, Hester," he said harshly. He would not listen as she resorted to name-calling. Fancy was not a hussy. She was a free spirit. "You're being unforgivably rude and disruptive. If you can't apologize, at least have the good grace to leave."

Hester's lips tightened, her gray-brown sausage curls quivering as she fought to contain a biting response. The rattling of the sheaf of papers crushed to her chest seemed to remind her of her mission. She held it out to Fancy. "Take it," she directed, defying Jeremiah's glower. "I'll gladly leave, Mr. Quick, as soon as I've conducted the business that has forced me to enter this den of iniquity."

Jeremiah's lips thinned, but Fancy stood and touched his hand. "Let me deal with this," she told him, approaching Hester as if the older woman were a ticking bomb. He saw she meant to handle the situation with a decorum Hester might've done well to mimic. "What have you got for me, Mrs. Hightower?"

Hester slapped the papers into Fancy's extended palm. "It's a petition," she said with a bit less fury. "I trust you'll find it self-explanatory." She drew herself up with a deep breath, slinging her heavy canvas bag over one shoulder. "If you'll excuse me, Mr. Quick? *Mr.* Mitchell?"

Mitch swabbed his brow with a napkin and Jeremiah shrugged, still glowering but aware that Fancy was watching his reaction with an interested air. "Good evening, Mrs. Hightower," Jeremiah said formally, and moved to hold out Fancy's chair. She favored him with a small smile as she sat. He breathed her scent of lavender, his tension easing.

Hester had nodded curtly at a seething Stella, swiveled, and marched to the front door. Jeremiah expected her to slam it but, instead, heard a gentle click.

"Well," Fancy murmured, tapping the papers against the table.

"I don't know what's gotten into that woman," Jeremiah commented as he held out Stella's chair. "She's always been cranky, but this was over the top. And why did Mitch's presence make her so angry?"

They turned to Mitch, who drained his wineglass in a gulp. "Hester and I went on a date," was his mumbled confession. "We saw *Arsenic and Old Lace*."

"Aha!" Stella grinned and a devious look crossed her face.

Mitch brightened. "I guess Hester was jealous!" The possibility seemed to please him.

"That's no excuse for her behavior," said Jeremiah, although his mouth was beginning to twitch.

"Oh, I rather enjoy being thought of as a wicked woman." Stella speared a succulent slice of meat. "More beef, Mitch?" she asked coquettishly.

"Why not? A man like me needs lots of red meat." Simpering, Stella loaded his plate.

Jeremiah and Fancy again exchanged amused glances. "What's in that petition?" he asked in a strangled voice.

Fancy smoothed the creased papers. "'We, the undersigned, wish to lodge our vehement protest against the reprehensible display of public nudity that occurred at the establishment known as Haute Water on Saturday... blah, blah, blah. Such lewd and indecent acts desecrate public morality, and we, the citizens of Webster Station, shall not allow... blah, blah, blah.'" She scanned the rest of the page. "It goes on like that for three-quarters of a page. Pure Hester rhetoric."

"How many signatures?" Stella asked grimly, picturing a boycott of Haute Water and future financial ruin.

Fancy flipped through several pages. "They've triple-spaced the signatures. Can't be more than twenty, tops." She looked to Jeremiah. "Is that enough to cause us trouble?"

"I suppose it depends on how much of a ruckus they create. You saw how the picketing fizzled out at your grand opening. The ladies in the Society for Decency are usually more bluster than substance."

"We'll fight her tooth and nail," Stella said with relish.

"I'm sure there's no need of that," Jeremiah drawled. He glanced at Fancy with hooded eyes. She squirmed. He'd been watching her squirm all evening and it had done his ego good to know that she might be as bamboozled as he. "If Fancy stays out of bathtubs, Hester and her ilk probably won't give you anymore trouble than you can handle."

"Huh," Stella grunted. "Just try and stop the girl."

Fancy poured herself a healthy glass of the excellent red Bordeaux Jeremiah had supplied. Intoxication of a different sort simmered inside him as he contemplated visions of Fancy and bathtubs and finding ways to direct her wild tendencies to a more private venue. "What do you say, Fancy?" he asked.

She set the bottle down with a thud. "I'm not making any promises."

IN THE BIG, cedar-shingled house next door, Mama Mitchell hefted herself up from a kitchen chair and gathered the detritus of her solo supper: a microwave-lasagna box, two drained bottles of wine cooler and a wilted ice-cream carton. Leaning heavily on her cane, she thrust the remains into the bottom of the trash can. Then she plucked Aubergine's soup off the stove and dumped it down the garbage disposal.

Satisfied that her tracks were covered, Mama lurched to her wheelchair, settling herself into it with a sigh. She wheeled through the dining room, the foyer and the uncarpeted front parlor, glancing with a practiced eye out each window as she passed. Cherry Street had been quiet since Hester had departed the O'Brien cottage.

Mama didn't turn on the light once she'd maneuvered into position in the glass-enclosed side porch. She peered out at the cottage, her excellent night vision seeking out anything of possible interest. They hadn't pulled the curtains in the dining area; she could easily pick out her son's chrome dome and Stella's gray head. Mama sighed heavily. You could bet the rent there'd be no action when Mitch was around. But where had the other pair gotten to?

There—a shadow had moved in the backyard. "I'm gonna gitcha," Mama whispered as she painstakingly searched each trunk and branch and leaf in the garden. They really should trim back some of those bushes. Maybe she'd suggest it to Stella, all innocentlike.

"Gotcha!" she cried triumphantly, snatching up the binoculars she kept clipped to the arm of her wheelchair. She focused on the couple in the garden, chuckling with glee. Her son thought she was into bird-watching. How much more thrilling to scout for cooing lovebirds of a different feather! Without lowering her binoculars, Mama lifted the phone she wore on a cord around her neck and punched out a number.

"M.J.?" she said with a hushed voice. "Hot Wheels here." The couple magnified by her high-powered binoculars moved closer together. "Have I got a live one for you!" she crowed.

STELLA AND MITCH were having dessert and coffee inside, but Jeremiah had said he'd prefer a breath of fresh air. He'd lured Fancy into the garden, and now they stood under the branches of a flowering cherry tree, sheltered by its pinky white flowers as if they'd been transported to a sweet-scented cloud. Except Fancy doubted that angels were allowed to feel the human, earthy, *lusty* things she was feeling.

Her resolution was rapidly becoming a distant memory. In fact, her brain, buzzing with the thrall of male-female interaction, was having a hard time recalling what it had been. Something about inappropriate men. Wasn't it?

Jeremiah Quick no longer seemed so terribly inappropriate.

"Um, Jeremiah?" she whispered huskily. "Are you feeling what I'm feeling?"

"Yeah." The garden was so dark she could barely make out his features; she used that as an excuse to move a step closer. "I feel like we're being watched."

"Oh." She looked toward the house, hoping he couldn't see her mortified face. No one was silhouetted against the window's yellow squares of light. "I don't think we're being watched."

"We are. There's a definite itch between my shoulder blades."

She nodded at the Mitchells' big barn of a house. "Do you think . . . Mama?"

"There's very little that happens in Webster Station without Mama's knowledge." Knuckles under her jaw, Jeremiah tilted Fancy's chin up. She was beginning to recognize the lilt that entered his voice whenever he was going to tease her. "You, sugar, are probably the best thing to happen to the town gossips since Bertie Lampkin ran off with the vacuum salesman."

"Is that so?" Fancy giggled nervously. His touch was again sending her emotions into confusion. She was skittish, wanting to dance away from her uncertainty about him. Yet she was also strongly attracted, yearning to feel his arms around her.

"You don't understand the magnitude of my statement." He paused for effect. "Bertie Lampkin is a man."

She snorted in amusement. "Well, Mama feels nothing but goodwill toward me. I'm sure she'll treat me kindly even when she gossips."

"Ah, yes. The miracle cure, according to Mitzi."

He sounded so cool! "A slight exaggeration. It was a simple chamomile-and-bittersweet wrap."

"Bittersweet," he repeated, his voice coming from deep in his chest, a little rough, a little thick. Maybe he wasn't as cool as she supposed.

"It's a plant. A nightshade."

Jeremiah's chuckle tumbled across her exquisitely acute senses. "And perhaps also the taste of your lips?" he murmured, one hand slipping around to the nape of her neck.

"I hope not," she still had the presence of mind to retort. "Bittersweet can be poisonous."

Jeremiah exerted a bit of pressure and she found herself nestled against him, her heavy aching breasts pressed to his hard chest. She made a tiny satisfied purring sound and, with her head cradled in his palm, trustingly offered him her parted lips.

"Maybe we can avoid the bitter and go straight for the sweet," Jeremiah whispered.

The screen door banged open. "Fanceee," Stella called. "Brett's on the phone for you."

Jeremiah didn't budge. Fancy turned her head sideways slightly, her eyes still locked on his. "Tell her I'm busy," she yelled.

"Indeed." Stella's arch voice floated out over the garden and the door swung shut. Moments later, the first strains of a mellow bluesy recording wafted from the house. A breeze stirred the cherry blossoms, catching the soft music and lifting it in invisible arms so the velvet night sky was rich with sound and perfume and desire.

Fancy released a long sigh. "Oh, Jeremiah, you were supposed to be my mother's date."

His mouth was against her hair, his words muffled by its thickness. "She didn't think so." His warm breath tickled her ear. "I didn't think so." The tip of his tongue flicked her sensitive lobe, and she shivered. "Only you thought so."

They began to sway back and forth to the music, less of a dance than a sensual caress of one body against another. A deep female satisfaction surged through Fancy. She'd never felt anything quite so potent.

"Okay, so I was wrong," she admitted softly. "Very, very wrong."

"Glad to hear it."

"Are you ever going to get around to kissing me?" she demanded, no longer caring if the whole world was watching.

He laughed. "Good things come to those who wait."

She stood on tiptoe to bring her lips closer to his, her hands clutching at his shoulders. "I've never been good at waiting."

"You probably open all your presents on Christmas Eve."

"And eat the frosting off the cake first."

"You're a scamp," Jeremiah teased, his fingertips gentle as they traced the bones of her face. "With the face of a mischievous angel," he whispered. She shivered with impatience as he slid his other hand to the small of her back. "Yes, I'm going to kiss you, Fancy. I'm going to kiss you more times than you can count."

Her dimple reappeared. "One will do for now," she said saucily.

"Oh, no. No. One will never be enough."

He bent his head and kissed her. It was a slow and deep kiss, the kind that sends a voluptuous sweetness plummeting through a woman's body until every inch of her knows she's been thoroughly and fantastically kissed. Fancy's head fairly whirled with the knowledge.

His tongue coaxed her lips open. "Mmm," she moaned, tasting a hint of red wine and then just Jeremiah. He was sweet, tart, warm, slick, male. Very male. She touched the tip of her tongue to the edge of his teeth and a razor-sharp thrill sliced through her.

His embrace tightened. She wanted to burrow into the hard lean length of him. She wanted it all. And, she knew he did, too. He was already aroused. With the last dazed shred of her reason, Fancy acknowledged that she was much too quickly losing all restraint. None of this had been in her plans. Yet her body clamored for his, her mouth eagerly confirming her desire. Despite her sporadic attempts at decorum, at that moment Fancy wanted nothing more than for Jeremiah to pick her up and carry her off into the deep dark night.

For Jeremiah, the point of no return was arriving more swiftly than he'd thought possible. It seemed that everything with this woman was immediate and irrepressible and impulsive. While that fact gladdened his heart, he knew he had to stop—it was now or never. Summoning his control, he eased his mouth from Fancy's with a slow delicious slide and one final quick nibble. She gave a tremulous sigh and rested her cheek against his chest, where he knew she had to be feeling the runaway thundering of his heart.

Jeremiah lifted his face to the cool night air and smiled, exultant. For him, meeting Fancy had been a *coup de foudre*. Love at first sight. He knew, absolutely knew without a sliver of a doubt, what he wanted—Fancy.

He also knew that he must proceed at a slow and easy pace. Although there'd been the quiver of surrender in Fancy's body—and in his the sudden mad urge to grab at quick gratification—Jeremiah knew he must possess her heart, as well as her body. Nothing less would suffice.

Fancy, so darlingly impulsive, thought she wanted to rush.

Jeremiah knew better.

And he would woo her until she knew it, too.

Webster Station Chronicle
Talk of the Town by Mitzi Janeway

And the Blind Shall See

You dear people! How sweet y'all are to be so concerned. After the flood of calls (a veritable deluge!) you made to my boss, your humble columnist is back in her place.

That's right. No more blind items! Of course, I *am* wondering why some of you couldn't figure them out, but for those of you still out of the loop, here're the answers:

Couple #1: Jessica Dandy and Beau Quick. Couple #2: Bart and Aubergine Rizzo (and the bun in her oven) Couple #3: Jeremiah Quick and Fancy O'Brien. Isn't this just like "Love Connection"?

Quick on the Draw

Oh, those dashing Quick brothers! What would my column be without them? Handsome Beauregard is cutting an absolute swath through the ranks of W.S.'s eligible ladies. Last week Jessica Dandy, this week Brett Randolph and Clarissa Boggs. My, my, Beau, how you do get around! I'm just awaitin' for the day you give us mature ladies a chance. Remember, a woman is like a fine wine—she must be properly aged. And full-bodied don't hurt none, either! Anyhoo, our Casanova was seen lunching with Brett and then out very publicly at the Loblolly with Miss Boggs. Clarissa shore do love them Singapore Slings! I did wonder what her fella of three years' standing, trooper Bobby Vernon (who's so adorable in his uniform), had to say about that. Then, *surprise*, who should stop Beau for speeding out on I-95 but you-know-who? I hear the ticket was a whopper!!

Meanwhile . . . Under the Cherry Tree

I've saved the best for last! It seems a mighty cozy foursome was caught red-handed when Mrs. Hester Hightower stormed their castle last Wednesday night. Who should La Prude barge in on but Stella and Fancy O'Brien having dinner with Mitch Mitchell and Jeremiah Quick!! How I'd have loved to be a fly on that particular wall!

Hester gave Fancy a petition protesting the goings-on in her bathtub. Fancy's tub, not Hester's. (I'm sure nothing happens in Hester's tub except a whole lot o' scrubbin'!) We all know (don't we?) that H.H. has set her cap for M.M., so Hester left the cottage with her bloomers in a bunch and steam coming from her ears! Then Stella calmly served Mitch a big old plate of cheesecake for dessert! The way to a man's heart, right, Stel?

And if that's not enough to set your tongues awagging, Jeremiah and Miss Fancy-pants had apparently retired to the garden. I'm not making this stuff up, folks—I have a very reliable witness! I'll leave it up to your imagination as to what the darling couple did under that cherry tree. (!!) Perhaps a touch of discretion will save my patootie from gettin' the bootie!

4

THE IDEA WAS STUCK in her head, going round and round in an infinite loop.

A totally inappropriate kick-up-your-heels affair. Fun, flagrant, flamboyant. The final fling of her carefree twenties.

What could it hurt?

Cradling a vase of hyacinths, Fancy leaned into the corner of the display area and looked toward the *Chronicle* building. Jeremiah's car had just pulled into the adjacent lot. She watched as he stepped out of the silver convertible, slammed the door, then reached inside for his briefcase. Maureen Rowe, the redheaded owner of the fabric store on Narcissus, stopped him in the middle of the sidewalk, forcing other pedestrians to go around them as she talked, fast and flirty. Even from her distant vantage point, Fancy could deduce that much.

She worried her lower lip between her teeth. No doubt about it, Jeremiah Quick was a desirable man. And she wasn't the only one who'd noticed.

Shortly Jeremiah disappeared into the building. The amazonian Mo continued on to Buy the Bolt, the persimmon peplum of her suit bouncing up and down on her swaying hips.

Fingering a hyacinth stem, Fancy continued to mull over the possibility of indulging in a very private spring fling. Last Wednesday's events had knocked her off kilter but good. Perhaps the only solution was to work this confoundingly improbable attraction out of her system. The idea did have its appeal.

Except . . .

Except every time she remembered the deep soul-stirring effect of Jeremiah's kisses, she began to have doubts. Doubts that a simple affair *could* occur between them. Doubts that she was emotionally prepared to deal with something more. And serious doubts that Jeremiah would be satisfied with the light frolicking sort of involvement to which she'd restricted past relationships.

He was not a man to be trifled with.

And she'd never done anything but.

Fancy sighed. All those doubts were enough to take the spring out of any fling. She was turning to place the fresh flowers in the display when she caught a suspicious movement out of the corner of her eye and froze.

Out on Dogwood Avenue, Mitzi Janeway sidled by, turning the corner and flattening herself against the Main Street window like a skulking cartoon spy—except that a cartoon spy would've worn a trench coat and fedora. Mitzi looked even more absurd in a chiffon dress and white gloves. Her bosom was mashed against the glass so that her cleavage was hoisted up to the vicinity of the triple-strand pearls clasped around her crepey neck. Fancy stood as motionless as a mannequin, fighting to hold back a laugh. Mitzi's bust dropped six inches when she stepped away from the window to set a straw hat crowned with a mass of silk roses atop her bouffant hairdo. Then she crouched to peer through Haute Water's glass door.

Fancy sneaked out of the display window. "Shh," she cautioned Brett, holding one finger to her lips as she scurried toward the door. Peeking from behind a rack of bathmats, she saw that Mitzi's face was pressed against the door at waist level. Beneath the hat's bent brim, her beady eyes examined every inch of the shop interior.

Fancy jumped out and yanked open the door. "Aha! Caught ya!"

Mitzi yelped and lost her balance. She stumbled over the threshold, ankles bowing outward above the wobbly stilts of her outrageously high heels. Fancy helped her upright. "Spot anything interesting?" she asked.

Mitzi repositioned her drooping hat with a jerk. She'd begun her career at twelve by catching Daddy Janeway snapping Cook's garter in the pantry. Since then, she'd become accustomed to the travails of eavesdropping. Determined to give no quarter, she adjusted her neckline and swallowed. The trick was to not admit anything, especially the obvious. "Bathrobes," she announced. "I've come to look at bathrobes. Mo tells me you have adorable ones."

Brett came out from behind the counter, pointing her finger. "You were spying—"

"Pshaw," Mitzi scoffed. "It's not polite to point, Miss Randolph." She fiddled with her ancient alligator purse, pulling out a wrinkled hanky and hastily tucking the bag beneath her arm before Fancy could spot the tiny cassette recorder she'd just switched to record.

"You were snooping," Fancy accused, leveling her own finger at Mitzi's plump painted face. "I caught you red-handed."

Mitzi waved the handkerchief. "La-di-da," she warbled, and swept toward the back of the store. "Let's take a gander at those robes."

Fancy shrugged helplessly and nudged Brett to follow. "Too bad there was nothing to see," she called after them.

Mitzi smiled mysteriously. "Oh, we'll see about *that*, dearie!"

Brett selected a voluminous gaudily striped caftan from the armoire. It was as stylish as a canvas awning. "This is you, Miss Janeway," she heartily insisted.

Fancy was relieved that Mitzi hadn't seen her at the window swooning over Jeremiah. Being reported as making out under a cherry tree had been embarrassing enough—even for her.

Brett was dropping yards of striped cotton over Mitzi's protesting head and Fancy was refilling the various baskets of potpourri when Betty Jo Dandy entered the shop. She looked somewhat forlorn, so Fancy greeted her extracheerfully.

"Do you realize that Jessica is only weeks away from her high-school graduation?" Betty Jo was soon confiding as she absently toyed with an assortment of scented soap. One after another, she lifted the soaps to her nose and inhaled, indiscriminately dropping them into the closest container. "Then she's off to New York for a summer of modeling before starting at the College of William and Mary in the fall." She made a tragic face and sniffed at an angel-shaped soap.

Despite the ongoing wreckage of her orderly displays, Fancy managed a clucking sound of commiseration.

"The modeling agency wanted to send her to Paris. I was to go along as her chaperon, since I knew Doctor could get along just fine without me," Betty Jo continued, referring to her husband, the town general practitioner. Snorting indelicately, she threw down a bar of black tar soap. "I can't imagine why Jessica prefers to go to New York alone. New York City at eighteen! Can you blame me for being in a dither?"

Mitzi walked out of the sapphire velvet robe Brett was holding up by the shoulders and set her open purse on a stack of towels. Brett hurried after her, flinging a hand-stitched antique chemise over Mitzi's head just as she started to speak.

Fancy unobtrusively steered Betty Jo in the opposite direction as Mitzi spat out a mouthful of batiste. "Jessica seems like a mature eighteen to me, Betty Jo. I'm sure she just wants to test her wings."

"And I'll be left with an empty nest," Betty Jo wailed, leaking mascara-tinted tears.

Ducking behind the counter for a box of tissues, Fancy made shooing motions at Brett. Brett pushed Mitzi into the dressing room, grabbing another gown from the armoire as she passed. "You've got to try this one, Miss Janeway," she said loudly. "The embroidered décolletage will do wonders for your cleavage."

Betty Jo dabbed at her eyes. "Dr. Dandy will be thrilled to have you all to himself," Fancy said soothingly.

Betty Jo's chin came up. Jessica had inherited her golden good looks from her mother; Betty Jo had been Webster Station's Miss Azalea in 1967. "That'll be the day. Doctor finds Maybelle Clark's bone spurs more interesting than me," she said haughtily, and then ruined the effect with another undistinguished snuffle.

"I see." So *that* was the lay of the land, so to speak. Fancy mentally inventoried the shop, searching for just the right product to solve Betty Jo's problem. "Massage oil," she blurted.

"Pardon?" Betty Jo's smeary eyes opened wide.

Fancy slipped her arm around the older woman's shoulders. "I've got exactly the thing for you," she said, maneuvering Betty Jo toward a pyramid of bottles. "Choose your fragrance. My own personal favorite is the orange-lavender—in the amethyst bottle."

Betty Jo's manicured hand reached out for one of the jewel-toned bottles, then hesitated. "I don't know . . ."

"Trust me." Fancy patted her on the back. "Do you have a big bathtub? Good. What you do is get your husband into a warm bath after a hard day at work—"

"All he wants is a highball and the newspaper."

"You're a woman. Lure him."

Betty Jo pursed her lips. "Maybe if I tuck the sports section in the tub caddy..."

Fancy smiled. "Nice trick. After the bath, lure him into the bedroom—preferably not with the business section. Dim the light, set out a few candles. Break out the massage oil and, well, I'm sure you know where to go from there."

Betty Jo blushed. "It's been a while."

"Just like riding a bike, Betty Jo. I promise."

Resolutely Betty Jo reached for a deep blue bottle with a French label. Fancy made her way to the boudoir section. "Do you have a nice negligee? Something elegant but a wee bit tarty?"

A new world was dawning in Betty Jo's eyes. "I've never done tarty."

"Then, if you'll pardon the expression, it's just what the doctor ordered."

The bell over the door chimed, and a beefy young man with a buzz cut entered. He looked around doubtfully. His gaze met Betty Jo's. "Hey, Mrs. Dandy," he said sheepishly, nervously turning his trooper's hat around and around in his massive hands.

Behind her back, Betty Jo dropped the bottle of massage oil into a basket on the floor, where it fortunately had a soft landing on a heap of sponges. She cleared her throat. "Good morning, Bobby."

Definite sounds of a skirmish came from the dressing room; Fancy decided it was crucial to keep Mitzi's nose for news away from the customers. She was removing the purse from the towel cart when Brett emerged, looking harassed.

"Can I let Mitzi out now?" she hissed at Fancy. "She's tried on every robe we have in her size—and some that weren't."

"Why don't you serve Bobby? I'll take care of Mitzi."

Brett smoothed her hair. "Bet you an hour of overtime she won't buy a thing. Robes ain't what she's shopping for."

Fancy crept on silent feet to the louvered half door of the first cubicle. Mitzi's feet were planted directly behind it, spike heels sinking into the plush carpeting. Fancy was positive the woman's nose was twitching with curiosity.

She impulsively grabbed the door, then released it just as fast. It swung inward, bopping Mitzi on the nose. She cried out in surprise and jumped up, banging her head against the hard-packed purse Fancy was now holding over the top of the door.

"Omigosh, Mitzi, I'm so sorry!" Fancy poked her head over the top of the door to examine the nose Mitzi was rubbing. "You know what? I've got just the thing for that. Chamomile cream! Of course, you'll have to leave it on your nose for at least twenty minutes, but you can sit in my office with a magazine. Do you like to read about plumbing supplies?"

JEREMIAH ARRIVED at Haute Water as Fancy was locking up for the day. She wasn't prepared for the deep pleasure the sight of him brought her. How, she wondered in amazement, could she have been willing to give him to her mother?

Her pulse beat double time as he walked toward her in that long-legged way he had. His grin was disarmingly sexy. His eyes—well, they were flatteringly focused on her. Fancy immediately forgot about her plan to soak her aching bones in a hot bath as soon as possible.

"Hi, Jeremiah," she said, her cheeks pinking. Again.

His warm eyes returned the greeting. "Did you have a good day?" he asked, nodding at the shop.

"Well, it was interesting." Brett had been right about Mitzi. After hanging around for nearly two hours, eavesdropping and forgetting her purse in some very odd nooks and crannies, she'd departed without so much as a bar of soap. Betty Jo Dandy, however, had selected several bottles of massage oil, a sexy black lace peignoir and a set of expensive damask towels.

"I came by to see if you'd like a ride home."

Fancy looked up and down the street. Pedestrian traffic had slowed to a trickle. A number of shopkeepers were closing up—most of them watching her and Jeremiah with unabashed curiosity. "I was going to walk," she answered, tossing her head with a return of her usual élan. Her dark hair skimmed her shoulders, the ends curved under to brush her jaw. She flashed a smile at the whole of Main Street. Let them watch. She didn't care!

"I'll walk with you." Jeremiah slid his hand down her lavender sleeve, his fingers seeking and finding hers. He took command of the satchel she'd slung over her right shoulder.

Just like teenage sweethearts walking home from school, Fancy thought with delight as they proceeded to the square, hands linked.

Mitch nodded as they passed. "Have a nice evening," he said, round face split by a broad grin. Mo Rowe rushed into the intersection, slumping noticeably when she saw that Fancy was with Jeremiah.

They walked along Azalea Avenue, where the azaleas were past their prime but still clinging to a few dark pink blossoms. Fancy took in everything. She'd chosen Webster Station just for this kind of cheerful ambience where everybody knew everybody else and she could walk hand in hand down the street with a man and not have a care in the world. It was worth all the gossips and the busybodies.

Two blocks later they were in the residential district. The tree-lined streets had fallen into a late-afternoon lull. Fancy looked through open curtains at the various comfortable domestic scenes with a pang of longing that was oddly disturbing. She halfheartedly scolded herself for being overly sentimental.

Two girls with flying pigtails whizzed by on their bikes, crowding the sidewalk so that Jeremiah had to pull Fancy close. Her body quickened at the contact, but when the walk was clear again they resumed their stroll as though nothing had happened.

Fancy started to chatter about her day at the shop, her voice bright and sharp in contrast to the mellow atmosphere. When they neared Cherry Street, she wound down. They turned the corner, walking beneath the white flowers of the cherry trees that lined the curb. The grass beneath the trees was carpeted in white petals—Fancy might have thought she was back in the Michigan snow except that the air was warm and as sweet as perfume. She slid Jeremiah an almost shy glance as they reached her gate, wondering if she should invite him in, wondering if he would kiss her goodbye.

They exchanged words of no great importance. He released her hand and returned her satchel, then turned to leave. Fancy, curiously caught up in the quiet magic of the moment, said nothing. With a bemused smile, she leaned against the picket fence and watched him walk away.

She went inside to soak in a fragrant bath, pretending what was happening to her body was the result of aromatherapy and herbs, and knowing all along that it wasn't.

Fancy had pulled on a pair of jeans and a slouchy sweater when she finally realized she'd been listening to unusual tinkling sounds for the past few minutes. Kneeling on her unmade bed, she opened the window and poked her head outside. As the breeze rippled through her hair, a silvery chiming filled the air.

Frowning, she yelled, "Mom, did you put up wind chimes?"

Stella answered from the kitchen. "Wind chimes?" Pots rattled. "We don't have any wind chimes, Fan."

"There are definitely wind chimes outside my window."

Stella came into the bedroom holding a stalk of celery. "Well, I'll be darned."

"Who hung them there?"

"Don't look at me. I've been out all day grocery shopping and hunting for the perfect kitchen curtains. I may have to investigate Buy the Bolt."

Fancy peered through the window again. The wind chimes hung from the porch eaves, all silver stars, flaming meteors and a big quarter-moon. "Webster Station must have a masked chime-hanger, then."

"Maybe there's an explanation in the note on your pillow."

"What note?"

"If you'd make your bed more often, dear, you'd see—"

Fancy whipped off the rumpled comforter, creating a gust of wind that blew a folded paper onto the carpet. She snatched it up, her reflexes a lot faster than her mother's. Stella conceded defeat and left the bedroom, waving the celery stick in time to "The Simple Joys of Maidenhood" from *Camelot*.

Fancy sat on the edge of the bed and unfolded the sheet of yellow foolscap. The large piece of paper contained very little writing:

Mischievous Angel—
May the song of these chimes accompany you through
nights sweet with dreams . . .

                                              J.

When Fancy closed her eyes, the note clutched to her
chest, what she saw was Jeremiah's face, a sight sweeter than
any dream. . . .

THE NEXT DAY, Jeremiah persuaded her to let Brett manage
the shop for the afternoon so they could drive to the Shen-
andoah Valley for a wine tasting. Jeremiah's company, the
stunning scenic vistas and a selection of award-winning
cabernet sauvignons went to Fancy's head. Or possibly her
heart, she decided when he delivered her back to her doorstep and touched his lips to hers in a kiss that was simple in
execution but devastatingly complicated to her emotions.

Thursday night, they went to Webster Station's only
movie theater, the Paragon, which happened to be showing a very *un*paragonlike lowbrow comedy. Fancy found
herself giggling, anyway—at least until she glanced over
and caught Jeremiah watching her with a look so loving she
dropped her popcorn.

Friday night. The Loblolly Club, a nondescript ware-
house-type building on the edge of town was rocking.
Smoke, escalating voices and thumping music poured from
the open windows in a cacophony that drowned out the
chorus of the peepers in the nearby swamp. Only the members of the Ladies' Society for Decency were missing the fun;
Hester's troops had been boycotting the Loblolly ever since
its experiment with wet T-shirt contests. In that case, decency had prevailed because the only woman willing to
compete had been Mitzi Janeway. Hester considered it a
dubious victory at best.

Although Jeremiah wasn't into the bar-and-club scene, Fancy had been eager to attend. As they sat in one of the booths in the so-called nonsmoking section, she told herself that Jeremiah Quick was no different than other men she'd dated and efficiently kept in their places. Perhaps he was a bit nicer, with his compliments, love notes and tender hand-holding, but she could handle that. And certainly he was sexier, with his devastating kisses and his mellow voice and hard body and soft eyes, but she could handle that, too.

What she had to remember was that no man was perfect. There was always a fatal flaw. Jeremiah's was probably the family he'd left behind in Atlanta. They'd done a lot of talking in the past week and he still hadn't mentioned them. If Mitzi hadn't told her otherwise, Fancy would have assumed he was an unencumbered bachelor and as close to perfect as she was going to get. That, she kept telling herself, should be reason enough to keep her heart firmly in place.

Then he asked her to dance.

Of course she said yes. And of course, as soon as they'd negotiated themselves into a space on the crowded floor, the band that had been churning out your basic Friday-night dance music with a country-and-western flavor down-shifted into something soft and slow. Jeremiah smiled as though he'd planned it and pulled Fancy close. The other couples began the clinging shuffle that barely qualified as dancing.

Jeremiah didn't shuffle. He glided and swayed, holding her properly. Fancy glided and swayed with him, perhaps only slightly missing being pressed together like Japanese commuters. Beau danced by, doing an R-rated grinding thing with a curvy blonde.

Fancy turned her eyes up to Jeremiah's, intending to make a caustic comment. Instead, she felt herself liquefying under the strength of his eyes. His right hand was splayed at the small of her back, radiating a potent heat that melted her insides like an ice-cream cone on a summer day.

"You're a wonderful dancer," she said. What a fantastic understatement!

"Thanks. So're you."

He had a frank way of making eye contact that had her imagination working overtime—even though she'd banished the little devil she usually blamed for such naughty ideas. Yet, after that first overwhelming kiss, he'd done nothing that was even remotely suggestive. The wild ideas were all in her own mind. Fancy felt another traitorous blush working itself up her throat. She ducked her chin, hiding her face against Jeremiah's chest.

Maybe the problem was that she felt so out of control. If she could make him feel even a modicum of the same, she might recover just a little.

"You know, you're much too buttoned-down for the Loblolly." She slid her hand from his and reached up to undo his patterned silk tie, leaving it hanging loose while she worked on the top three buttons of his shirt.

"As a matter of fact, you're usually too dressed up." Her fingernails skimmed the ridge of his collarbone as she spread his starched collar. The up-and-down motion of his Adam's apple told her that her touch was having an effect. Good. She smiled bewitchingly.

"I probably haven't totally relinquished my city habits," he said, and slid his hands from her waist to the flare of her hips, his long fingers briefly pressing into the soft curve of her derriere.

A tiny gasp escaped Fancy's parted lips. This wouldn't do. Not at all. Jeremiah was drawing her closer and closer. She was going to go up in flames.

Mitzi Janeway shuffled by in the arms of Hamish Hightower, avid eyes cataloging their position for future reference. "Yoo-hoo," she called to Jeremiah. "Save me a dance, honeybuns!"

He shrugged helplessly. "Ms. O'Brien has me all booked up." Before Mitzi could protest, Ham launched her into a fancy dance step that sent them reeling into the crowd. "Close call," Jeremiah said with relief.

Fancy had used the distraction to put a few inches between them. But she still had to hit on a humdrum topic of conversation. "How nice that we both ended up in Webster Station. I always knew I wouldn't stay in D.C. I'm not a city person." If she could discover his reasons for leaving Atlanta, her raging imagination would be stopped cold. "What about you?"

"Atlanta born and bred."

"So what made you leave?"

She thought there was a hard edge to his smile, but all he said was, "Had an inkling I'd meet the woman of my dreams here." Suddenly he swung her in a wide circle as the band picked up the tempo. When Fancy finally spun to a stop, he leaned over and planted a big smacker on her breathless lips. The dancers near them cheered.

The band's lead singer, a bleached and permed woman in a Western-cut shirt and tight jeans, began to sing in a surprisingly good cigarette-and-whiskey-rough voice. Fancy recognized the song: Bonnie Raitt's "Something to Talk About." Ideal.

The tempo was faster now, catching Jeremiah and Fancy in its wake. Someone near the bandstand whooped, and Jeremiah pulled off a tricky move that had her bent back over his arm. He leaned down to whisper in her ear. "Do you get the feeling all eyes are on us?"

Fancy puffed to catch her breath. "We've got your gossip columnist to thank for that."

"Should we really give them something to talk about?" he asked wickedly, paraphrasing a line of the song.

"I don't think that's necessary!"

He set her upright and moved in very close. She could feel the heat and hardness of his body, see up close the gleam in his amber eyes. "How about love?" he murmured, and the singer echoed his words.

Fancy's heart cartwheeled.

When the crowd began to organize itself into rows for line dancing, Fancy escaped to the bar. She'd left Jeremiah in their booth with a promise that she'd bring back a beer. *After I've gotten myself a little bit drunk*, she thought, ordering herself a Negroni. She sat on a stool next to Clarissa Boggs, who was stirring a pink concoction with a straw. "Hi, Clary. I saw you dancing with Bobby."

Clarissa pushed a thick wad of brown bangs out of her eyes. "I know, I know. I swore up and down I wouldn't go out with him until he proposed, but he showed up at the café this morning looking so sorry and smelling so good I couldn't resist. I dunno, I'm feeling so dang hot tonight he must've snuck an aphrodisiac into my drink. Or something."

"Or something," Fancy agreed. It wouldn't be discreet to blurt out what it was Bobby had bought from Haute Water.

"Maybe if I play up to Beau again, Bobby'll really come through."

"I'd give him a little more time if I were you."

"Three years is plenty long enough." Clarissa chugged her drink until the ice rattled against her teeth. When the band started to play again she hopped off the stool. "The Tush Push," she cried. "I gotta go find Bobby!"

Swiveling back toward the bar, Fancy came face-to-face with Mitzi, who'd been sitting on the other side of Clarissa. She smiled toothily and pushed back her ten-gallon hat. "Betcha Clary would give a day's tips to know what ol' Bob got from Haute Water. She could use it to wangle a ring out of that boy right quick."

"M-Mitzi," Fancy sputtered. "Please tell me you won't."

"Inquiring minds want to know."

"Mitzi, you can't. I won't have any customers if their every purchase winds up in 'Talk of the Town.' You wouldn't do that to me, would you?"

"We could make a deal . . ."

"I could ban you from my store."

Mitzi pouted. Fancy stared her down. Mitzi shrugged as if she'd given up, although Fancy wasn't fooled, and went off to attach herself to a line of pseudocowboys. Fancy smiled weakly at the bartender, who set Jeremiah's beer before her. She pressed it against her hot forehead, knowing that Mitzi was the least of her problems. In the past week she and Jeremiah had grown close—dangerously close. It was time to make a decision.

Fancy sipped her drink and made one. Fun and games she could handle. Mutual attraction she could handle. But love...love was too much. Love she could not handle, and a smart woman knows her limitations.

So she'd offer Jeremiah what she'd first planned—a little carefree involvement with an expiration date. They could get together, turn each other inside out, turn back to normal people again and that would be it. She could still stick to her snoring-boring resolution. Jeremiah Quick would no longer be an issue.

Simple, no?

Ignoring the *no!* that screamed inside her head, Fancy laid a bill on the bar. Then she went to rescue her man from Mo Rowe, who was pushing her tush in his direction.

HE'D BEEN extremely tempted to drive directly to his building, sweep Fancy into his arms and carry her up to his apartment. He'd even aimed the convertible in that direction—only at the last second making a squealing turn onto Azalea and stopping in front of the darkened Garden Club headquarters. Not a bad location, as it turned out. Fancy was amenable to whiling away a few minutes on one of the wrought-iron benches that were tucked into various leafy vantage points of Fuzzy Frewer park.

She looked up at the stars, her profile creamy against the dark red of a Japanese maple. To Jeremiah, she appeared peaceful and untroubled, her brow as smooth as silk. But she'd been alternately jittery, seductive and boisterous at the Loblolly. At no time had he been sure what was going on behind those blue-gray eyes.

He took a deep breath and put his arm across the back of the bench. "So how did you find your first Loblolly Club experience?"

She turned to him. "I thought it was fun." She paused thoughtfully. "But not your cup of tea, hmm?"

"I loved dancing with you." He put his hand on the back of her head, letting his fingers sink into her hair. "In general, I have to admit I prefer a more peaceful environment."

She tilted her head back, making a satisfied purring sound in her throat. His fingers caressed her nape. "Like right here?" she asked, lashes lowering. "Or did you have an even more private place in mind?"

It would be so easy... He gritted his teeth. "There is a private place I'd like to take you to see one morning soon. I'll surprise you."

Her eyes flashed open with the realization that they weren't speaking of the same thing. "Ohh-kay. I love surprises." Flirtatiously she leaned her cheek against his shoulder. "But I hate to wait for them."

"I believe you've already told me that." *And I want to be the one to teach you the sweet agony of anticipation.* He shifted, recrossing his legs. Yup, agony was the word for what was happening to him right now.

Fancy peered over his shoulder. "I keep expecting Mitzi to spring out from behind a bush."

"I didn't think you minded being the 'talk of the town.'"

"Well," she said doubtfully, "maybe I've been feeling and doing several things lately that I wouldn't normally do. Or feel."

His eyebrows lifted a devilish quarter inch. "Sounds promising."

"I'm not used to being...wishy-washy." Jeremiah watched as several thoughts passed through her expressive eyes like clouds in a wintry sky. Then, brightening, she stood. "I did make a decision tonight."

"Anything I should know about?"

She put her hand to her mouth to muffle a giggle. "That would probably be helpful," she said, but when he started to ask why, she put out her arms, looking up at the sky as she twirled off along one of the paths. He watched as she drifted past a copse of birches, the filmy skirt of her dress floating on a breeze. He got up and followed her to the fountain.

"Is this what's called being led a merry chase?" he asked when she eluded his reach by slipping away to the other side of the round fountain. "You're being very enticing."

"En-tic-ing," she breathed, stepping up onto the base of the fountain. Jeremiah saw that she was dangling her shoes by their straps.

"Fancy, what are you doing?" he scolded, mentally adding up how much alcohol she'd consumed that evening. Not that much.

"Enticing you of course!" she sang out. Standing on her toes, she did ballerinalike turns around the circumference of the fountain until she'd returned to face him.

Jeremiah put his arms around her legs. They were damp from the spray of the water. Under her wind-wafted dress, his hands were on the backs of her thighs, and he found the feel of her firm flesh and silky stockings exciting. "I'm extremely enticed," he said gruffly. "You can come down now."

With a teasing smile, she stepped backward into the water. It was cold. She shivered, marring her attempt to appear carefree and adventuresome. "Hasn't anyone but Mitzi and Hester played in this fountain?"

Jeremiah tried to look stern. "Casey Swertlow and Lulu Grenville. They're five."

Fancy tossed her head and flung her arms apart in an imitation of Dottie the Mermaid. Although she was laughing, Jeremiah sensed something else motivating her frivolity. Again there was a jittery tension about her. He wondered if she was dancing in the fountain simply because that was what she'd always done—and wasn't prepared to change.

The spout of splashing water had wet her dress up to the waist. The sheer fabric clung to her hips and thighs, delineating every curve, revealing even the fact that her panties were edged with lace. Jeremiah reached in and pulled her out, lifting her over the stone base and into his arms.

She looked into his face as her body slid down the length of his in a rush of delicious heat and friction, despite the chilliness of her damp dress. "Everyone already thinks we're . . ."

"A couple?"

She shook her head. "Lovers," she breathed.

He couldn't think of anything to say—only of something to do.

Fancy tilted her head and gave him a long assessing look. "Let's have an affair," she said suddenly, and there was a feeling in his chest, a pressure, as if a balloon had just inflated and was pressing against his ribs. Maybe it was just his heart, expanding to contain the hugeness of his feelings for Fancy.

"Let's have an affair, for a few glorious, wild, sizzling weeks," she continued. "Let's really give this town something to talk about!"

He deflated. He liked the glorious, wild, sizzling part. It was the "few weeks" he'd prefer to change. Trying not to show his immense disappointment that an affair was all she was ready to offer, he tried to evaluate Fancy's forced expression of delight, and the underlying edge of desperation he didn't quite understand.

"Do you love me?" The question had emerged of its own volition. When she winced, his stomach dropped precipitously—although the heat in his loins was still throbbing and insistent. Having 120 pounds of luscious, bikinipantied, almost-as-good-as-nude mermaid plastered to your body did that to a guy.

Fancy peeled herself off him and plopped down onto the edge of the fountain with a squelching sound. She picked up one of her sandals and jammed her foot into it, fumbling with the tiny silver buckle for an interminable ten seconds before conceding that her numbed clumsy fingers weren't working. Bereft and confused, Jeremiah watched in silence as she slumped in defeat.

"Damn," she moaned softly. One shaky hand swept back the dark silk curtain of her hair. Jeremiah saw the deep blotch of red that stained her pale cheek. She turned to look up at him, lips quivering.

From cold? he wondered. Temper? Desire? Or... fear?

"No, Jeremiah," she said tonelessly. "I don't love you." Then she stood up, looked blankly at the sandal in her hand and walked out of the park, leaving him there alone.

Webster Station Chronicle
Talk of the Town by Mitzi Janeway

Do the Bump

Y'all were probably wondering: Where's our Mitzi? We want Mitzi! Betcha were scared stiff that I got the sackerooni. Well, don't fuss your li'l heads any longer—I wasn't booted, I was just bumped! The powers that be decided to run an in-depth report on our town's need to expand its recycling program and bumped *moi* instead of something boring like Eudora Vincent's recipe column! Now, as mayor I'm rah-rah for recycling (I always fish Fritzi's schnapps bottles out of the garbage pail!), but I know how much you folks rely on my pearls of wisdom... so let's all make sure it *never* happens again!!

So Much Gossip, So Little Space

Since there's a whole week's worth of hot stuff abubblin' in the pot, let's get to it. First off, Maureen Rowe asked me to announce that she's broken it off (we all know how assertive Mo can be, but I don't believe she meant that literally!) with her steady beau, Ernest Groves of Cloud River. Which means Mo is on the loose, guys, so *watch out!!* Could the dashing Quick bros. have anything to do with Mo's decision? (Just wondering!)

I also bumped into (literally!) a rumor of rumblings in the Dandy household. Seems Doctor hasn't been making any house calls on his own sweet wife! Y'all know and love Betty Jo, so how's about giving her a break? Eudora, no more midnight sciatica emergencies! Boyd, stop whining about your tinnitus! As for me, I'll sacrifice my flu shot appointment—gladly!!

No Ring, No Schwing

I've saved the juiciest for last (and boy-oh-boy were the juices runnin' last Friday night at the Loblolly!!) The biggest clamorama: Bobby Vernon and Clarissa Boggs are once more joined at the hip—though Clary's ring finger is still *au naturel!* Really, Bob, three years is plenty long enough. Frankly, I'm betting on something I heard Clary tell Melinda Willis in the ladies' room (and I quote): "If I don't get a ring, he ain't gonna schwing!" And what of Clary's dumpee, Beau-be-nimble? Whoa, doggie! That ol' hound don't waste time. I spotted him sniffin' 'round Rita Bellingham (whose parents still don't know their darling sneaks out after they go off to bed) and dirty dancing with the opportune Miss Willis. No moss grows on *her* caboose.

Also tripping the light fantastic were our fave-rave couple, Fancy-pants O'Brien and Jeremiah Quick-the-boss-is-coming, seen smooching in the middle of the dance floor. They've also been spotted holding hands on Azalea Avenue and at the Paragon (ain't love sweet?). Wild rumors are currently sweeping the town about Fancy doing the cancan in Frewer fountain. Personally, I think it was Fuzzy's ghost come to haunt the members of the Garden Club!

Speaking of the Garden Club, there I was all gussied up last Monday morning (hat and gloves and everything), when apparently someone canceled the meeting! What gives, folks? Explanations, please! Could it be that a certain faction of the membership's still smarting over my critique of their entries in the Great Azalea Festival Exhibition? And I was *so* looking forward to Oliver Sidley's presentation of "Kudzu: Taming Our Creeping Enemy With Kindness"!!

5

KISSES FEATHERED over her face.

Fancy sighed in contentment and rolled over in bed, her
face turned to the window to welcome the cool morning
breeze.

Kisses, sweet and gentle . . .

Lashes fluttering, she began to realize she wasn't dream-
ing. The breeze was real. The kisses . . . yes, they were real,
too. She made a moue with her lips and received another.
A kiss, a hint of warm tongue, the brush of a hard jaw.
Without opening her eyes, she put her hand to the back of
the kisser's head, her fingertips detailing the shape of the
skull, the downy fuzz at the nape, a protruding ear.

Only when the kiss ended did she open her eyes. And
there was Jeremiah. There was his wonderful face with its
chiseled nose and desirable lips, his elbows on the sill of her
opened window, the sleeves of his brushed twill shirt rolled
up to reveal tanned forearms. She murmured a sleepy hello.

"I see you're awake."

Fancy blinked behind a crisscrossed web of morning hair.
"Must be having a relapse. I'm hallucinating."

"Oh, I'm quite real, I assure you."

She smiled at his accent and burrowed into the warm co-
coon of her bed. The sheets and blankets were all freshly
washed, scented by the sun and wind from being hung out
on Mama Mitchell's clotheslines. For the past few days,
Fancy had been sick in bed with a cold, the result of her im-

promptu wade in the fountain. Maybe she was too old for such foolishness.

The first day, she'd suffered mightily, alone and grumpy with only Aubergine's chicken soup for company. The second day, doped on cold medicine, she'd been weepily grateful for Jeremiah's arrival, bearing the results of a clean sweep of Mitch's magazines, tissues and cough drops. On the third day, after a long, hot seaweed soak and the delivery of a dozen pink roses, she'd begun to recover. This morning Fancy wanted to relish the simple pleasures of good health and a comfortable bed, but Jeremiah was presenting too good a reason to get up.

She pushed herself to a sitting position and leaned her own elbows on the sill so they were face-to-face. She kissed the tip of his nose. "Morning, handsome."

"You're feeling better."

"Uh-huh. I even made it into the shop for a few hours yesterday."

"Then what you need now is exercise."

She sat back, aware that the strap of her ivory batiste nightgown had slipped off one shoulder. She made a sultry expression and did her best Mae West. "What kinda exercise didja have in mind, big boy?"

Brows lifting, he considered the cozy nest of her bed. "Not that kind, sorry to say." His eyes held a glint of both wishful amusement and caution. "I had in mind something more wholesome—a walk."

"A walk?" Fancy peered out at the dull sky, tinted an ashy rose at the horizon. "So early?"

"Have you ever walked through the dawn?" Jeremiah asked, and she admitted she hadn't. "Then it's an experience you don't want to miss."

"Okay, I'm up for it." And she was, out of bed and on her feet. A torch began to burn behind Jeremiah's half-lidded eyes. Her pin-tucked, tissue-thin gown was almost transparent in the light slanting through the window.

Let him suffer, she thought with a return of her old verve. He'd asked for it. Or hadn't asked, if one got technical. "Ten minutes," she said on her way to the bathroom, knowing he was watching the movement of her hips and legs through the sheer fabric. She gave him an extra wiggle and was rewarded with a soulful moan.

She took a hasty shower and put on a set of plain cotton underwear, thick socks, baggy muslin pants in a sort of oatmeal noncolor and an oversize sea-foam green blouse. After a vigorous brushing, she anchored her hair at the top of her head with a green velvet scrunchie. She was feeling a little cocky and a little wild after too many days of inactivity. How had Jeremiah known this was the number-one thing—make that number-two—she needed? Chuckling, she tied a soft green mohair sweater around her shoulders.

Explaining that Stella might be awakened by the door, she wiggled out through the open window, landing with a soft thunk on the wooden porch. The chimes tinkled as she quietly closed the window.

"That made me feel sixteen again," she told Jeremiah, who was waiting on the back steps with an interestingly bulgy backpack.

He laughed. "Of course. You used to sneak out of the—"

"Shh," she cautioned, motioning toward the house. They linked hands to tiptoe through the yard like runaways.

Once they were safely away, Fancy tossed her head, her ponytail bouncing like the tail of a high-stepping Arabian mare. "I was in love with a gorgeous drummer. He had inch-long eyelashes and a better sneer than Billy Idol. I used to sneak out of the house with my fake ID to see his band play in local dives."

"Was this before the Mohawk or after?"

"I never had a Mohawk! But it was after my punk phase. I was *much* more mature at sixteen, don'tcha know?"

"Sure sounds like it," Jeremiah agreed, eyes dancing.

Leaving the alley, they followed the sidewalk past neat rows of quiet houses until it stopped and Rockridge Road began. The sky had lightened to a pearly gray with a wash of pink in the east.

"What were you like at sixteen?" Fancy asked as they walked along the road that sloped upward to the top of Rockridge Hill.

"A rock-and-roll babe like you would've never noticed me," he answered. "I was studious."

She tried to imagine an adolescent Jeremiah. She could picture him gangly and maybe a bit awkward, but she had a hard time imagining that even a babe would miss his essential good-heartedness. On second thought, maybe good-heartedness wasn't high on a babe's list. But what about his gorgeous amber eyes? *She* certainly would have noticed.

"I wore loafers and pressed clothing when the fringed, tie-dyed, Indian-bedspread look was coming into style. My hair was shorter than the high-school principal's. I looked ridiculous in a headband." He sent her an I'm-gonna-trust-you look. "My nickname was Frog."

"Frog?" Fancy pressed her lips together and concentrated on the crest of the hill, where sunrise was gilding a stand of beeches. "As in Jeremiah was a . . . ?"

"Bullfrog," he finished with a nod. "Only I wasn't bull-ish, so it became just Frog."

"It's kinda cute."

His expression was pained. "Do *not* tell Mitzi."

She had to laugh. "Just imagine!"

"The garbled metaphors and screwy similes would be a publisher's nightmare." He tugged on her hand. "Let's turn off here."

She obediently complied as he picked a path through a hedgerow at the side of the road. Beyond was a small pasture of green grass rising to a line of dark pines. "Are you sure you know where you're going?"

"As long as you don't mind getting damp. The grass is still dewy."

She fell back a few paces as they walked. Going up the hillside, she got to watch the flex of the muscles in his thighs and to allow her gaze to linger on the breadth of his shoulders. It was the first time she'd seen him in such casual clothes—a pine-colored shirt and khakis. His pants were loose (Jeremiah definitely wasn't the tight, tight jeans type), but they looked just fine. She found herself wanting to slide her hands into his back pockets to give him a lusty squeeze. Wouldn't *that* make her Frog Prince jump?

"Look," Jeremiah said when they'd reached the trees, putting his arm around Fancy's shoulders to turn her around so she could look back the way they'd come. Webster Station was set out below them like a miniature toy village. Fancy picked out the white spire of the Episcopal church and the redbrick campanile of the town hall. The pretty houses were swathed in the pink, white, yellow and green of spring. It all seemed so tidy and uncomplicated that Fancy sighed a little as she leaned back against Jeremiah's chest. His hands squeezed her shoulders.

"I wonder if life in Webster Station is active enough to hold your interest," he commented in a suspiciously detached tone.

She was yanked out of her own contemplation of the complexities of her not-so-tidy life. "What makes you say that?"

"You're so lively. An extrovert. Is there enough excitement here for you?"

"Maybe *excitement* isn't the word I'd use, but, yes, there's plenty here to keep me involved and busy." She couldn't read his expression. "Enough to keep anyone interested."

He shrugged. "Not *anyone*," he said softly, turning away.

They entered the grove of pines, where it was dark and cool. Jeremiah held a branch out of the way and motioned for Fancy to go ahead. "I wouldn't have moved here if I'd needed the pace of a city," she explained, no longer sure whom they were discussing.

They headed uphill again and soon came to the edge of the forest. "It's beautiful," Fancy said reverently. The rounded green hills of the Virginia countryside were layered before them, cut here and there by dark green forests and slashes of red earth. Far off were the hazy foothills of the Blue Ridge Mountains.

"Why would I prefer city smog to this?" asked Fancy.

"I know. When I came here, I felt as though I'd finally found my own small patch of heaven on earth," Jeremiah said. She looked at him questioningly, but he was suddenly concerned with less esoteric details. "Did you get wet? Are you feeling okay? Should we turn back now or go on?"

"Let's keep walking, please," she was quick to answer. "I'm loving this."

"If we cut through here," he said, pointing, "we'll eventually hook up with Rockridge Road again. I've brought provisions, so we can stop for a break any time you need one."

"I knew you were the type to think of everything."

The wind ruffled Jeremiah's hair, making it look like dark velvet shot with silver threads. "We studious types can be useful to have around."

Fancy grinned engagingly and took his hand. "While we flighty types provide the entertainment."

She began to tell a joke as they followed a thicket of elderberry bushes that skirted a ravine. They didn't stop walking until they'd reached a hilltop that overlooked the far pasture of a horse farm. Its white board fence was pristine against the emerald grass. The sun had burned off the dew long before, so they sat comfortably on the ground beneath a blooming dogwood tree.

Fancy, weakened by her bout with the cold, sank to the ground with a moan of exhausted pleasure. "Does that feel good," she sighed, legs flopping in an unladylike way.

Jeremiah patted her calf. "Poor baby." He unzipped the backpack, found a foil package of muffins and offered her one.

"You know this country well," she commented, clasping an apple muffin between her palms. It was fresh and still warm. "I would've been lost any number of times, but you always knew your way."

"I walk almost every day."

"Alone?"

He poured them each a cup of coffee from a thermos. "Usually."

"Hmm." Fancy broke off a chunk of muffin and popped it into her mouth. Brown sugar and cinnamon melted on her tongue and she rolled her eyes in appreciation. She was curious about all aspects of Jeremiah's life. So far, he'd not been very forthcoming. "Why'd you move to Webster Station?" she blurted.

Jeremiah took a long swallow of coffee before answering. "Same reason you did, I suppose. My business was here."

"Sure, but why did you buy the *Chronicle?*" She flashed him an apologetic grin. "Mitzi told me, even before you did, that you were an editor at a huge Atlanta daily."

"I wanted to get out of the rat race."

"Yes, of course." Fancy drew up her legs and rested her chin on her knees. Was she imagining it, or was Jeremiah more than a bit terse? Three tiny gray birds flitted through the branches of the dogwood, and she squinted at them as if she was more interested in bird-watching than the on-going interview. Well, why shouldn't she come right out and ask him? "Were you married? Before, I mean, when you lived in Atlanta?"

"That's right. I'm sure Mitzi already told you that. Also that the marriage produced three children and a divorce, too."

"Oh? Three?" she said airily, leaving it up to interpretation as to whether she'd already known. The birds were juncos. Their beady black eyes and twittering reminded her of Mitzi.

"You want the whole sordid tale, right?"

Fancy winced. A sordid tale. Was that how her father referred to his ex-family when exchanging vital stats with another prospective wife? She shrugged and gulped the strong black coffee, needing the caffeine.

"All right. The life of Jeremiah Peterson Quick, abridged version." The crow's-feet around his eyes deepened as he stared in the direction of the sun. "I told you about the solemn, studious, serious Frog. Same thing in college—"

"But why were you so studious?" she interrupted. "Beau certainly doesn't seem so—"

"Well, there are nine years between us. I was the older brother, the straight-A achiever. Also . . ." His face was emotionless as his gaze turned inward. Fancy had noticed that his eyes, which could express so much, became veiled when he spoke of himself. He showed the world an aura of smooth control and grace. She wanted to know what lay beneath it.

"My father was the rigid demanding type. He expected a lot of his sons, but Beau was only eleven when Dad was killed in an airplane accident, so he grew up with different expectations."

Fancy watched an emotion flicker across his face and disappear. Perhaps, she mused, the grief he'd channeled into sterling achievement? "Go on," she urged.

"Yeah. Then I met Diana."

Diana. Fancy hesitated, then again murmured, "Go on."

"Diana was arresting. She had a glossy, well-taken-care-of look. She didn't know the meaning of failure because everything she touched turned to gold. I thought the same would apply to me and our life together." He cleared his throat, looking uncomfortable about revealing so much. "We were married right out of college and not much more than the required nine months later became parents. Diana produced magnificent babies of course. Two of them. Twins."

Fancy was frowning over her image of a perfect Diana Quick and wondering why a man would choose to leave such a woman. She hadn't expected to be envious of Jeremiah's ex. Sympathy was more convenient. "It probably wasn't easy, managing twins at such a young age."

"Not if you're the average struggling newlyweds. Diana, however, had a trust fund and Nanny Billbrough."

"Oh."

"We had our first major fight when I insisted on joining the staff of the *Atlanta Courier*, instead of filling the son-in-law slot at Daddy's conglomerate."

"Wait a minute." Fancy had leaned her forehead against her knees, but now her head popped back up. "If you became a father at age—"

"Twenty-two," he supplied.

"That makes your twins—"

"Twenty-one, last March."

"Good grief." She calculated quickly. Jeremiah's children, whom she'd been picturing as no older than teenagers and desperate for a father's influence, were actually legal adults and less than nine years younger than herself. It was something of a shock. She'd have to redo all her preconceptions!

"There's also my youngest daughter, who's thirteen."

Fancy abruptly decided she didn't want to hear this sordid tale, after all. Now the only image in her mind's eye was of herself at thirteen. After her father had absconded, she'd become a rebel without a pause, her newly punk attitude giving Stella major grief at a time Fancy now realized must have already been difficult enough. She made a mental note to buy an extravagant gift for Mother's Day.

She fell back, crushing the grass flat. Did Jeremiah's daughter sport a shaved head and a nose ring?

His face loomed into her field of vision. "I see the story of Jeremiah Peterson Quick, water-under-the-abridged version, has prostrated you. Do you require nourishment?" A peeled orange floated past her nose.

She opened her mouth and he placed a plump section on her tongue. Chewing, she turned her face to the sun. Juice dripped down her throat. "Do you have visitation rights?" she asked right out of the blue, blue sky.

Jeremiah had no problem following her train of thought. "Yes. And if this is a game, that's your nineteenth question. You get one more."

There were a hundred crowding her brain: Do you *use* your visitation rights? Do your children still recognize you? How many of their birthdays and graduations have you missed? And how can I possibly become involved with you when I made a fervent vow—as only a thirteen-year-old can—that I would never, never, *never* find myself on the "wrong" side of a broken family?

"So what's the Peterson?" she asked, not able to articulate more important questions. She opened her mouth like a baby bird.

"My mother's maiden name."

He dropped another orange section into her mouth and she bit down hard, the sweet-tart sensation flooding her tastebuds. Sweet and sour, she thought. Bittersweet. *Like my feelings for Jeremiah.*

But then he leaned over her and she was overwhelmed by longing and affection. Every time her doubts grew, she had only to look at him to forget them. All she remembered was the question he'd asked in the park. *Do you love me?*

She *could* love him. For something so complicated, it seemed astoundingly easy.

The contrast between the jewel-bright sky and the pink dogwood blossoms hurt her eyes. She squeezed them shut as Jeremiah braced his arms on either side of her shoulders and leaned down to kiss her. She felt his shadow fall over her skin like a gossamer veil and then the tenderness of his lips on hers.

"You taste like oranges and sunshine," he whispered.

Fancy framed his face with her hands, her skin pale against his tan, smooth against rough. They looked into each other's eyes and were quiet among the rustling leaves and sighing wind. *You taste like love,* she thought. *And I'm hungry for more.*

The slightest tightening of her hands brought his lips down to hers. This time the kiss was longer, more thorough. Jeremiah's chest pressed against her breasts as his hands skimmed upward, loosing her ponytail so her hair fanned across the grass. He stroked her cheeks, her jaw, tipping it up so his mouth had access to the arch of her throat. She squirmed, caught between the sweet pressure of his weight and the warm earth, pulled in different directions by the implacability of her resolutions, both recent and not so, and the powerful attraction that demanded her surrender.

"Jeremiah . . ." His name was her anchor.

He plucked at her almost sheer blouse. "Have you any idea what this looks like when it's clinging to your body in the wind?" he asked, undoing several buttons and sweeping aside the pale green gauze. She shuddered under his touch as he pressed his mouth to the inside curve of her left breast. Fancy felt as though her heart had risen up to meet his lips. It hammered against her skin, threatening to burst through.

She herself undid the rest of the buttons. While Jeremiah paused to look his fill, the sun and wind caressed her skin, hot and cool at the same time. They were soon replaced by his hands and mouth, only hot, very hot. She arched against him as he pushed up her bra, catching her naked breasts in his palms. She called his name again, urgently this time, and he answered with his mouth, taking hers, his tongue thrusting inside to stroke and taste and savor.

It was too good, too fast. She couldn't think, couldn't evaluate, couldn't rationalize.

His hands were like streaks of lightning, setting her on fire wherever they touched. One was at her breast, teasing her diamond-hard nipple; the other he laid across her navel, just inside the waistband of her pants. The muscles in her stomach twitched.

She had to retaliate. Unwinding her arms from around his neck, she slowly stroked her hands down his back, memorizing the lithe muscles. Jeremiah muttered something triumphant but unintelligible into the damp skin at the nape of her neck as she twisted beneath him. She slid her hands lower, into his back pockets, and squeezed.

His dark head lifted, then lowered. He used his lips and tongue like an artist with a paintbrush, layering kiss upon kiss, painting her skin with magic strokes, skillfully drawing her bottomless need out into the sunlit sky.

"Jeremiah . . ." She didn't recognize her own voice.

"Beautiful Fancy."

She licked her tingling, bee-stung lips. "Jeremiah, I can't . . ." Her dazzled brain struggled with the idea that, yes, she *could*. "This is too much. I can't handle it."

He studied her face for a moment, his eyes darkened but still sparking with amber light. "I thought you wanted to have an affair?"

She caught her breath. "But you didn't."

He touched his lips to her soft cheek. "I wanted to love you. I wanted us to be making love."

Was he saying that *now* they would be? When only days ago she'd been on the brink of sending him away for good? They hadn't actually come to an understanding since that night in the park, not in so many words, but something had certainly changed between them. Was this the mature relationship she was supposed to find as soon as she'd turned thirty?

Her thoughts whizzed. She was ahead of schedule, but out of line. She was out of whack, out of control, out of her mind. She was falling in love. Falling in love with an entirely inappropriate man.

Or so she'd supposed. She could no longer be sure. There were too many shadings of gray in what she'd been certain was black and white.

Fancy rolled sideways and sat up, hastily adjusting her clothing. Prickly awareness danced a jitterbug across the surface of her skin. She pressed her palms against her aching breasts, snapping the bra's elastic band back into place. "We're both going to be late for work," she said, only a tiny catch in her voice betraying her surface calm.

Through the airy blouse, Jeremiah's index finger traced the ridge of her spine. "Undoubtedly."

For such a studious responsible type, he didn't sound bothered. She glanced over her shoulder. "I thought you always stuck to the rules."

He'd begun to pack up the remains of their breakfast. "Ah, but I came to Webster Station to get away from the rules."

"Is that so?" Exactly what did he mean?

"A whole new life," he murmured, speaking his thoughts aloud.

Fancy's heart contracted. "I see."

"Do you?"

She nodded once, briskly. "More than you know."

Webster Station Chronicle
Talk of the Town by Mitzi Janeway

Tootsie de Suite

Seems I stepped on a few oh-so-sensitive toes in my last few columns. The truth hurts, don't it? Nonetheless, I'm being forced to issue a one-size-fits-all apology to Fritzi, Boyd, Eudora and anyone else who feels offended (or offensive). I don't know why my yearly mea culpa (traditionally printed the last week of December) couldn't suffice—but who'm I to argue? My own tootsies took a bruising when (as my vaunted investigative skills uncovered) the ipso facto *el presidente* of the Garden Club, one Janice Bellingham, pulled a switcheroo and held the last meeting at her manse on Rockridge Hill. She claims she "forgot" to inform *moi*—even though I *am* the club secretary!! Does that sound kosher to you? I thought not!

Parties: Young & Old & Very, Very Private
Lupy Hapgood's birthday party at the Emerald Square retirement village (what Fritzi and I used to call "the home" when we visited crazy old Grammy Hattie) was a total washout when the candles on Lupy's cake set off the emergency sprinkler system! All attendees were drenched and even the cake became a casualty when Etta Ipswich—on her way to the fire exit—ran over it with her wheelchair!! It was the wildest b-day I'd attended since my own sweet-sixteen soiree at the Janeway-mansion pool with the high school swim team (Fritzi refused to come out of her bedroom!). Is this what my life has come to? Whaddaya think? Am I hanging out with the wrong crowd?

One of my top-secret operatives spotted Fancy O'Brien and Jeremiah Quick sneaking through Cherry Street's back alley at dawn. No, your bifocals ain't cracked—*dawn!!* When I stay out all night I have to spend the next day in bed. Mebbe that's what F&J do, too. (Tee-hee-hee!!) And speaking of dawn, Dawn Ohlmeyer wishes to inform all who attended her daughter's birthday party that little Dawna hasn't come down with the measles, after all. Seems that Quint Jr. was only experimenting with a red felt-tip. Too cute for words.

A Fairy of a Tale

Since this has become my column for announcements and disclaimers, I'll finish up with one more: Oliver Sidley, who's on May grounds-keeper duty at Fuzzy Frewer, wishes to announce that the owner of the size-7 sandal found near (rumor has it *in??*) the mermaid fountain may claim her (or since anything goes in the gay '90s, even his) shoe at the Garden Club headquarters. P'raps we ought to do a door-to-door search, à la Cinderella, to find the shoeless lass! (Although I've got an inkling that our mysterious Cindy's ash is in some very haute water!) Unfortunately, Mitzi J. can't lay claim. Because of my bunions, I wear a 9!!

6

JEREMIAH WAS HAVING déjà vu.

"Someone must be held accountable," Hester declared, pacing before his desk.

Why me? he wondered, then steadied himself. He could ride out this storm. Hester's sturdy legs drove like pistons; the floor should've been shaking beneath her wrath. When she reached into her canvas bag he almost expected her to withdraw a thunderbolt to hurl at his head.

She pulled out a thick manila envelope.

"Here's a copy of our petition protesting Miss O'Brien's actions at her—" Hester lifted her lip in a sneer "—place of business. And this is an editorial I'm submitting for publication in the *Chronicle*." She slapped a thick wad of papers on the blotter and dropped into the chair cater-cornered from Jeremiah's desk—effectively blocking his only escape route. She wriggled her ample behind into a comfortable position and crossed her arms over her chest.

He examined the papers. The "editorial" was neatly typed, double-spaced and—he saw at a glance—packed with hyperbole and vituperation. It was also twenty pages too long. "You've put a lot of work into this."

"As you haven't seen fit to defend Webster Station from the influence of that she-devil in pastel skirts, I must!"

"Mrs. Hightower, I don't set community standards. The newspaper is a vehicle for reporting news, not making it." He tapped together the corners of the much-handled petition. "If you have a problem with our coverage—and I think we've adequately represented both sides—I'll be happy to discuss it with you. Otherwise, I'd suggest that you present this petition to the mayor and town council."

Hester snorted in disgust. "Mayor! Mitzi Janeway—mayor!"

Jeremiah suppressed a grin. "Well, Mrs. Hightower, thanks for stopping in . . ." *For twenty minutes.*

"But what about the editorial? You wrote one lambasting the society for merely attempting to remove pornographic materials from the library. Is that what you call fair?"

Damn, another twenty. He hoped they wouldn't have to rehash the whole art-book fiasco; Hester had called Lucy Brandenburg's degree in library science a "license to corrupt public morality." Lucy, not your stereotypical meek librarian, had thrown a stamp pad at Hester's head. "That's why it's called the op-ed page, Mrs. Hightower. Editorials are opinions—the personal opinion of the writer. But I can't print something libelous."

"Well, this one is my personal opinion." Hester resettled herself, clearly not planning to budge.

Jeremiah felt a bitter thread of stress uncoil itself in his chest. He'd come to Webster Station to get away from such tension. His decisions at the *Chronicle* were supposed to be innocuous: should he send Leo Bean to the high school basketball game or the bowling-league playoffs? Alice Ann to the Scoutorama or the Downtown Merchants Association meeting? What had happened to the worry-free life he was supposed to have in Webster Station?

Hurricane Francine O'Brien, of course.

And he was glad of it, even if it meant reaching for the antacids again, because along with the turmoil came her brio and refreshingly simple love of life.

"I pray you don't allow your personal relationship with that hussy to influence your decision," Hester said, heavy on the sarcasm.

"Shall we refrain from name-calling, Mrs. Hightower?" Jeremiah included himself in the politely couched but steely question; a few choice names were running through his head just now.

Hester smiled poisonously. Jeremiah studied her for a moment, realizing that Webster Station's turbulent spring had wrought changes even in the Widow Hightower. Her hair was now a uniform rich brown, stiffly haloing her face. She was wearing makeup: a smear of iridescent green on each eyelid, a circle of pink on each cheek.

He smiled. She blinked in confusion. *Stick around, Hester,* he thought. *Fancy will soon have you frolicking in the mermaid fountain* without *a raincoat and galoshes.* "As long as you accept that there'll be editing involved, I'll be happy to consider your piece as a guest editorial."

She squinted suspiciously. "I suppose that will have to do."

The tightness in Jeremiah's abdomen eased. "All right, Mrs. Hightower," he said, slowly rising. "Let's take a look at Fancy's new window display."

Although the temperature was fifteen degrees warmer and there were no balloons decorating the front of Haute Water, Jeremiah felt another wave of déjà vu as he and Hester walked toward the bath boutique. He'd heard the chanting picketers the moment they'd stepped out of the *Chronicle*'s door.

The crowd was smaller than the one Fancy's infamous bath had drawn. Aside from a knot of Main Street regulars, most of the curious bypassers glanced at the picketers, stopped to look into the window and, after a second or two, stepped back in what appeared to be amusement,

shock or perhaps insult. Jeremiah's curiosity grew. He only
hoped Fancy wasn't doing something that involved an excessive amount of nudity. He'd have to defend her honor,
and there would go his neutral newsman stance.

The members of the society shook their picket signs at
him as he approached. "Good afternoon, ladies. Fritzi,
Maybelle, Dawn, Margaret," he said in acknowledgment.
He put his head down—Maybelle waved a mean sign—and
plowed through the picket line.

At first glance, the window display seemed harmless
enough. He was relieved to see that Fancy had no part in it,
although it did feature another bath. A big Jacuzzi this time,
filled with bubbling water. The rest of the space had been
redone in a slick Art Deco style, with a sleek black marble
sink and gilded swan-shaped fixtures, and a black, red and
silver zigzag wallpaper.

The Jacuzzi drew his attention. A blond mannequin was
perched in the far corner, her arms stretched along the sides
as though she was enjoying her soak. Her mouth formed an
"oh!" of delight, eyebrows arching above wide blue eyes.

Jeremiah glanced at Hester beside him. Her face was white
under the blotches of clownish blush. "I don't see anything
too scandalous," he started to say.

Then he saw the snorkel.

And the legs of a male mannequin poking out of the roil-
ing water, feet covered by shiny black flippers that flopped
over the side of the Jacuzzi. He stifled a laugh that would've
sent Hester into orbit and examined the Jacuzzi's occu-
pants more closely. Just beneath the surface of the water was
the pale shape of the male mannequin's buttocks. The rest
of the body wasn't visible, but the snorkel was attached to
a head, its synthetic brown hair cresting the water. The top
edge of a pair of goggles made it very clear what undersea
attraction the diver was exploring.

Which gave a whole new meaning to the female manne-quin's expression.

Which in turn explained why Hester had stormed into his office. Jeremiah swiped his hand across his face, hiding his eyes, biting the inside of his cheek so Hester wouldn't no-tice the silent laughter that shook his shoulders.

"It's obscene. Absolutely obscene! We can't have it in our town!" Hester snatched up her placard—My Birthday Suit Is A Dress—and hurried off to head the line. Working her arms, as well as her lungs, she rounded up the ladies and resumed their chant.

Elmer had seen enough. "Maybelle's marching," he said slyly to one of his Main Street cronies. "That means Clary's in charge at the café . . ."

"Holy, yuh, let's go get us some pie! Clary cuts 'em way bigger than Maybelle."

The two took off, passing a couple of women who'd just come from Mitch's. "Oh, look," the younger one said. "There's a new window display over at Haute Water."

Jeremiah recognized Janice Bellingham and her daugh-ter, Rita. "Why is the society picketing?" Janice wondered aloud as they neared. She looked at the window. Three seconds later, she tried to push Rita away.

"Wait, Mother. I want to see . . ." Rita peered into the Ja-cuzzi, realized what was in it, realized that Jeremiah was watching, and blushed.

"I may join the society. That window is...is...indecent," Janice sputtered as she towed her daughter away. "It's no wonder you're running wild, Rita Marie. The bad influ-ences in this town have managed to taint even you."

Jeremiah watched them go, then turned back to the win-dow display. Beside the gleaming black Jacuzzi was a card on an easel. Within its stylized border was a slogan: Ja-cuzzi. It's Not Just A Bath—It's An Adventure!

Jeremiah had to smile. Fancy certainly knew how to draw attention to a selling point. He considered the new window nothing but good-natured naughtiness until two young boys rode by on their bicycles. Seeing the fuss and noise, they veered onto the sidewalk and peered through the window. Then Jeremiah began to wonder if Hester was right. Perhaps the scene *was* improper for public viewing.

But the boys glanced with mild interest at the blond mannequin, with puzzled nonchalance at the flippers, and read the sign aloud. "I don't get it," one of them said as they wheeled past the picketers. "What're the flippers for?"

Jeremiah decided a chat with Fancy was in order. Stella was standing just inside the shop door, fuming as she looked out at the marching ladies. "You'd think those dames could find something better to do," she said in lieu of a greeting. "I should hook up a hose. Give 'em a good soaking. Dampen their spirits."

A couple of customers were oohing over a rainbow-shaded display of bath beads. Brett Randolph was busily polishing a grouping of mirrors, making faces at herself in each one. "Jeremiah," she said with a tilt of a bottle of glass cleaner. "Fancy's in her office, but watch out. She's in a snit."

"Thanks, Brett. I'll consider myself warned." He passed through the flowery boudoir with only a quick glance at a sexy white-lace undergarment draped on the armoire's open door. *Did Fancy ever wear…?* Abandoning that thought—for now—he knocked on the door of her minuscule office.

"Come," Fancy said, biting the word off with the snap of an alligator. She didn't look up from the ledger and papers layered across the surface of her desk. "What are they doing now?"

"Running through the village with burning torches, coming to batter down the castle door."

She looked up. "Funny," she said out of the side of her mouth, then took a cigarette from the other side. "Real funny."

He pulled over the flimsy stool that had been paired with the dressing table in the previous window display. It tilted precariously when he sat on it. "Since when do you smoke?"

Fancy squinted one eye at the end of the unlit cigarette. "I don't see any smoke. Do you see any smoke?" She rolled the white cylinder between her fingertips. "I don't smoke. Anymore. But there's something about Hester that brings out the oral fixation in me."

"Ah. Well, would you consider substituting an oral fixation of another sort?"

Her skeptical look wasn't exactly welcoming, but he leaned over the writing desk to kiss her. They'd been slightly touchy with each other in the past week, cautious, each wondering how to define their relationship and waiting for the other to make a move. Fancy's lips were pressed firmly together, but it wasn't long before they softened and parted. There was no question of their physical attraction for each other.

"Let's make a date," Jeremiah whispered in her ear, taking the opportunity to nibble on her lobe. "It's been much too long since I've seen you immersed in water of one sort or another."

"Mmm," she hummed sexily. "What did you have in mind? I've always had fantasies about the reflecting pool in D.C." She crumbled the cigarette and dropped it into the wastebasket beside her desk.

"What about the fountain at Lincoln Center?"

"Oh, yes. Not to mention the pools at Versailles." They kissed again, amused with themselves, and settled back in their chairs. "By the way, thanks for retrieving my sandal from the Garden Club."

"It wasn't easy convincing Oliver that I wear a size seven."

Her smile turned rueful. "Did you really come by to talk about the intersection of our social schedules?"

"Unfortunately, no. I've just been subjected to half an hour of Hester Hightower."

"She went to you to complain?" Fancy waved a hand in dismissal. "She should be talking to the mayor."

"She doesn't find Mitzi a receptive listener."

"And you are?"

"I'm trying to stay impartial."

"How noble of you."

"I do have a certain standing in the community, a responsibility to—"

"Wait a minute." She shuffled her papers together, closing the ledger with a snap. "Let's start at the beginning. What did you think of my new window?"

"It's amusing."

She cocked her head. "But?"

"It's also somewhat . . . inappropriate."

"Inappropriate," she repeated in a cutting tone that told him her temper had flared. "It's attracting a lot of attention. Already this morning one person has ordered the fixtures featured in the window lock, stock and barrel."

"Does that include the snorkel and flippers?"

The office went silent. Outside it, Jeremiah could hear the jingle of the bell over the shop door, even the faint chanting from the protesters outside. Suddenly Fancy shot up, shoving her chair back so vehemently it hit the wall behind her desk. She paced agitatedly, three steps to the wall, three steps back. Jeremiah thought she looked quite fetching in her dusty-pink skirt and white blouse touched with lace. Too bad she was frowning.

He tried to remember that he'd adopted a neutral-newsman stance. It wasn't easy when he wanted to take her into his arms and kiss her frown away. "Hester may have a point in saying that the window is too risqué for the general public."

"Oh, come on!" She rolled her eyes. "Lighten up a little, Froggie. Don't take it so seriously."

"Fancy..." he said warningly.

She came back to the desk and leaned across it so they were face-to-face. "You wouldn't really agree with Hester and the Ladies' Society for Decency, would you?" She reflected on their acronym. "The LSD," she said acidly. "How inappropriate."

A smile quirked the corners of Jeremiah's mouth. "I told you, I'm attempting to stay impartial."

Eyelids lowering, she used his tie to tug him a few inches closer. "Impartial, Jeremiah? Really?"

Not when he was staring at that cute little dimple, he realized. And probably not even when he wasn't. "Maybe that's not possible," he conceded. "That's why I'll have Alice Ann edit the piece Hester submitted for the editorial page."

Fancy stood upright again, her shoulders squaring and her outrage flaring. "Let me guess. It's all about my heathenish influence corrupting the moral fabric of this community. Does she call me a pornographic vixen? Or just a Jezebel?"

"I didn't get that close a look at it. But she did call you a she-devil in pastel skirts during our chat."

Fancy looked down at her skirt, her short bark of a laugh not terribly sincere. "I'm surprised she hasn't declared you depraved for consorting with me!"

"She'd probably like to, except that I own the only newspaper in town. She needs me."

"Yesss," Fancy hissed. "And you're going to obligingly supply her an outlet to smear me."

He stood, wanting to reach across the desk for her, even though she was probably packing the voltage of a live wire. "You can be sure I won't print anything libelous."

"Don't worry," she said, tossing her head defiantly. "I can take it."

"Mitzi will stick up for you in her column."

"I'm so glad someone will."

Jeremiah didn't think she was being fair. He certainly wasn't going to be told what to print in his own newspaper—not by Hester, not by Fancy. "Fine. Then I guess we have nothing else to discuss."

"Fine by me."

He turned back at the door. "You never did say when we'd go out . . ." he ventured.

Fancy smiled icily. "When Hester freezes over."

FIVE MINUTES after Jeremiah left Haute Water, Fancy came out of the office, her face cross. Stella was outside arguing with the picketers, but Brett was there to sniff suspiciously. "Is that smoke I smell? Do tell. You and Jeremiah are such a hot item y'all started a bonfire."

"Blow it out your ear," Fancy said out of the side of her mouth. Brett laughed merrily and went back to polishing the mirrors.

The doorbell jangled. For some ridiculous reason Fancy's spirits soared, hoping Jeremiah had returned to defend her honor, come hell or Hightower.

It was only Willa Clark, his secretary. She sidled into the shop, eyes lowered demurely. She was wearing a beige sweater over a blouse with a Peter Pan collar. No makeup, no adornment except for a headband holding her ash blond hair out of her face.

Fancy came forward. "May I help you, Willa?"

"Hi, Fancy. I want . . . I think I want . . ." Fancy tried to smile encouragingly as Willa took a steadying breath. "Some of the women at the *Chronicle* were . . . I've heard you might have—" she ducked her pointed little chin and whispered down the front of her sweater "—aphrodisiacs?"

"I see. Well, there's a line of what are called beauty aphrodisiacs. I carry them in several forms—bath gels, perfume, body lotion, incense. Was that want you wanted?"

Willa looked confused. "I don't know . . ." She ran her pinkie over the neckline of the sweater as if it was choking her. "Alice Ann told me that Mitzi told her that there's something you, uh, mix?"

"Oh. The essential oils." Fancy moved behind the sales counter, waving at the rows of tiny bottles beneath the glass. "Calendula, lavender, rosemary, mint, eucalyptus. Take your pick."

While Willa was taking tentative sniffs of the bottles set out for sampling, Fancy reflected on Jeremiah. First she told herself he wasn't the man for her. Then she tried to remember she'd have to give him up by her thirtieth birthday, now just over a month away. Although the affair idea hadn't worked out, neither would a more serious involvement.

Along with all the other complications, there was the LSD. Fancy knew Jeremiah was on the spot and that she and Hester had put him there. Would he really print Hester's diatribe against Haute Water? Could her window display actually be offensive?

Willa was hemming and hawing again. "Fancy? Is it, uh, do you sort of, you know, mix these? To make an aphrodisiac?"

"Sure, I can mix a personal scent, Willa. But I can't make any promises about what it'll do for you."

"Oh, please do," Willa breathed. Her rounded eyes were shining, making her pretty in a waifish sort of way.

"Okay. Why don't you tell me which ones you prefer?" Fancy took out one of the pretty glass bottles she kept on hand and began to concoct a custom blend. Rosemary and lemon for energy. Twelve drops of ylang-ylang. And, because it wouldn't hurt to bolster Willa's confidence, she made a show of reaching under the counter for the "secret ingredient," the oil that *did* seem to spark the interest of the opposite sex, although calling it an aphrodisiac was a stretch.

As she manipulated an eyedropper over the tiny bottles, Fancy's thoughts returned to Jeremiah. She wasn't actually angry with him. By now he must realize she found a bit of snappy repartee invigorating. When all was said and done, she knew he'd never betray her.

She froze, mentally repeating herself. Jeremiah would never betray her.

Was that true? she wondered as the eyedropper continued to drip the "secret" oil into Willa's bottle. Could she trust Jeremiah? With not only her reputation but her *heart*?

And if the answer was yes, how would that change her feelings . . . and their future?

With a start, Fancy came out of her reverie, hastily turning her attention back to the task at hand. Capping the bottle, she explained that the oil could be used in several ways: in a bath, in body cream, as a room-scenting infusion. She wrote Willa's name on a blank label, then paused, waiting for inspiration to strike. She always named the custom mixes. Bobby Vernon's had been "Commitment."

The nib of the pen hovered above the label. Willa waited in breathless suspense. Finally, without a conscious decision, Fancy wrote one word. "Irresistible." She didn't think it fit Willa Clark, but there it was.

Willa sighed.

STELLA WAS RUNNING through the entire Broadway recording of *Fiddler on the Roof*. Fancy had peeled potatoes to "Sunrise, Sunset," scraped carrots to "Tradition" and chopped celery to the "daidle-deedle-daidle-digguh-digguh-deedle-daidle-dum" from "If I Were a Rich Man." She'd half expected her mother to grab a bottle from the wine rack and balance it on her head as she stomped through the house doing the Russian bottle dance.

Instead, Stella stirred the stew and sang her way through every villager's part in "Anatevka."

Fancy was drying the dishes and trying to remember why she'd thought it a good idea for them to live together. Hadn't she planned to marry her mother off? Stella, being Stella, was acting contrary. She'd even turned down Jeremiah! Fancy shook her head. Amazing.

Someone knocked at the kitchen door. Stella was up to her elbows in dishwater, so Fancy put down her towel and went to answer it.

Expecting Mitch, who'd taken to dropping by to moon after Stella, she was startled to open the door to Jeremiah. She blinked, pupils dilating as she absorbed the magnificent sight of him. If he really was such an inappropriate man, shouldn't she be able to take him or leave him? Or was this a case of wanting exactly the thing you shouldn't have?

"Hell-o, Jeremiah," Stella caroled.

"Good evening, Stella," he said, but his gaze didn't leave Fancy's. "Am I too late to offer you dessert?"

His voice was low, resonant, insinuating itself into Fancy's very pores. "Oh..." she said softly, realizing he was holding two plastic spoons and a pint of ice cream. His fingertips were melting through the icy coating on the carton, and his golden brown eyes were melting Fancy's lingering contrariness into a warm thick syrup that drugged her brain. Being sensible was altogether impossible.

The water in the sink gurgled as it was sucked down the drain. Stella dried her hands, looking upon them with an indulgent smile. "I believe I'll go next door to visit Mama," she said on her way to the front door. *"L'chaim!"*

Jeremiah's brow furrowed. "Are you part Jewish?"

"Just tonight," Fancy said dryly. Strains of "Matchmaker, Matchmaker" floated across the yards as Stella made her way to the Mitchells'.

Fancy was intensely aware of her ragged denim cutoffs, bare legs and feet, her uncombed hair. Then again, maybe it didn't matter. Jeremiah was looking at her as if she was the most beautiful woman in the world. The man truly was a treasure.

"Why don't we sit out on the porch?" she suggested, not trusting her somewhat shaky sense of decorum if they were in the house alone. "As long as you don't mind that Stella and Mama will probably have binoculars trained on us the entire time." Which was probably a good thing. She'd have to restrain herself from jumping him.

Jeremiah acceded with good grace. "So that's how Mitzi does it."

"I understand she has a vast network of spies. Considering the population of this town, I'd say they spy on each other, too." The screen door swished shut as they moved to the porch. Fancy hadn't turned on the light; it was shadowy and still. Earlier Stella had set the ferns out on the railings, and their feathery green bower gave some semblance of privacy.

They sat on the steps, and Jeremiah handed Fancy a spoon and pried off the lid of the carton. "On the walk over here, I made a detour to the ice-cream parlor. Hester and Mitch were there, slurping ice-cream sodas."

Not even Hester's name could sour Fancy's first taste of the peach ice cream. "Mmm," she murmured. "So Hester is my mother's rival for Mitch's affection?"

Jeremiah dipped his spoon into the carton. "It appears so." He studied Fancy's profile. "May I point out that Hester has, in a manner of speaking, frozen over?"

Her glance flicked over him and back to the ice cream. "Actually," she said loftily, "it sounds more like she's melting."

"Like the witch in *Wizard of Oz*?"

Fancy laughed, although she'd really been speaking in terms of a melting, shivering attraction and seduction. And not necessarily Hester's. "I'm sorry I was such a snippy little snot this afternoon," she said after a while. She lowered her eyes and concentrated on digging out a frozen chunk of peach. "Of course you have every right to print Hester's editorial."

"You could write one of your own," he suggested. "I could run them side by side."

"Point, counterpoint? Pleasing both sides at once?" Fancy made a face. "You're right about your 'standing in the community.' There are quite a few people waiting to see where you'll stand when the chips fall. And if the LSD continues to escalate this war, the chips will be falling, Jeremiah."

He wasn't going to let her get away with that. "I believe it was the creator of Haute Water's risqué window who escalated the Great Webster Station War for Decency," he said. "Just out of curiosity, what propelled you to do it?"

Eyes flashing, she stabbed the plastic spoon into the softened ice cream. "I'll have you know it was *your* fault, Mr. Jeremiah Quick!"

He was nonplussed. "My fault? I don't think so, sugar."

"You installed those damn wind chimes outside my bedroom!"

"What does one have to do with the other?"

"They're keeping me up at night." She wiggled her bare toes in the cool grass that grew long beside the steps. "I can't sleep. I'm on edge. The . . . sheer aggravation drove me to the brink of creative anarchy!"

His husky knowing chuckle cut to the heart of the matter. "Are you certain it's the wind chimes keeping you up at night?"

Fancy thought of her restless nights and hot wrinkled sheets. She thought of the way she'd felt both sensual and edgy after her supposedly relaxing evening bath. She thought of whom she'd been thinking of when she came up with her idea for the new window display. "What else could it be?" she boldly lied, hoping she sounded totally innocent of lascivious thoughts.

He didn't buy it. "I know what's been keeping *me* up at night."

He set the ice-cream carton on the porch floor and reached for Fancy's hand. She shivered at the touch of his icy-cold fingertips and lifted his hand to her lips. Tingling iciness and the immediacy of hot desire warred for supremacy. Her tongue darted out and touched each of his fingertips in turn, warming them with tiny flicking licks. Jeremiah hummed roughly with pleasure, letting two of his fingers curl past her parted lips. She sucked on them, her tongue weaving back and forth, then slowly, deliberately, scraped her teeth across his fingers so he'd feel the bite of the attraction that had flared inside her.

Jeremiah smoothed Fancy's cheek in a butterfly caress. She smiled, looking at him through the screen of her lowered lashes. He leaned closer, bestowing a kiss of such exquisite tenderness that she knew she was cherished. At the same time, there was so much careful control in his movements that she also knew he was exerting iron willpower to withhold the fiercer desire that was always ready to sweep them into an erotic oblivion. She loved that thoughtful controlled part of Jeremiah, and she hated it.

She wasn't thirty yet; there was still time to indulge.

She nuzzled his ear, then peppered small kisses along the sharp line of his jaw until she came to his chin. Her tongue slid up over its sandpapery texture, finding and kissing his lower lip. She took it between her teeth, giving it an almost painful nip that she instantly soothed with another kiss. Jeremiah groaned, his grip on her upper arms tightening.

"You are purposely trying to tempt me beyond endurance," he accused.

"Who, me?" she whispered into his mouth, aware that he was doing the same to her, though in a different way. But his careful courting had been too difficult to resist, even once she'd realized he was trying to make her fall irrevocably in love with him. Which she was awfully, dangerously, gloriously close to doing.

"I was thinking..." he began, his breath catching when she put her hand on his thigh. He plucked her hand off his leg, holding it tight. A man had his limits.

Fancy's head lolled against his shoulder. "You were thinking?" she prompted, deciding to behave. For the moment.

"Right. I have to admit that window of yours gave me a few ideas..." It was Fancy's turn to chuckle knowingly. "My place is still in the middle of being remodeled. Actually, it's a wreck. I thought I might order one of those Jacuzzis myself."

"Oh, that's a *very* good idea."

"Would you be interested in designing a deluxe bath for my apartment?"

The businesswoman part of her brain forced her to sit up a bit straighter. "I'm not an interior designer."

"You have a knack for it. That window is probably going to sell a Jacuzzi to every man in town."

Her giggle was very unbusinesslike. "Don't be sexist. My first order came from a woman."

"I bet Mitzi would love to see your client list," he said with a laugh. "Are you interested in the job?"

She thought about if for three seconds. "I'd love to, on one condition."

"Which is?"

"I have to be invited to the inaugural bath," she said, without evaluating what such an interlude would do to her self-imposed birthday deadline.

His beautiful eyes made her a promise. "That, my sweet spring Fancy, is most definitely a date."

Webster Station Chronicle
Talk of the Town by Mitzi Janeway
Love Is in the Air

Y'all who suffer with allergies may think there's nothing but pollen in the air, but Mitzi is here to tell you better. L-O-V-E is in the air, folks, and it's wreaking havoc! There has never been a spring like this one in the entire history of good ol' W.S.—*never!* My only regret is that none of the fairy dust seems to have landed on me. Anyone out there want to volunteer to remedy the situation?

Makeover Takeover

We all know the Loblolly is the place to party, but Umberto's is *the* place to see and be seen (and to treat yourself to some of Umberto's dee-vine pasta at the same time). The only problem last Friday night was that some of you may not have realized whom you were seeing! Beauregard Quick (I regard *him* as lip-smacking!) was spotted at the lovers' table with a gorgeous mystery woman, and who should she turn out to be but *Willa Clark!* Who'da thunk it? Miss Willa was derked out in a sinfully sexy, slinky red dress that showed off her *très* slender figure to its utmost deliciousness! Inside info tells me that the Curly Girly's Melinda Willis was the beauty operator (make me an appointment—quick!) who did Willa's hair in all those cunning ringlets. "Curly" Sue Swertlow did the to-die-for makeup and nails. I am *dying* to know what prompted the transformation. Beau looks kinda thunderstruck and Willa ain't talking! But she shore does giggle a lot!!

Willa's wasn't the only miraculous transformation. Did any of you happen to spot Missy Prissy Hightower at Ice Scream U Scream with Mitch (he must have an itch!) Mitchell? Didn't Hester's hair used to be *gray?!* Anyhoo, Hester must've figured out that the way to Mitch's heart is coated in chocolate syrup—I wonder what Stella O'Brien will have to say about that!! Ain't this lovey-dovey stuff *fun?*

Brouhaha-Ha-Ha-Ha-Ha

Haute Water was the site of another set-to between those vivacious O'Briens and the Ladies' Society for Decency when Fancy unveiled a very naughty window display. I won't describe it (this is a family paper), but it certainly has turned a few heads! Word is that the LSD plans a boycott. To each her own, but let me tell you, darlings, you haven't lived until you've tried Fancy's honey-and-almond facial mask recipe. It's a free handout (is this a woman we should be boycotting?) and it'll make your skin look 15 years younger. I swear by it! (Compare my skin to Fritzi's and you'll swear by it, too!)

Two final announcements: Oliver Sidley will present "Killing Kudzu: The Kamikaze Method" at next Monday's Garden Club meeting. And Dr. Dandy has reduced his office hours, so if any of you are overdosing on lovesickness, you'll hafta work it out of your system on your own! I know a good method, but it's not printable!!!

7

"THIS TOWN IS twitterpated!" Brett Randolph declared as she entered Haute Water.

Fancy was opening a carton that had just been delivered. "Twitter-what?"

"Twitterpated," Brett repeated firmly. "Lovesick. Gaga. Suffering from a major epidemic of spring fancy."

"Are you hinting I have something to do with this affliction?"

"Maybe. Probably." Brett held back the flaps as Fancy reached inside the carton. "I swear, I just saw Oliver and Gillian Sidley smooching in the gazebo on the green. They've been married for at least forty years. Shouldn't they have outgrown such nonsense by now?"

"It sounds rather sweet," Fancy said, glancing at the packing receipt. "They were more cross than smoochy when they came into the shop the other day. I'm glad things are working out." She reached into a heap of foam chips and pulled out a plastic sea-monster soap dish. It was hot pink, with a yawning snaggle-toothed mouth. "Is this tacky?"

"Terribly." Brett picked up an electric blue one. "I love it. I'll have to take one home for Chloe." She hoisted the box off the counter and carried it to the storage room.

"What about you, Brett?" Fancy asked when she came back. "Have you been twitterpated?" While Brett had the proper family background, thick honey-colored hair and peachy complexion, her skewed outlook and offbeat style prevented her from being a true Southern belle. A quirky sense of humor and the fact that she'd needed an employer flexible enough to work around the demands of her three-year-old daughter had persuaded Fancy to hire her.

Brett set her hands on her hips. Today she'd combined a chic black dress with magenta leggings, fringed go-go boots and a macaroni brooch Chloe had made at day care. "The only thing I know about being twitterpated is what I've read in Chloe's storybooks."

"What about Beau? Mitzi reported that you had lunch with him."

"Beau schmeau! I'm not looking to become another notch on his . . . well, Beau doesn't even have a bedpost to call his own, does he? I can't think of a better reason to steer clear."

While Brett busied herself with sorting out the baskets of soap, Fancy wondered whether she protested too much. Beau was cute, but something of a Lothario. Brett needed a man with dash to sustain her interest and the ability to be a good father to Chloe. If Beau was half as grounded as his brother, he'd be perfect.

Fancy's eyes grew round. *Jeremiah* was spirited but settled, passionate but controlled, responsible but certainly not dull. He was perfect, the very man she'd envisioned as the ideal husband for her thirty-year-old self.

Almost, she reminded herself. *You've already lost your heart. Don't lose your head, too. Remember the family he left behind, even if he apparently doesn't. Probably Miss Cherry Blossom, Kaitlin and Heather thought they were marrying the perfect man, too. Charming men have that way about them. . . .*

The chiming of the doorbell interrupted her thoughts. Fancy shook her head. Experience had taught her early and well, yet her strong feelings for Jeremiah had come awfully close to erasing those hard-learned lessons. She had to get a grip.

Alice Ann stepped up to the counter. "Okay, you broke me."

"Pardon?"

"I give in. Let me have some of those essential oils."

"I see." Fancy's dimple appeared as she tried to hold on to a businesslike detachment. Forthright, down-to-earth Alice Ann Keating had herself a hankering for a fella. Well, why not? Fancy knew she herself wouldn't entirely lose her interest in the opposite sex, even after she'd turned into the most sensible thirty-year-old since Doris Day. "Tell me about him," she said.

"You know him." Alice Ann straightened her cuffs, hesitating uncharacteristically. "He's . . . a photographer."

Not another Beau devotee! Fancy gulped as she reached for the "secret ingredient," dismayed that even Alice Ann had succumbed. By the time she'd filled all her orders, Beau would be in olfactory heaven. Or hell. "Are you sure about this, Alice Ann? Maybe you should start off slow—"

"I know what I want," Alice Ann said staunchly.

Fancy gave the eyedropper a good squeeze.

"I know he's sought-after, but we'd make a very good team," Alice Ann elaborated. "When I saw him hanging around Willa's desk this morning, I realized I couldn't wait for him to notice me. It's now or never."

After Fancy had finished the blend and issued her customary spiel, which now included the admonition that this was most definitely not an aphrodisiac, she inked in *Alice Ann Keating* and the name that had come to her: "Reckless."

There was no lollygagging with Alice Ann. She paid at the cash register and marched to the door. "Have fun," a doubtful Fancy called after her.

Alice Ann, who approached even fun in a no-nonsense manner, nodded crisply. "I intend to."

FANCY HAD an appointment to meet Jeremiah at the *Chronicle* at three. He was on the phone when she arrived, so she passed the time with Willa. After Mitzi's last column, Fancy had expected the secretary's new style. What she wasn't prepared for was the glow of confidence that emanated from Willa's inner self. In the ten minutes that Fancy loitered near the desk, Pringle, Ham and a clean-cut college intern found excuses to approach.

Alice Ann watched dubiously from behind her terminal. Even Fancy had a momentary doubt. Was it possible that Willa's sudden reversal had come from that tiny bottle of essential oil? No. While aromatherapy had its uses, transforming Willa Clark into a femme fatale wasn't one of them.

Jeremiah emerged from his office with apologies for the delay and directed Fancy to the stairway that led up past the second-floor composing room to his apartment on the top floor.

She was surprised by the vast emptiness of the loft. Although there were polished wood floors and handsome oak doors, the walls were unpainted and the few furnishings were yard-sale shabby.

"Where's all your furniture, furniture, furniture...?" she asked, mocking the emptiness with a self-made echo.

Jeremiah playfully tugged her French braid. "This is it, but my ex-wife has a whole houseful in Atlanta."

"Oh." Oh, these helpless bachelor types! "Did you ever hear of something called shopping?"

He shrugged. "I've got what I need." He pointed over the half wall that partitioned off the kitchen, where the appliances looked virtually unused. "Eating," he said. A stack of grease-stained Chinese take-out containers were all that marred the pristine countertops.

Jeremiah walked past the grouping of a long low-slung couch, a sagging armchair, a moving box with coffee-mug rings and a television on wheels. "Living."

Fancy surveyed the space. The basketball hoop bolted to the bare brick wall seemed appropriate. "This place looks like a YMCA."

"Is it that bad?" he asked innocently.

"This is a terrible cliché, but what you need is a woman's touch."

He winked and disappeared behind a three-quarters-high wall. His rich voice drifted over the top. "As long as it's the touch of the right woman..."

Fancy's knees turned to mush. Woozy from the reaction he could set off in her at will, she managed to sidle over to the wall, pretending she was simply going to look at the artwork that leaned against it. She fumbled with a framed print, seeing only Jeremiah. In a bed. What the heck, one little peek couldn't hurt.

With too much curiosity for her own good, she walked past the partition and into the bedroom area. Jeremiah, darkly handsome in his customary business suit, sat on the edge of a king-size bed covered with a puffy plum duvet. He spread his hands, indicating the bed, a black metal lamp and a library of books arranged in precarious stacks on the floor. "Sleeping," he said, looking levelly at Fancy in a way that made her nervous. And even more aroused.

She edged closer. "Sleeping? Is that all?"

"Since you came to town, yes." He reached out, snagging her around the legs to pull her closer. Her wilting knees knocked against the edge of the mattress as she leaned her weight into him. The thin fabric of her palazzo pants was no match for the heat that radiated from his hands. He was probably leaving scorch marks on her derriere.

"That's your own fault," she whispered. "I offered—"

"An affair of very short duration," he said reproach-fully. "I want more."

I want more, too, she admitted. Finally. "Yes," she agreed softly.

He looked up into her face. "Yes?"

"Oh yes," she said. "Yes, yes, yes."

Jeremiah pulled her down onto his lap. About to kiss her, he stopped and said, instead, "Are you sure?"

She straddled his hard thigh. "Just kiss me, you fool."

But he didn't. "You have to be certain. Because I love you. Once you're mine, I'm not letting go."

Couldn't you have simply shut up and kissed me? she wanted to rail, because rather than being reassured, she was turning doubtful. Her head moved in a reaction that was as much a shiver as a shake. He loved her. He promised for-ever. Wasn't such a vow what she'd been waiting for? A thousand emotions churned through her, but the strongest were the ones that propelled her to and then away from Jeremiah. For every *yes* was an unfortunate *no*.

And Jeremiah had to see the uncertainty in her eyes.

He released her, and she tumbled onto the bed. "You're not ready," he said, the air between them thick with frus-trated desire. Jeremiah stood, dignified and restrained, but Fancy recognized the pain of rejection in his stiff spine and controlled movements.

"I guess not yet," she mumbled inadequately. "Sorry." She jumped up, making a production of smoothing her slacks and matching blouse to hurry the moment of dismissal—both his and hers—along. What they needed was a neutral topic. Although she was supposed to be here on business, her gaze returned again and again to Jeremiah's bed. It was huge. And empty. "What do you do when your kids visit?" she asked, unthinkingly blundering into another area of contention. "Put them in sleeping bags on the floor?"

"That hasn't been a problem—"

"Or sling hammocks from the beams?" she continued, her tor. too bright to be true.

"—because they haven't been here."

Fancy's face went blank. Jeremiah had been in Webster Station for more than a year, and he hadn't seen his kids in all that time? A wicked wind whistled through her suddenly hollow insides, chilling her to the bone. She had to clench her jaw to stop it from howling up out of her mouth. She stumbled away from him, one hand closing around the black lacquer spire of the bed's headboard. "Your children haven't visited, not even once?" she asked tightly. Maybe she'd heard wrong.

Jeremiah was looking at her oddly. She probably did look peculiar, but couldn't he see how shocked she was? "Well, my son showed up for a long weekend last Thanksgiving. He bunked on the couch, like Beau's doing now."

"That's—" Turning away, Fancy snapped her teeth together to stop herself from blurting out exactly what she thought of the long-distance version of fatherhood. And she'd begun to think that Jeremiah was different!

When she released her grip on the headboard and turned back to him, her expression was calm. Pale, closed, distant, but, superficially at least, calm. "I came to give you an estimate on the bathroom," she said. "I may as well take a look, but this is a bigger job than I'd figured on. Maybe I should bow out." *Of more than the bathroom overhaul,* she thought bitterly.

Reassuring her that she could handle the job, he led her to the bathroom, the only room in the loft that was completely enclosed. Woodenly circling a space as large as a master bedroom, Fancy dispassionately saw that it could've been made into a dream bath. Take away the water-stained fixtures and prefab shower stall, and she could really do things with the curving glass brick wall, the high ceiling and tall windows. Through half-closed eyes, she pictured a modern but faintly Roman bath . . .

No. It wasn't going to happen. *You've got to find a way to get out of this,* she told herself with a pang of regret. *And the relationship. Jeremiah's flaw is fatal, at least to you. And don't look at him or you'll be changing your mind!*

He checked his watch. "I have to get back downstairs."

Fancy stared straight forward with a bleak concentration. "I'll stay. I can . . . take a few measurements."

"Sure," he said blandly, as if nothing had happened between them. But she knew he wasn't that insensitive.

Fancy risked a quick glance at him, some persistent part of her still hoping. Jeremiah was a good man. Perhaps he only needed someone to point out the error of his— *Stop that!* Unsteady on her feet, she kneeled to examine a curling corner of the ugly linoleum as she lectured herself. She mustn't fall into that way of thinking. The only reclamation project she could handle was a simple bathroom redo.

After the front door had closed behind Jeremiah, Fancy allowed herself a groan of despair. Hurt raged through her—a hurt she'd thought she'd never have to feel again after finally accepting the limited relationship that was all her father cared to offer. She pressed her palms to the floor, hanging her head as if physically ill, but what was rising in her throat had the bitter taste of heartbreak.

Except for his son's brief visit months before, Jeremiah hadn't seen his children in more than a year. Maybe he could be forgiven for the twins. They were adults. But what about his daughter? His needy, lonely, vulnerable thirteen-year-old daughter?

She swiped at her eyes, not knowing for which thirteen-year-old she cried.

After a minute, Fancy pushed herself up off the floor, realizing that she didn't even know the names of Jeremiah's children. In all the time they'd spent together, talking over things both trivial and significant, he'd never bothered to speak their names. If they were trivial to him, that was very, very significant to her!

She had to get out of his apartment.

Before she could go, footsteps pounded up the stairs. The door opened and closed. She was looking wildly around the room as if she had to find a place to hide when she recognized the sound of a bouncing basketball, then the metallic ring of it hitting the metal hoop and rebounding across the loft.

She crept out of the bathroom. Beau was sprawled across the couch, a folded sports section in hand. "Hey, little Miss Fancy-free," he hailed. He shifted his legs and politely stood, gesturing at the worn armchair. "Take a load off, sweet stuff."

Fancy managed a weak grin, dropping into the chair like a sack of cement. She closed her eyes to summon up the wherewithal for a few minutes of small talk. "So," she began, her eyes blinking open, sheened with emotion, "you're not going to break Willa's heart, are you?" So much for small talk.

Beau kicked the basketball and slumped back down on the couch. He laid one melodramatic hand on his chest. "It's Willa who's toying with *my* heart. I invited her out again, but that gal is suddenly as booked up as Willie the Weasel on Derby Day."

"Willa's all dated up?" Fancy said wonderingly. There was something off about the situation. Even if the "magic elixir" had provided Willa with a major dose of self-confidence, should she have become quite so completely irresistible?

"Sure does beat all." Beau scratched his head, ruffling the dark brown hair that was a shade lighter than his brother's. His velvety brown eyes, a shade darker than his brother's, were lazily sexy. Bedroom eyes, Fancy thought, but still nowhere near as potent as Jeremiah's. And when he talked, in a Southern accent slightly thicker than his brother's, not even one square inch of her felt like melting.

"I can't figure it out," Beau said, speaking of Willa.

I'm afraid I can, Fancy realized, definitely not thinking of Willa.

"For weeks, I didn't give that gal a second look. She was as timid as a mouse. Then one day her presence hits me between the eyes like a brick. I found myself canceling out on a hot honey from Tylerville so I could take Willa to Umberio's. It was the damnedest thing."

"Sometimes it happens like that," Fancy whispered. *Your mind goes numb and you lose your senses and it's too late to protest. You're in love.*

"Damn straight."

Fancy's stricken gaze swept the room as a useless wail built up inside of her. How could she have fallen in love with such an intrinsically inappropriate man on the very brink of her descent into maturity? Now she was only several measly weeks away from her thirtieth birthday and her life was in a bigger mess than ever! "Oh, Beau," she moaned, putting her head in her hands. "Why? Can you explain it to me? Why has Jeremiah abandoned his kids?"

Beau leaned forward, baffled. "What're you talking about, Fancy?"

"He told me that, except for one weekend, they haven't been to Webster Station in all the time he's lived here." She lifted her head, hands clenched into tight fists under her chin. "Doesn't he even care?"

"It appears you've been led astray somewhere along the line. I'd say Jeremiah's a right fine father."

The roar in her head was cut off in midhowl. "What?"

Beau shook his head as he studied her with a shame-on-you expression in his eyes. "I don't know 'bout his kids visiting here. What I do know is that Jeremiah will hop on a plane without so much as a toothbrush if he's got a chance to visit Libby. One time the airport was closed for bad weather and he drove straight through to Georgia without stopping 'cause he didn't want to miss her birthday. As for Andrew, he's in college most of the year, and Allison got herself married last summer."

"Allison and Andrew are the twins?" Fancy asked faintly. "And Libby . . . ?"

"Jeremiah's youngest daughter. If Lib hasn't come to Virginia, I can promise you it's of her own choice. She's a headstrong gal and has got a sulk on her that's wicked to behold. Lib knows how to hold a grudge." He flashed a rakish grin. "'Course, she adores her uncle Beau."

Fancy's brain wasn't quite up to speed. "Jeremiah has visited them since he moved to Webster Station?"

Beau lifted an eyebrow. "What kinda man do you take my brother for?"

There was a strange emotion flooding Fancy's body, swamping her, yet at the same time making her feel as light as air. It was more than relief, more than guilt, more than happiness. It was even more than love. She drew a deep tremulous breath. "Maybe you'd better tell me the whole story—about Jeremiah and his children and his divorce."

"Sure you don't want to hear this from him?"

"It seems we haven't been communicating too well."

"Yeah, I can believe that. Jer's s'posed to be working on letting his feelings out, not keeping them all bottled up inside, y'know?"

Fancy shook her head. "No, Beau. I don't know." A slow smile was working its way out to the corners of her lips. "Tell me. Tell me everything, please."

Webster Station Chronicle
Talk of the Town by Mitzi Janeway

A Prayer to St. Joan

It's getting so difficult to keep track of all these spring romances that I'm going to have to beg the Q-man for an assistant. My *own* dainties have been in a dervish what with the way new developments keep apoppin' up like mushrooms after a rain! It's either keep up with Talk of the Town or see to my duties as mayor. Which is more important—garbage restrictions or as my heroine would say, gossip, gossip, gossip?

The Pleasures of Newlywed Bliss

Of course, the absolutely hottest of the hot-off-the-presses news is the elopement of Clarissa Boggs and Bobby Vernon!! Yup, Clary done finally roped her man! The lovebirds ran off last Friday night and got hitched in fine style—I hear both of them were still in uniform! I always did ascribe to the homily that there's nothing as sexy as a man in uniform. (Except one who's out of it!) Immediately after the ceremony, the honeymooners checked into the Heart 'n' Hearth Motel, where each room is decked out with a faux fireplace, a heart-shaped bed and a cupid motif! (Now how did Miss Mitzi know that?!) So Clary's got her ring, Bobby's got back his schwing, and y'all got to read about the whole dang thing! Don't you just love it when things work out so well? Congrats, newlyweds!!!

Telltale Hearts

Willa Clark continues to be the hottest ticket in town—she's even too busy for Beau! For one dizzy second, I thought Maybelle was following in her daughter's footsteps when I stumbled on her and Leo Bean sharing the same bench in Fuzzy Frewer. But, alas, 'twas not to be! It seems that ever since J.Q. declared the newsroom a smoke-free zone, Leo's been sneaking out for ciggie breaks, and so does Maybelle when the café's not busy. P'raps love will bloom among the butts! *Très romantique*, huh?

Another fella who continues to be extrabusy in the love department is Mitch Mitchell, seen one night with Stella at the Paragon and the next with Hester at the church's potluck dinner! Not only was Hessie sporting her fancy hairdo (the girls at Curly Girly's swear they didn't touch it, but there are some *mighty* familiar wigs at Luck's—you make the call!), she also had a new dress (50 percent off at Dress-up Duds) featuring a V-neckline. Way to go, Hester! Next thing we know, La Prude will be showing *cleavage!!* And that (coming from one who's seen Hester's brassieres flapping on the clothesline), would be a date for the record books, fellas!!

There's just enuff room for one quick whisper. What sweet young thing has been spotted going up to a nameless publishing mogul's digs almost every afternoon this week? Could it be they've discovered the pleasures of afternoon delight?

8

"VA-CA-TION!" Fancy shouted happily to Jeremiah as she ran down her front walk and hopped into his snazzy silver convertible. She wasn't in a mood to sit. Instead, she planted her feet on the seat and propped her behind on the headrest, posing like a beauty queen on parade. "Let's get going."

"The sooner the better," he responded, swinging her weekend bag into the back seat and his long legs into the front.

As the car pulled away from the curb, Fancy waved. "Goodbye, Mama! Not even your binoculars can follow us," she said as they passed the Mitchells' house. "So long, Cherry Street!"

It took them only a few minutes to drive through Webster Station; in that time, she waved goodbye to a number of early risers. When they zipped past the town-limits sign, she swiveled around and saluted the diminishing town. "Goodbye, Webster Station!"

Jeremiah was both laughing and shaking his head as he reached up and snagged the waistband of her white linen shorts. "And goodbye to fifty bucks if Bobby Vernon catches you riding that way," he said, yanking her down into the seat.

She settled down with a bounce and fastened her seat belt. Her hair was already wild and tangled, so she stuck her head out over the door to blow it back from her face.

"I take it riding in a windy convertible doesn't bother you," Jeremiah observed.

"It's great. It's glorious," she replied, her voice lost in the rush of air and the roar of the engine. She reached over to squeeze his arm. "Thanks for inviting me to your beach house. You're a brilliant man."

"You don't mind leaving the store?"

"Are you kidding?" She was punching buttons on the radio, hoping to find Springsteen singing "Born to Run" or something equally appropriate. "Stella and Brett were squabbling over who gets to be boss. And Hester won't make trouble—lately she's been more concerned with the battle for Mitch than the War for Decency." Fancy beamed. For the past week, ever since her talk with Beau, she'd been feeling as free as the wind, as happy as a clam, as bright as the sun, as gooey as a jellyfish. How convenient that they were going to the beach!

She wanted to pop up and shout her glee to the wind, but the seat belt effectively held her in place. She had to content herself with running her palm along Jeremiah's thigh. He was wearing jeans. They were fairly tight, very faded, and there was even a cute, strategic rip along the right seam. He'd probably borrowed them from Beau, she thought with an inner grin. Oh, well, that didn't mean she couldn't slip her thumb inside the rip and trace her nail across his tanned flank . . .

"I'm trying to drive here," he protested, but not too strenuously.

"What about you?" she asked. Bless his hardworking heart. "Did you leave the *Chronicle* in capable hands?"

"As capable as yours?" Her forefinger had joined her thumb; her small caresses were doing insidious things to his concentration. "Er, Alice Ann is nothing if not capable."

Fancy frowned fleetingly, hoping Alice Ann wouldn't choose this weekend to turn *reckless*. "Tell me about the beach house," she said. "I can't wait to get there."

He took one hand off the wheel and pulled hers off his leg, lacing their fingers together. "It was built way back when by Great-Grandfather Quick. At present Beau and I share ownership. It's rustic, but there's plumbing and electricity."

"I'm glad you didn't lose custody of it after your divorce."

"The beach house was a nonnegotiable item. Diana didn't care—she got the Atlanta house and half of everything else."

Fancy sensed he was in a more expansive mood than usual. She wasn't above taking advantage. "You got the *Chronicle*," she commented. Beau had told her that Jeremiah had liquidated heavily to finance the purchase. "I hear you rescued it from the brink of bankruptcy."

"Fancy, sugar, the *Chronicle* had gone over the brink. It was splat on the ground when I bought the thing. I streamlined like mad and cut to only two editions a week. Webster Station's too small to support a daily."

"So if I'm dead set on finding myself a wealthy man, I'd better look elsewhere?"

"Don't you dare." He pulled out to pass a pickup, never removing his hand from hers. "I'm currently newspaper-rich and cash-poor. If the *Chronicle* breaks even this year I'll be satisfied." He glanced significantly at her. "But my prospects are good."

Fancy leaned over to kiss him on the cheek. "And looking better all the time as long as we keep supplying Mitzi with fresh gossip!"

"I wasn't speaking strictly of business."

Fancy smiled wisely. She knew that. And her nerves did, too. Adrenaline was coursing through her at his merest hint of their future together, making her blood run warm. Now that Beau had spilled the truth, she knew that Jeremiah was eminently qualified to be a part of the life she'd planned for herself. She still had some questions. And she still had to find a way to mold herself into a woman who'd fit into *his* life. Surely turning thirty would do it; the mere fact of being irrevocably adult should be enough to keep her feet on the ground. But for now, she was planning to thoroughly enjoy this sky-high elation.

"Do your kids use the beach house?" she asked, returning to the previous subject.

"Well, Allison and Andrew are busy with their own lives. I'm hoping to spend part of the summer there with Libby."

She mulled that over for a minute and decided it was time to clear the air. "You know, when you told me your kids hadn't been to Webster Station, I thought you meant you hadn't seen them in over a year." She paused as his grip on her hand tightened. She squeezed back. "I was afraid you were one of those absentee dads who don't give their children another thought after the divorce." He glanced at her with skeptically arched brows. "I know. I was being incredibly stupid."

"Truth is," he said slowly, "I've been feeling sort of guilty about Libby, especially when I realized that first night at your house, how the same situation had affected you as a teenager. So I didn't particularly want to get into it with you." Jeremiah frowned. "Libby's had a tough time dealing with the divorce. She didn't want me to leave Atlanta, and that's why she hasn't been to Virginia—she's punishing me for moving away."

"You're probably right," Fancy agreed. "Although I wanted badly to visit my father in D.C., I was downright surly to him the few times I did. It wasn't until I grew up that we stopped having a love-hate relationship." Right. Now they were cordial strangers.

"I hope Libby and I won't have to wait that long."

Fancy's smile was encouraging. "You won't. You love and care for Libby. She has to know that. Keep trying, and that will make all the difference."

He glanced at her with admiration. "Will you take it as a compliment if I say you're sounding very wise?"

She laughed in surprise. "Oh, sure. You're the only person in the world who'd call *me* wise."

He glanced at her again. "Maybe that's because I know you best."

There was such an intensity of emotion and appreciation in his voice that she was forced to see herself in a new way, too. Maybe her plan was working. Or maybe—her throat tightened—it was just because he loved her as she was? "Keep your eyes on the road, Froggie," she said hoarsely. "I don't want to get in an accident and die before I've really begun to live." Now where had that come from? The whole idea was that by her thirtieth birthday she'd *stop* living it up.

He gave a disbelieving snort. "Ha! I'd say you've packed more living into your near-thirty years than most people do in a lifetime."

"Maybe so," she murmured. *And maybe not.* Maybe she'd been trying so hard to live a manic, footloose and fancy-free life that she'd missed all those things she'd grown up believing were hopelessly beyond her reach. *Like family. Like stability. Like love.*

THE QUICKS' beach house was on Virginia's wild and windswept Eastern Shore. Their journey took them down the Northern Neck, the peninsula bordered by the Rappahannock and Potomac rivers, and across the Chesapeake Bay by ferry before finally ending on the narrow peninsula that separated mainland Virginia from the Atlantic.

It was late afternoon by the time they pulled up in front of a simple weathered house set among the dunes. The house was spare and unassuming, bleached like a bone by the harsh wind and sun. All around it, dune grass grew long, rippled by the wind into waves that mimicked the real thing. Fancy immediately adored it.

Excitedly she jabbered at Jeremiah as they took their baggage and entered through the screened porch that sagged off one end of the house like a dilapidated caboose.

The door opened directly into a plain serviceable kitchen. A big square table topped by a piece of gnarled driftwood sat in the middle of it.

The living room was large, cluttered by several generations' worth of summer leftovers and well-used sports equipment. Shelves were stuffed with paperbacks, stacks of magazines, games and shell collections. Fancy was drawn to the wall of windows that overlooked the ocean. Falling into silence, she put an admiring hand up to the glass.

Beyond the dunes of sea oats and beach grass, beyond the long stretch of sandy beach, was the ocean, fairly calm, mirroring the sky with its vast deep blueness. Gentle combers rolled in, breaking into white swirls of froth along the shoreline. Huge clouds scudded across the sky, looking, if one was imaginative, like ghosts of the wind-filled sails of the ships that had once plied these waters. Fancy, not lacking in the imagination department, found the analogy stirring and appropriately romantic.

A movement from Jeremiah drew her attention. He held up her suitcase. "You may have your pick of the bedrooms."

Fancy knew he was in his gentleman mode, quite ready to allow her to make the decision, but she longed to see him lose his formidable cool.

She trailed him quietly as he showed her one bedroom with wall-to-wall bunk beds and another with lavender walls and twin beds. He set down her bag and she picked it up. "Where do you sleep?" she asked, deciding to force the issue.

"Usually in the loft if—"

"I want to see that one."

He led her to the addition that jutted from the back of the living room. A spiral staircase led up to a loft bedroom. It wasn't a large space, but it had a magnificent view through a big half-circle window.

"This is where I want to—" she hesitated long enough for him to become aware of what she might say "—sleep," she finished docilely, and set her bag on the double bed. Was that obvious enough? Feeling Jeremiah's questioning gaze follow her as she lifted out a pile of underwear and dumped it into the top drawer of a knotty pine dresser, she added, "We can share."

His exhale was audible, but he began to unpack as matter-of-factly as she. When she came to the last item in her bag, she hesitated, wondering just how bold she was prepared to be. She glanced at the rickety bedside table. It had a drawer. It was just a few steps away. She could unobtrusively sidle over there and slip the box—

"What's that?" asked Jeremiah.

Fancy turned pink. Too late to be coy. She held up the box and said, "Condoms."

Jeremiah's eyebrows lifted. She thought he might say something suggestive or maybe embarrassing. Instead, he reached into his gym bag and pulled out a box exactly like hers—almost.

"The jumbo pack?" she squeaked, recognizing the drug-store price sticker. "Mitch must think we're going at it like minks!"

FANCY FELL BEHIND as they strolled along the beach. Jeremiah walked with his chin up, gaze skimming the distant blue horizon. She was more interested in dodging in and out of the water, splashing in the shallows, stooping to check out interesting shells or tracks in the wet sand.

Finally she raced to catch up to him. With her legs slim and bare beneath her mud-smudged shorts, he thought she looked like a spindly-legged seabird. "Let's go back," she said, sliding her arm around his waist. "I'm absolutely starving, aren't you?" After they turned and started off in the opposite direction, she had another thought. "Unless you wanted to walk farther? You must be stressed after the long drive."

"Stressed?" He looked sideways at her, appreciating the several inches of sun-flushed abdomen revealed by the briefness of her top. Her breasts tented the fabric, making him want to slide his hand up under it to feel the contrast of those shaded curves and the hot firm skin of her midriff.

"Beau told me you're supposed to walk . . ."

Jeremiah chuckled at the "I know what's good for you" seriousness of her tone. "I don't have a prescription to walk five-point-three miles a day or anything like that," he said.

"Maybe I misunderstood."

His expression turned wry. "What exactly did my big-mouth brother tell you?"

"He was more informative in thirty minutes than you'd been in thirty days!" Fancy set her lips primly and looked ahead to the house. "You said you came to Webster Station to get out of the rat race, but you didn't explain that a doctor had advised you to make a change in life-style."

"It was only one suggestion on how to reduce the stress I was under." The several years previous to his move to Virginia had not been the greatest time of his life. His marriage had become a social convenience for Diana, and meaningless—but for the crucial connection to Libby—for himself. Once purposeful and animate, his job had turned into a source of tension and dissatisfaction. Jeremiah stared out over the ocean and knew beyond doubt that he was extremely glad he'd made the change, despite what he'd lost. He looked at Fancy. In return, he'd gained more than he'd dared to dream.

"It's not important why I came to Webster Station, only that I did," he murmured as her face turned toward his, vivid with an innate joy even when cast with serious intent, as now. "And found you," he concluded.

"Of course it's important," she said vehemently. "It matters, because I thought you were a deadbeat dad! Practically, anyhow."

Although he regarded her with an appalled censure, he wasn't angry. By now, he'd come to realize that Fancy tended not to see the trees for the forest. "Why would you choose to think the worst of me, instead of the best?" he asked, but of course he knew the answer.

She stopped on the stairway that led up to the deck, looking shamefacedly back at him. "I'm sorry. I already admitted it was dumb of me. My only excuse is that it was a learned response."

His eyes softened. Her expression was vulnerable and trusting. That trust had been slow in coming—but well worth the wait. Only in the past week had it been clear she was finally ready to commit to him, fully and wholeheartedly and with a promise of forever.

"Let me put your mind at ease," he murmured, spanning her waist with his hands. "After all those years of striving for success, I'd reached the peak of my personal mountain and all I saw on the other side was more of the same. I didn't abandon my family as your father did—I asked them to come to Virginia with me. Diana thought I was going through a midlife crisis and wouldn't consider it."

Fancy looked relieved and then wary. "You didn't want a divorce?" she asked, eyes widening.

"I'd say it was a mutual decision. Even as I was asking her, I knew Diana wasn't interested. Webster Station wasn't her style and never will be. I think I was inviting Libby more than my ex-wife."

"I see," she said, relief obvious in her small voice.

"The only reason I wasn't the first to suggest a divorce was Libby. Eventually I realized that this way was better for all of us." He paused for a moment, thinking of his stubbornly recalcitrant daughter, and added softly, "Now if only Libby could understand that."

Fancy put her hands over his. "I wish I could say that she will, and soon. But I'm afraid that daughters can be selfish, preferring to have their parents together, unhappy, rather than happily split. Because that seems to mean your father is also happy being apart from *you*." She shrugged sadly and turned to tromp up the wooden stairs.

Jeremiah watched, sensing the hurt that still lurked within her, wishing he could be the one to cure it. He'd like to say a few choice things to Richard O'Brien.

"I hope you'll meet Libby soon," he told Fancy, joining her on the deck. "It sounds like you two have a lot in common."

"Yes, I'd like to get to know her," Fancy said with a certain irony. "But I doubt Libby would say the same."

AFTER DINNER—Jeremiah was even less of a cook than she, but they'd managed to cobble together paella using a cookbook, a box of instant rice and the fresh shrimp they'd bought earlier—Fancy took her glass of white wine and went down to the beach. Sunset had come and gone, and stars were beginning to sparkle in the clear blue-black evening sky. Although she'd dressed for dinner in an ivory silk blouse and a pastel-flowered challis skirt, she chose to sit in the sand, wrapping the long skirt and its eyelet-trimmed petticoat around her folded legs.

After a sip, she sunk the base of the wineglass into the sand, digging it in good and solid so it wouldn't spill. She sunk her bare feet into the sand, too. A faint heat still lingered on the surface, and underneath, the sand felt silky and cool. She wiggled her toes contentedly, wrapping her arms around her upraised knees. *All's right with the world*, she thought.

Then she remembered the destruction of the rain forests, skinheads and the vast disappointment of Euro Disney. So she amended that thought to *All's right with my little patch of the world*. And that was good enough for now. Very good, she amended again as Jeremiah joined her. She rested her head on his shoulder. It didn't seem as though there could be anything wrong in a world that had given her Jeremiah Quick.

He sighed contentedly. "It's been a long day."

"Mmm. Pleasantly so." She considered, and asked solicitously, "Are you tired?"

"Is this another inquiry into my health?" he teased. "If so, let me again assure you that I'm as healthy as a horse. The only pressure I'm under now is what I get from Hester Hightower. Don't say it! I can handle that woman's bombast just fine."

"Okay, okay," she replied with a soft laugh.

"If I wasn't in tip-top condition—"

"Oh, you are, you are," she interrupted, rubbing his muscled shoulder.

"If I wasn't, I would've had a heart attack when you showed up on Main Street naked in a bathtub."

She raised her head and stuck out her tongue, but a cozy warmth enveloped her heart. They were a couple. A full-fledged couple. They had memories, they had a future, they had endearing nicknames and private jokes. "I wasn't naked. But you're the only one who knows for sure."

"You were as good as naked." Jeremiah's eyes narrowed. "It pleases Elmer to believe you were. I guess we can let him have his fantasies."

Fancy was starting to get just the tiniest bit nervous. She knew what was going to happen next—it was what this weekend away was for. And the thought of it was making her hot and cold and shivery all at once.

"No, on second thought, I'd better set Elmer straight," Jeremiah continued. "I don't want even a toothless old man entertaining fantasies about my sweet spring Fancy."

"Getting jealous, are we?"

"I don't know about you, angel, but I sure can be." He cocked his head, staring at her in silence until she was unbearably flooded with expectation. She was getting ready to tell him the suspense was killing her when he made a sudden move that had her on her back in the sand. Neither noticed the overturned glass and the pool of spilled wine, quickly soaked up by the sand.

Fancy laughed nervously as his face loomed over hers. "I'm beginning to think you like this position."

"It has its advantages," he agreed, inserting his knee between her legs.

Fancy had a few swift moves of her own, and she'd recovered enough to use them. She put her hands on his chest, rolling out from beneath him, and pushed hard so he toppled over. She clambered atop him and looked gloatingly down at his handsome face. "We women no longer allow men to always have the upper hand."

He made an upward motion of his hips that sent a shock wave of sensual knowledge rippling through her. "And we men are perfectly willing to let you women think you're in charge."

Fancy made a sinuous movement of her own, a sexy wiggle that rubbed her body against the entire long hard length of his. His arms were stretched out across the sand. She eased her palms along them until she'd manacled his wrists. "*Think* we're in charge?" she asked as she slid around to sit astride him.

Jeremiah grinned, his teeth silvered by starlight. "Go ahead, torture me, baby."

"I'll torture you, all right." Pressing hard on his wrists to keep him locked against the sand, she lowered her lips to within a quarter inch of his. And stopped.

He tried to flick her lower lip with his tongue and she pulled back another quarter inch to avoid it. She bared her teeth in a soundless growl of domination. "How does it feel?"

"If this is torture, don't stop."

She licked her lips. "I suppose I'll have to escalate the torment," she whispered, and closed the gap between them. If she'd thought she was in control, the notion vanished as soon as their lips touched. Jeremiah's mouth was deliciously warm and greedy, and it drank ravenously from hers. In a flash, her entire being was centered on the point of their intimate connection.

Fancy didn't realize she'd released his hands until he brought them down on her upthrust derriere and snugged her hips to his. Then her concentration splintered, half of it on the white-hot blaze that drove her to twist her lower body against the saddle of Jeremiah's upraised thigh, half on the wild intensity of their kisses—kisses that continued for long hot hungry minutes until they weren't enough. She wanted more. Needed more.

She scrambled up out of the sand, giving Jeremiah no time to protest as she tugged him up after her. "The house," she said in a rush. "Let's go to the house." She charged breathlessly up the deck stairs, throwing open the door with such force it banged against the wall.

As he allowed her to lead him across the living room, Jeremiah's amusement was released in a rough-edged chuckle. He put his hands on her hips with an intimate lover's possession and followed her and her curvy behind up the winding staircase. She was yanking her blouse out of the waistband of her skirt even before they reached the loft.

"Impetuous Fancy," he murmured, sinking his hands into her wind-ruffled hair as he kissed her again. Cheek to cheek, he whispered, "Haven't I yet taught you the pleasure of sweet slow anticipation?"

She had his shirt unbuttoned and hanging off his shoulders in the instant before she answered. "I've had enough anticipation to last me a lifetime!" With both hands, she caressed his smooth muscled chest, burying her face between his pectorals and reveling in the intoxicating taste of his skin.

She lowered one hand to the hard bulge beneath his fly, and it was her turn to find his excitement amusing. "Anticipation has nothing on consummation, does it?" she taunted playfully, her bold fingers squeezing.

He sucked in a lungful of air, trying to concentrate on the full moon shining through the window as he deliberately forced her hand away. He wasn't going to lose all control until she had. "Ladies first," he said, and, as impetuous as Fancy, undid only enough buttons to expediently lift the silk blouse over her head. "Not another layer," he said plaintively when he'd revealed her full white petticoat.

Fancy shimmied her skirt down her legs, bending to step out of it, her breasts cupped enticingly in the petticoat's low scooped neckline. Jeremiah, forgetting all about anticipation, picked her up and put her on the bed. She started to laugh as he crawled between her thighs, indiscriminately flinging the folds of the voluminous petticoat out of the way.

"Wait, wait. There are buttons." With fumbling fingers, she undid them as fast as possible.

He parted the cotton, looking like a man who'd never known the meaning of the word *control* as he stared hungrily at her curves, contained only by a few tiny lace rosettes, narrow satin straps and triangles of almost transparent pink silk.

Oh, my goodness, Fancy thought dazedly as his eyes burned a path across her skin. His gaze made a slow sensuous journey from the dark shadow beneath the wisp of her panties up to her nipples, poking against the scratchy rosettes.

"You make the most erotic picture," he murmured.

She shivered, and was amazed by the depth of the thrill that sang through her, curling her toes, throbbing between her thighs, dancing across her breasts, parting her hungry lips. She had the power to make Jeremiah's eyes burn, the ability to seduce him into total abandon, and that was as satisfying as the sensations he likewise produced in her. They were an even match, but so delightfully different.

She unhooked her skimpy bra and let it fall away, the satin straps slipping down her arms as she lifted her upper body off the pillows.

"You are truly beautiful," Jeremiah breathed, reaching for her.

Fancy eagerly arched to meet him, but the shock of his hands on her breasts flattened her back against the mattress. She sighed with deep pleasure, sliding her palms over his dark hair and down to his flexing shoulders as he took turns suckling each of her taut nipples, gentle with his teeth, fervent with his tongue and lips.

She submitted until it became impossible to lie still. Then she writhed beneath him, alive with the need to move, to touch, to see. They were kissing, tongues matching stroke for stroke, when she wedged her hand between their bodies to reach his zipper. She eased it down, pleased to find how aroused he was. How much he wanted her.

In a lovers' tangle, they rolled across the bed sideways, arms and legs twisting and twining. He gasped. She giggled. They pulled off their last few pieces of clothing, flinging them away haphazardly because kissing and caressing took every bit of their concentration.

Jeremiah reached over to the bedside table. Fancy grabbed the box out of his hand, tossed it aside and took the other out of the drawer. "Break out the jumbo pack," she urged, voice shaking. "We're going to need it!"

She was too aroused to lie back and wait for him as he violently ripped the box open, the tiny packets flying in all directions. She knelt behind him, hands all over his skin, marveling at its texture and the lean elegant composition of bone and muscle and tendon. She adored the jutting bones of his shoulder blades, the smooth skin of his tapering back. He turned, and she adored the urgent virility of his thrusting erection and the golden light that burned in his eyes when she took him in her hands.

He pushed her back against the mound of pillows and in one smooth motion buried himself in her eagerly accepting body. Fancy's eyes went round at the suddenness of the deep thrust. She'd imagined Jeremiah as a gentle lover, but maybe they were too far gone for that.

He felt exquisitely deliciously right. She clung to him, legs wrapping around his thighs as he began the first slow excruciating withdrawal and thrust. She was already on the edge, nerve endings demanding the bliss of release. But Jeremiah wouldn't yet let her go—he was kissing her wildly, stroking her intimately. When she opened her mouth, his was there to swallow her cry. They moved against each other, with each other, meeting and mating and sliding and pushing, making friction, making music. Making love.

Fancy gritted her teeth, then couldn't contain herself another second. She cried out, perhaps saying Jeremiah's name, perhaps gasping only the unintelligible sounds of sweet fulfillment. She was beyond knowing.

"*Yes*, sweet Fancy, sweet sugar," Jeremiah crooned, coaxing every last whimper of her shattering climax out of her. He drove into her one last time, deep lines etched in his face as his own release came on a surge of wild abandon.

"WHAT DID YOU SAY?" he whispered, some time later.

"That a jumbo pack might not be enough?"

"No, before that."

"Ooh, ooh, ooh, *ahh?*"

"Right after that."

"Umm . . ."

"*Fancy.*"

"Oh, all right. I said, 'I love you,' okay?"

"No, what I think you said was, 'I LOVE YOU!'"

"Mm-hmm."

"I knew it all along."

"Oh, don't be so smug, Froggie."

"That's a male prerogative after—"

"Point taken."

"And I love you, too."

"Damn straight."

Webster Station Chronicle
Talk of the Town by Mitzi Janeway

The Big Cheese

When the Big Cheese is away, the mice will play! And since my own Boss Cheddar is out of town, this little mouse has got some squeakin' to do. If only I had something more exciting on my calendar than Oliver Sidley's next-in-the-series Garden Club speech "Kudzu: Tear Them Suckers Out by The Roots." Gilda Lampkin and I are thinking of starting a Still Sexy at Sixty club but we can't find any male members!! (Does that read the way I think it reads? Ah, well. 'Tis the hard truth!!)

So y'all are wondering where-oh-where ol' J.Q. has gone, right? The silly man—did he think he could sneak out of town without *moi* knowing? Of course not! Sources report that the scoundrel kidnapped his ladylove and drove off into the sunrise. Destination: the Quick beach house on the Eastern Shore. Beau calls it the Love Shack!! Knowing those dashing Quicks, Miss Fancy-charmed-outta-her-pants isn't the first young lovely to be swept away for a weekend of sea and sand. Just one warning: Careful where you get the sand!!!

The Big Ham

Something of a skirmish is developing within the ranks of the Webster Station Players. After *Arsenic* was such a rousing success (if I do say so myself, my Martha was Tony calibre!), the Players want to attempt something more ambitious. Director Paul Woodman has discov-

ered a star-on-the-rise in Stella O'Brien. It seems she
can really belt out a tune! He wants to do *Fiddler on the
Roof*. Mo Rowe (the biggest ham in a company of
hams!) can't carry a tune far enough to walk around
her ego and is thus leading the vocally inhibited op-
posing faction. I, as your trusty objective reporter,
shall be watching from the wings as the skirmish es-
calates. Stay tuned!

And Two Slices of White Bread

The *Chronicle* newsroom has turned into the town's
hottest swinging-singles scene. Beau is a bit agitated
lately 'cause Li'l Miss Willa-Won'tcha *won't!!* While I
was at my desk slaving away on this very column, Alice Ann Keating, editor pro tem, disappeared into
Pringle's darkroom for a *very* long conference (one
hour and 14 minutes for those of you who keep track
of such things). Whaddaya think "developed"?! While
the Pringlemeister is a bit too skinny (and pale!) for my
taste, I guess Alice Ann could fatten him up. (Personal
note to A.A.: Check out Eudora's page-six Choco-
holic Cake Supreme recipe.) Sometimes a woman has
to work with the limited material available!

9

FANCY SNIFFED the fresh salty air and rolled over, stretching like a cat. She looked at Jeremiah through the tangled skeins of her hair and smiled. What a delightful sight to wake up to. Even though the sunshine flooding the window told her it was at least ten, he was still sound asleep, skin tawny against the crisp white cotton sheet. She carefully eased herself off his left arm and slid out of bed.

The rhythmic whoosh of the ocean beckoned her. She grabbed her bikini and tiptoed from the loft, bare bottom flashing her unseeing lover.

In the downstairs bath, she discovered that her breasts were tender and whisker-burned. She gloated, then winced as she pulled on the pale lemon bikini that she hoped would make Jeremiah forget all about her infamous bathtub getup. Barefoot, she wandered out to the kitchen even though she was too edgy to eat. There was a funny rolling feeling in her stomach—as if she'd hitched a ride on a roller coaster.

Was that love? she wondered, drinking a glass of ice-cold water.

It felt more like Brett's definition of being twitterpated. Fancy had known the heady thrill of infatuation. She'd expected love to be steadier and maybe a teeny bit dull—ideal for mature thirty-year-olds with responsibilities and mortgages.

But now she wondered if the two feelings could be combined into the kind of love that lasts a lifetime. Certainly Jeremiah thrilled her to the core. If they'd ridden that first

rush of sexual attraction straight to the bedroom, maybe
that would've been it. Jeremiah, however, had taken the
time—very wise of him—to let the more lasting emotions
build.

Fancy went out through the sliding glass doors of the living room, squinting at the glare of the sun on the water and
sand. Eleven o'clock, she decided. She and Jeremiah had
been in bed for more than twelve hours, but had slept for
only half of that.

And she'd told him she loved him.

Which was true. The problem was that in the bright light
of day she could see the complications of their relationship
more clearly.

"Another fine predicament you've gotten yourself into,"
she muttered, bounding through the hot sand. Her nose
wrinkled in self-deprecation. Was she, of all people, labeling Jeremiah's daughter a complication? Would she turn out
to be as selfish and possessive as her stepmothers had been?
Or, she amended fairly, as they'd seemed to a mixed-up
teenager, anyway.

With a sigh of relief, she stepped onto the hard-packed
sand of the shoreline. A wavelet washed over her toes,
turning the sand to wet satin. She stepped into the water,
savoring the chill as the surf foamed around her calves.
Technically, mid-June was still spring. It felt like summer to
Fancy.

Thinking of summer reminded her of her upcoming
birthday—thirteen days away. If she was stubborn enough
to stick to her original plan, she'd have only thirteen more
days with Jeremiah!

But she could no longer conceive of giving him up for the
ideal, never-married, never-*alive* Ken doll of her foolish
prejudices. That had definitely been one of her more ridic-

ulous ideas, right up there with the lime-Jell-O mermaid jump.

She hadn't won the Alaskan cruise then; she wasn't going to lose Jeremiah now.

She waded deeper into the ocean and dove in. She surfaced with a shout on her lips and threw herself into a rolling wave, coasting on its swell like a lithe porpoise until it broke and she was thrust again into the cold depths.

Strong arms wrapped around her chest, lifting her upward. "Look what I've found," Jeremiah said. "I thought mermaids could handle ocean waves, no problem."

Fancy pushed her hair out of her face. "I'm very good in the water." Her palms slid across his sun-warmed muscles. "So are frogs, I understand."

He kissed her salty lips. "We make quite a pair."

"Oh, yes," she agreed, eyes reflecting the deep blue of the ocean as they looked up into his. "In water or out of it."

He grinned a cocky morning-after grin. "Why don't you demonstrate the 'in water' part of that theory?" he challenged.

She wasn't one to back down from a dare and he knew it. Since she was buoyed by the ocean and his feet were firmly planted, she wrapped herself around him like a piece of clinging seaweed and kissed him long and hard.

"Not bad," he said when they came up for air.

"Not bad?" she repeated haughtily. "I believe I hear an insult!"

He shrugged. "You can do better."

"If you insist." She released her grip on his shoulders and let one hand descend, scoring one of his dusky puckered nipples with her fingernail. His eyes narrowed to a glint of topaz beneath dark lashes. Wriggling out of his embrace, she floated in the swell and reached for him beneath the water, thrusting her hand under the waistband of his trunks.

Although a large wave buffeted Jeremiah, he stood his ground. "I didn't know mermaids were so daring," he groaned as she caressed him. The water was very cold. He, however, was growing very hot.

Fancy peeked up at him through water-spiked lashes. "We're the temptresses of the sea." She began to kiss away the salt on his chest, journeying lower and lower until her chin was in the water as her tongue darted in and out of his navel.

Did she dare?

Yes. She yanked down his trunks. Before he realized what she had in mind, she'd taken a deep breath and sunk below the waves.

Jeremiah's eyes closed as she took him into her mouth. The feeling was incredibly erotic—the contrast of her warm mouth and the cold sea, the liquid caress of the water and the tightening stroke of her cupping hands. His fingers threaded through her floating hair, cradling her head to his loins for just an instant, and then he lifted her high.

Fancy's face was streaming with water, her mouth open and laughing. "Sea siren," he murmured, desire tightening his throat. "I love you."

She clung to him, her mouth on his. He wrapped his hands around her hips, pulling her so close there was only a thin scrap of yellow bikini between them. "And I love you, Froggie," she promised breathlessly.

Their declarations were seared into her mind by the flaming touch of his deft fingertips between her thighs. His caress was teasing at first, delicately probing. When he felt her liquid heat, two of his fingers slid boldly upward, making her squirm and gasp his name.

He answered her unspoken request by stretching wide the leg opening of her bikini and slowly lowering her onto him. She released a long sigh, tightening her thighs around his flanks. The ocean foamed around them, swelling and receding in a rhythm that matched their own.

He surged up into her and she arched against him, bending way, way back until her hair trailed into the sea. The arc of her throat was turned up to the sun, vibrating as her climax coursed through her in wave after tremulous wave. Moments later, Jeremiah joined her with a shout and a deep quaking shudder.

A wave slammed into them. They were thrown into the water in a tangled knot. Fancy bobbed to the surface, secure in Jeremiah's arms. "You see," she said, chilly and hot, buoyant and replete all at once. "I told you—I'm very good in the water!"

AFTER THEY'D GONE for a long walk to dry off and returned to sit on the deck, their arms wrapped around each other, they realized they were ravenous. For food, this time.

Fancy was on the porch trying to shake sand out of her bikini bottom when Jeremiah called from the kitchen. "Do you often eat peanut butter for breakfast? You'd better tell me now, while I can still dump you."

"Is that a threat?" she asked, entering the kitchen with an odd wiggle. He was dangling a sticky knife between two fingers. An open package of bread lay on the counter. Fancy frowned. "I didn't eat peanut butter for breakfast. Not this morning, anyway."

"No?"

She shook her head at the milky glass in the sink. "If I didn't and you didn't . . ."

"We must have an intruder," Jeremiah said softly.

"A burglar! But what kind of burglar breaks for lunch?" It seemed too absurd to be frightening, but then again . . . "Should we call the cops?"

"The phone's not connected yet." He cocked his head, listening to the silent house. "Fancy, go outside for a minute, will you? Just in case." He ducked into the living room and picked out a baseball bat from the array of sports equipment.

Fancy selected a table-tennis paddle, holding it at shoulder height as she closely followed his stealthy footsteps. "Shh, listen," she hissed.

Thunk thunk thunk. The sound came from one of the bedrooms. Jeremiah crept closer. There was a jouncing noise—bedsprings?—and then the resumption of the thunking. "Who's been sleeping in my bed?" Fancy whispered.

One of the bedroom doors was open an inch. Jeremiah reached out with the head of the bat and nudged it farther. Fancy raised her paddle, ready to leap out with the "Aha!" that had caught Mitzi. Jeremiah simply looked inside.

His baseball bat hit the floor with a thud. "Libby!"

Libby? Fancy stuck her head past the door and saw a girl sprawled on one of the twin beds, her head bobbing to the tune playing in her earphones, one foot stamping a rhythm out on the cast-iron headboard. *Thunk thunk thunk.*

Jeremiah leaned the bat against the jamb. "My daughter," he explained. "Libby," he said loudly, going over to the bed and touching her shoulder.

She opened her eyes. "Hey, Dad."

He pulled the earphones off. "Libby, what are you doing at the beach? How'd you get here? Did you run away?"

Libby got off the bed. "I'm not a baby, Dad." She rolled her eyes. "I took a bus, then the ferry of course." She snapped her fingers, not yet noticing Fancy in the doorway. "Nothing to it."

"Does your mother know where you are?"

Her sharp chin quivered. "She doesn't care."

Goldilocks, Fancy thought. Libby was very slender, with the gawky arms and legs of a tall adolescent. Her topaz eyes and honey blond hair declared her to be a beauty-in-waiting. Once curves had replaced her angles, Jeremiah's hands would be fuller than they already were.

"Sounds like you ran away to me," he said sternly. "First thing we've got to do is let your mother know you're safe." He pulled her to him in a bear hug. "You shouldn't be here, but I'm glad to see you just the same."

Libby's head burrowed into her father's shoulder. Fancy's heart contracted at the sight. But then the girl's eyes opened and her gaze shot straight to Fancy. Libby jerked out of Jeremiah's arms. "Who is *she?*"

Wincing at her harshness, Jeremiah extended his arm to Fancy. She had no choice but to walk into the bedroom, crossing her arms over her half-naked body. It was one of those impossibly awkward moments. Note for future reference, she thought: Never hunt burglars in a bikini.

"Fancy," Jeremiah said, "this is my runaway daughter, Libby. Libby, this is Fancy O'Brien."

Fancy knew enough not to extend her hand to someone who'd just as soon bite it off. "Glad to meet you, Libby. I hope we can be friends." Oh, jeez, wasn't that what stepmother number two had once said simperingly to her?

Libby's body had grown as taut as a bowstring. She looked as though she'd happily send a poison arrow Fancy's way. "What's she doing here?" she asked shrilly.

"We drove over for the weekend," Jeremiah patiently explained.

"That's why you don't want me here! I'm interrupting your weekend with your stupid girlfriend!"

I think I resent that, Fancy thought, unobtrusively withdrawing.

"Lib, I'm angry that you left home on your own, not that you're here with me," Jeremiah was saying in a soothing tone as Fancy slipped out of the room.

A strategic retreat, she figured, not the coward's way out. Still, she cringed halfway up the spiral staircase when Libby's soprano rang out with obvious disdain. "Why'd you have to bring *her* to our beach house?"

Fancy scurried upstairs in a turmoil. This was terrible. But how ironic that she was on the brink of becoming exactly what she'd always sworn she wouldn't—a wicked stepmother!

Twenty minutes later, both Fancy and Libby had calmed down. Sitting on the bed, Fancy had listened to the conciliatory murmur of Jeremiah's voice, Libby's high-pitched rejoinders and the accompanying banging of doors and slamming of drawers. When a relative peace had finally descended, she'd risen to change into the least objectionable outfit she could concoct: white denims and a sleeveless but demure fuschia cotton blouse. She buttoned all but the top button, remembering her own reaction to Miss Cherry Blossom, who'd bounced through the house in body-hugging spandex when Fancy had been going through a "chocolate is my only solace" pudgy period. Like Libby, she'd staged a getaway—hopping a midnight bus in the middle of her scheduled week with her father. Flat broke after the ticket, she'd starved through the long trip, a jump start on the diet that had turned her into a sexy rock-and-roll babe. Go figure.

Fancy sighed and brushed her hair. This situation called for no makeup, so it was time to head back into the fray.

Before she could, an unfamiliar car pulled up beside the convertible, honking raucously. From the loft, Fancy watched as a young man and woman emerged. Jeremiah came from the house and they gathered for a group hug. Fancy became numb. It seemed she and Jeremiah were about to have a full-fledged family affair.

She inched out onto the landing, hanging her head over the railing to watch as Quicks filled the house, laughing and gabbing and carrying on. *Wait'll they get a look at me,* Fancy thought morosely as she started down the curving stairs.

Libby shuffled out of the bedroom. "Lib, you rascal," said the male twin.

"You've caused us no end of trouble!" chimed the female.

They gathered in front of the smoke-blackened stone fireplace. Libby slouched, her lower lip sticking out a mile. Andrew was tall, with a boyish frame just beginning to fill out. Allison was as bandbox perfect as Fancy had imagined Diana Quick to be: neat dark brown hair anchored at her nape with a grosgrain bow, a billowing blouse, stirrup pants and practical shoes, all color-coordinated in shades of blue.

"...all because Mother wouldn't let her attend a Pearl Jam concert," Allison was saying to Jeremiah. "Mother made us drive up here to get her and it's not fair. My plans are ruined. We were going to shop for the baby's layette." Belatedly Fancy realized why Allison was wearing a billowing blouse.

"So-o-o sorry I upset your big plans," Libby sneered. "Just like I interrupted Dad's love life!" She marched off, slamming the bedroom door behind her.

"What did she mean by that?" Allison asked.

Andrew's gaze lifted to where Fancy was frozen in place on the staircase. "Well, look at that, will you?" he said. "Way to go, Dad!"

Allison stared, bug-eyed. "Dad, how could you? She looks younger than me!"

JEREMIAH SAVED the day by keeping everyone busy and organized. Libby and Andrew were sent off to find a telephone and more groceries. After a swim and a game of Scrabble, he commandeered Allison and Fancy as his kitchen crew. He was outside lighting the charcoal when Allison smiled sweetly over the pepper she was seeding and slicing. "Just think, Fancy, if you marry my father, you'll be a stepgrandmother at age thirty."

Fancy almost sliced off her thumb. "How...unique," she managed. "When is your baby due?"

"And then if you get pregnant, my baby'll be older than her own aunt or uncle," Allison continued. "I never thought the Quicks would turn into a sitcom family!"

Smiling determinedly, Fancy stabbed a zucchini. She planned to keep on smiling until it killed her or gave her wrinkles, whichever came first. Wrinkles would be good. A stepgrandma could use a few.

A while later she was sitting out on the deck, watching as Jeremiah tried to juggle the cooking times of all the meat and vegetables he'd thrown on the grill. A halved tomato had already split its skin and fallen into the coals.

Andrew came up from the beach, his unbuttoned shirt hanging open. He looked uncertainly from his father to Fancy, then came to sit beside her. With a charming lopsided grin, he put his arm on the railing behind her shoulders. "Why're you hanging around an old fogey like my dear old dad?" he asked, adding insinuatingly, "I bet we'd get along real well."

Flames shot up as Jeremiah lost a shrimp. "Who's an old fogey, Andy?" he roared.

Fancy tried to laugh—not easy to do through a gritted-teeth smile.

Andrew flashed her a lady-killer-in-training look. "Do you like younger men?"

She patted his cheek as if he were a baby in a bassinet. "Aren't you cute?" she said, and firmly removed his arm from her shoulders. Andrew looked doubtful for only a second or two before his face cleared and he favored her with another smile. Genuine, this time.

The tightness in Fancy's throat eased enough to allow her to eat some of her charred dinner. Thankfully, Jeremiah was in control of the conversation, making his children tell him everything they'd been doing since he'd last talked to them. Fancy learned that Allison's husband was in law school at the same Texas college Andrew attended. The twins had driven to Atlanta for a short visit with their mother before returning for the summer session and preparations for the baby's arrival.

Uncommunicative Libby glopped three huge spoonfuls of sour cream on every vegetable but her baked potato, eliciting an "Ew!" from her sister. When Jeremiah pushed, she grudgingly admitted that she and her mother had been clashing over the proper behavior for a young lady of thirteen.

Now that sounds familiar, Fancy thought with some sympathy. Maybe she and Libby could find a way to be friends. However, judging by the sullen looks Libby kept shooting at her over the table, Fancy knew the girl considered her more of an enemy.

What goes around comes around, Fancy's little devil whispered gleefully. She entertained herself by envisioning sticking a fork in it and roasting it over the coals.

After dinner, Jeremiah and Andrew began to play basketball in the driveway, and Allison went to take a short nap. Ten restless minutes later, Fancy screwed up her fortitude and followed Libby down to the seashore.

She was scuffling along the tide line, kicking up clots of wet sand, her head hanging low, her jeans wet up to the knees. Fancy rolled her white denims up to her calves and strode purposefully across the sand. "Hi, there," she chirped. "Looking for seashells?"

Glowering, Libby tossed a pebble into the ocean. "Is this the part where you try to be my buddy?"

Fancy smile determinedly, her jaw starting to hurt. "I wouldn't dream of it. But there's no reason we can't be polite acquaintances."

Libby shrugged and dug her toes into the sand. Despite the girl's rudeness, or maybe because of it, Fancy again felt a surge of empathy. "What grade are you in?" she blurted, and immediately winced. How incredibly lame!

"I'll be a freshman," Libby said with a put-upon sigh.

"That should be fun."

"Yeah, sure," Libby replied, infusing her words with the heavy ennui only a teenager can manage. Rolling her eyes, she turned to face the ocean.

Fancy took a deep breath and tried again. "When I was thirteen, punk was cool. I hacked off half my hair, dyed some of it blue and wore safety pins through my ears."

Libby looked mildly interested. "My mother would kill me if I did that."

"My mother would've if she'd caught me."

Libby scowled when she realized they'd been having a conversation. "The punk look is *so* dead." She bent to scratch in the mud.

"What's that? A periwinkle?"

Libby tossed the little brown shell into the water. "It was chipped."

"My father sent me some beautiful shells—cowries and conchs, I think—when he was honeymooning in the South Seas with my first stepmother. I decided I wanted to be like a mollusk." Fancy paused, but Libby didn't ask why. She appeared to be listening, though. "Mollusks make their shells from lime, did you know that?"

"I've taken biology."

Fancy persisted. "So, anyway, I admired the mollusk. It builds and transports its own shell, an invulnerable defense for its very vulnerable body. Everywhere it goes, it's home, if you see what I mean."

"Does this story have a moral?" Libby asked, trying to be surly, but there was a slight tremble in her voice.

"Uh..." Great. A moral. She had to come up with a moral. "Well, maybe just that we humans aren't mollusks, no matter how tough our shells. But we can still learn that home is where the heart is."

Libby snorted. Fancy recognized the wounded look in her eyes. "Libby, your father cares about you. He worries about you."

Libby turned on Fancy, tension radiating from her fragile body. "I could tell him not to marry you. I could. And he *wouldn't!*"

"Maybe you're right, Libby, but think about it. What does that tell you about his feelings for you? Do you really believe that a few hundred miles diminishes those kind of feelings?"

Libby uttered a small harsh cry and spun around, her long Quick legs sending her soaring across the beach, sand spraying behind her.

Fancy followed a minute later, trudging through the sand with her average-length O'Brien legs. However, her *heart* was soaring. Despite the complications, despite her upcoming birthday, she was for some odd reason suddenly sure that she and Jeremiah were meant to be together.

Webster Station Chronicle
Talk of the Town by Mitzi Janeway

Broadway Baby

The die is cast and the cast will die. Or mebbe it's only Mo Rowe who'll die—because Stella O'Brien is our Tevye!! Stella assures me she looks *mucho* macho in a long gray beard! Since she had the strongest voice of all who tried out for *Fiddler,* Director Woodman went the gender-bender route. Dustin Hoffman and Jaye Davidson did it in Oscar style, so why not Stella? *My* only reservation is being cast as Yenta the Matchmaker. Do I look like a nosy, meddling, gossipy old hag? I *do?!!*

Baby on Board

On other affronts, Hester and the LSD have proceeded with their boycott of Haute Water—but the only women obeying are those without a boy in their cot! (And no hope of getting one?) I suspect Hessie herself would dearly love to try out one of Fancy's magic elixirs on the boy she's trying to lure into *her* cot. Too bad she's painted herself into a corner!

I'm not s'posed to tell this next juicy bit, but I just can't help myself. (Insert fanfare here.) Betty Jo Dandy is in the family way!! Betty Jo may be a few (!) years past this column's age deadline, but the grand conception doesn't quite fall into the miracle category. Since her own momma had a change-of-life baby (B.J. herself, and didn't that cause big sis Hester some embarrassment!), Betty Jo's just continuing a family tradition. Doctor is looking mighty proud and Jessica thinks it's Jim-dandy (how's that for a name if it's a boy?). The way this spring has gone, I wouldn't be surprised if nine months from now W.S. is reaping a bumper crop of bouncing babies!!

Ooh Baby, Baby

Since we're speaking *en famille*, I must announce another arrival to Our Town. We last left Fancy and Jeremiah romping in the surf. I don't know what those two got up to, but I do know they returned with a bouncing baby girl of their own—only she's a wee bit sassier than your average infant. There I was at the *Chronicle*, writing my fingers to the bone, when who should drive up but J.Q. and his *thirteen*-year-old daughter, Libby! Fancy was squeezed next to a cooler behind them (talk about taking a back seat!). Libby, something of a give-'em-hell Southern belle (a gal after my own heart!), looks like very promising material for future columns. I'm keeping my eye on her!!

10

JEREMIAH STUDIED the intriguing tangle of naked limbs and torsos, wondering what Fancy was planning now. She was standing in the display window, tearing down long strips of wallpaper, looking both cute and workmanlike in a tight delphinium blue tube top and white painter's overalls. He rapped on the glass.

She waved at the shop door. "Come on in," she mouthed. "It's not locked."

He walked through the darkened store and climbed up into the lighted display. "Hi, Fancy," he said, weighing the rigidity of her turned back and deciding it was safe to kiss her. "Stella told me you were staying after hours to work on a new window." He paused significantly. "Does this have anything to do with Hester's editorial?" Hester's piece, a mere shadow of its former verbiage, had appeared in that afternoon's *Chronicle*.

"Not at all," she insisted. *Rip.*

"You sure?" Alice Ann had excised the most blatant swipes at Haute Water. Still, everyone in town had to know to whom the phrase "lawless, godless, soulless destroyer of public morality" referred.

"Positive. I'd heard it all before. The whole town has heard it all before." She shrugged. "The LSD boycott doesn't worry me, either—even Fritzi Janeway came in on the sly for some skin-care products."

"Then why the new window?"

Fancy scratched at a section of stubborn paper. "I needed an outlet for my excess energy."

"The wind chimes again?"

She raised an eyebrow. "Wind chimes are the least of it."

"Ah." He allowed himself a satisfying burst of male pride, then surveyed the display area. The fixtures had been removed and now the space was thick with plants: bushy ferns, potted trees, palms of several varieties. "It's a jungle in here."

Fancy was opening cans of gray and blue paint. "That's the idea."

"Can I help?"

She wiped her hands on her thighs. "Want to untangle Santa Maria?" She nodded at the mannequins. "She goes into storage."

"I see." He sure did. And so would anyone passing by on Main Street. Between the shadows of the foliage and the contortions of the nude mannequins as he untangled them, it had to look as if something "utterly obscene" was once again happening at Haute Water. As he separated Santa Maria's torso from the legs of the second mannequin, her blond head swiveled around to stare up at him with a familiar wide-eyed expression. "What about the other one?"

"Pinta stays here. I have plans for him."

That was what he was afraid of. But he held his tongue and slung Maria over his shoulder for the trip to the storage room. Fancy was stirring paint when he returned. He watched for a minute, then said, "About Libby." She kept stirring. "I'm sorry we haven't had much time together lately. It's been one thing after another with Libby. I'm not sure where that girl's head is at . . ."

Fancy knew. She stopped stirring and straightened. So far, Libby had smoked in the *Chronicle's* smoke-free newsroom, dumped red dye into Dottie the Mermaid's water-

circulation system and called Hester a bossy old bag when
Hester scolded her for wearing makeup. Fancy, clinging to
her soaring moment of hope on the beach, had made over-
tures of friendship each time she was in and out of Jeremiah's apartment to work on the bathroom. Libby's
reactions had run from hot anger to cold disdain—only now
and then hinting that a more temperate climate existed.

"It's okay, Jeremiah. I understand. Libby comes first just
now, and that's as it should be."

"I've been on the phone with Diana, trying to persuade
her to rearrange the visitation schedule. Turns out what
Libby really ran away from was being sent off to tennis
camp while her mother and new stepfather toured Eu-
rope."

"Oh . . . poor kid." Although she could sympathize, the
idea of putting their relationship on ice for the next few
weeks didn't sound so great, either. Every time she remembered how Jeremiah had held her in the night, whispering
intimate midnight words, Fancy knew she couldn't give him
up for anything. Not even to please the thirteen-year-old girl
of her present. Or her past.

Seeing the soft glimmer in her eyes, Jeremiah walked over
and took the dripping paint stick from her hand. He
dropped it on the sheet of newsprint that contained Hester's guest editorial. "There's one thing to be set straight,
Fancy. I don't assign places of importance to the women in
my life."

As he put his arms around her, a little shiver ran up her
spine. No matter how many times she heard it, his smooth
voice had the same intoxicating effect. "My heart is big
enough for all of you," he murmured, and she knew it was
so.

"Promise?"

He kissed her. "I promise."

"Even though Libby hates me?"

He grinned against her lips. "I know she acts like a brat around you, but she doesn't hate you. Just yesterday we were discussing Smashing Pumpkins and Red Hot Chili Peppers, and Libby was quite impressed that you knew all their songs. She told me you were punk when punk was cool."

"She did?" Fancy's eyes brightened as she put her arms around his shoulders, getting a smear of paint on his pristine shirt. "And what would you know about the Red Hot Chili Peppers?"

"They're hot and spicy?" he guessed. "So are you." He waggled his eyebrows. "Wanna get pickled?"

She giggled. "So long as it's by you, Froggie, any time. But what about Libby?"

"She can't stand hot pickled peppers."

"What the heck are we talking about?" Fancy asked, even though it didn't matter as long as Jeremiah kept on kissing her. He really knew how to kiss. He did a thing with his tongue that made her hotter than a jalapeño.

"Beau is on baby-sitting duty tonight."

"And my mother's gone to rehearsal by now. We can have the house all to ourselves. You won't even have to sneak in through the window."

"Can I, anyway?" His hand slipped under the bib of her overalls. His fingers were playing a sensual tune over her ribs, thumb nudging under the stretchy tube top, when someone knocked on the window.

They'd forgotten they were on display. Bobby Vernon stood on the sidewalk looking in at them. A police car idled at the curb. He mouthed something that contained the word *Libby*.

Jeremiah was outside in two seconds flat. Fancy followed almost as quickly. Bobby explained that Libby was

fine, just causing trouble because she'd crashed the Loblolly, swaggered up to the bar and ordered a martini. Beau's
motorcycle had been found in the parking lot; Beau had
been found snoozing on Jeremiah's couch. "All those late
nights must've finally caught up with him," Bobby gloated.

"Maybe I should have you stick the both of them in jail,"
Jeremiah said, shaken by the stark terror of fearing Libby
had been hurt—or worse. He turned to Fancy. "Sorry, but
I've got to—"

"Go on," she urged, having also been jolted. She touched
her palm to his cheek. "It'll be okay. Libby's looking for attention—even the negative kind." Gosh, why did that ring
a bell of familiarity even now?

He kissed her again, only a quick peck. "See, I told you
you're wise." He hurried off toward his car.

Fancy watched him run down the middle of the empty
street, remembering what Stella had said with a jolly laugh
of retribution after she'd met Libby: "Consider this your
comeuppance, Fan. I just hope Libby doesn't give you as
many gray hairs as you gave me!"

ALTHOUGH THE BACKYARD appeared undisturbed, Stella
flicked on the light and opened the door, listening. Except
for the hum of the bugs gathering around the glowing bulb,
all was quiet.

Stella wasn't fooled. She'd developed an instinct for these
things in the days when Fancy had thought sneaking out to
join her black-leathered rock-and-roll boyfriend was the
height of rebellion. What her daughter had never suspected was that Stella had paid young the drummer—he'd
had his eye on a pricey snare—to see that Fancy drank
nothing more intoxicating than Coke and was home within
ninety minutes of curfew. Not even the drummer had
known that Stella had purposely set curfew earlier so that

Fancy could think she was breaking it. Convoluted, yes, but it had worked.

Stella stepped onto the porch, sure there was something—and there was. The screen from Fancy's bedroom window had been removed and propped against the porch railing.

The wind chimes tinkled in the breeze. Stella stepped toward the window, coming close enough to hear Jeremiah's low tones and her daughter's answering giggle. Then she went back into the house, directly to the kitchen cupboard where she'd secreted her colorful travel pamphlets behind a sack of lima beans. It was finally time to make her plans.

"NO NUDITY! No nudity! No nudity!"

Fancy was sure she'd hear the chant even in her dreams. It was much louder than usual because Hester's troops had swelled. The LSD had been recruiting among the more conservative residents of nearby Cloud River. They'd been joined this fine morning by a fresh-scrubbed baby-faced youth group who were ardent supporters of the cause.

"No nudity! No nudity! No nudity!"

Stella threw down her dusting cloth. "That chanting is driving me up the wall. I can't take it anymore! Let's have them arrested for disturbing the peace." She marched out of the store, eyes blazing. Fancy followed. There was going to be trouble.

Stella stomped past Fancy's jungle tableau. It featured a nude Tarzan—Pinta with his back to the window—bathing under a thin stream of water spraying from a nozzle hidden among a pile of fake rocks painted to look lichen-covered. The back wall was sky blue, the floor a fuzzy green carpet scattered with real rocks. Tucked among the foliage were the bottles, tubes and jars of the ecologically friendly line of bath products Fancy was pushing.

The picketers shouted and jeered when the O'Briens emerged from Haute Water. Hester lifted her sign. Cover Up! was scrawled across it in jagged black letters. Fancy glanced at poor Pinta's bare buns. Perfectly unobjectionable fiberglass buns, she'd thought, as smooth and hard as globes. Besides, they were barely visible through the spikes of a monster yucca and the fronds of a lush maidenhair fern.

"Im-moral! Im-modest! Im-pure!" Hester bellowed, aiming one stubby finger at Fancy's alarmed face.

"Im-becile," retorted Stella.

"It's not ladylike to point," Mitzi said, joining Stella and Fancy on the sidewalk. Despite the eighty-degree weather, she was wearing a sturdy safari jacket and what appeared to be combat boots over a flamingo pink pantsuit and a trailing chiffon scarf. She hugged Fancy around the shoulders. "Don't worry. As mayor of this town, I pledge my support to your cause."

"I don't have a cause—" Fancy tried to protest, but Mitzi had drawn Stella over so the three of them stood abreast. She began to sing "We Shall Overcome" in her reedy warbling voice.

The escalating clamor had drawn most of the Main Street shopkeepers outside. Mitch came from the drugstore. His gaze darted between Stella, singing in unison with Mitzi, and Hester at the head of the picket line. His bald pate began to sweat.

Hester circled around to him. "Albert," she ordered, "grab a sign and join the group!" He shuffled his feet indecisively.

Alice Ann arrived, accompanied by Pringle and his camera. Elmer and his buddies watched avidly from a safe position—no fools they—across the street. Out of the corner of her eye, Fancy even spotted Libby. She was leaning against a mailbox, watching the commotion in amusement.

Hester turned to address her troops, waving at the window of Haute Water. "What do we *say* to such a flagrant display?"

"No!" they answered, and took up the chant again: "No nudity! No nudity! No nudity!"

"Jeez," Fancy said to no one in particular. "All this because of Tarzan's buns? I thought 'no nudity' applied only to live flesh."

Several tourists approached with triple-scoop ice-cream cones and looks of curiosity. The society broke formation and swarmed the sidewalk. "Boycott! Boycott!" Hester boomed as she whipped the picket sign in frenzied circles overhead.

Stella stepped forward, trying to clear a path so the tourists could reach Haute Water. "Clear the sidewalk," she shouted at the protesters. "You're violating the peaceful-protest ordinance, Hester. Police! Police!"

Crouching, Stella dug one shoulder into Hester's backside to push her out of the way. Hester gasped with indignation and planted her feet, in the process losing her grip on the wobbling picket sign. It swung downward like the blade of a guillotine, aimed at Stella's exposed neck.

Fancy leapt forward, grabbing the sign a split second before it could do a Marie Antoinette on her mother's head. Hester yanked violently on her end, but Fancy's grip was stronger and Hester lurched backward, slipping on a puddle of melting ice cream and bowling into her troops as if they were pins in an alley. "Stee-rike!" an onlooker yelled gleefully.

Maybelle Clark charged up and slammed her picket sign into the side of Fancy's head. With a banshee-screech, Stella rammed her shoulder into Maybelle's midriff. "Take *that*, you old crow."

Reeling, Fancy put her hands over her ringing ears and sank to the sidewalk, not sure if she should laugh or cry. Through a forest of flailing arms, stomping legs and well-padded rear ends, she saw Libby Quick rounding up the dumbstruck youth group. She was talking excitedly. Amongst a cacophony of shrieks, grunts and cries of "No nudity!" it sounded like "Let's all go to my place and listen to some Amy Grant and Barry Manilow!" Fancy decided to laugh.

Suddenly two strong male hands were lifting her up. She didn't have to turn to know her knight in shining armor had galloped into the fray.

"*Stop!*" Jeremiah yelled, more forcefully than one would think a gentleman could. Clutched protectively against him, Fancy felt the thunder in his voice right up her spine. The fine hairs at the back of her neck prickled as an abrupt total silence descended upon Main Street.

In the shocking silence, Maybelle groaned and slid to the ground.

Mitch straightened Hester's wig.

Stella hoisted Mitzi out of the gutter, and Mitzi handed her twin sister, Fritzi, the other half of a torn picket sign.

And Fancy and Libby exchanged shaky smiles.

JEREMIAH LOOKED UP from the antiseptic he was uncapping. "My hero," Fancy cooed, batting her eyelashes at him as a thin line of blood trickled down her left temple. He shook his head in exasperation. The woman was irrepressible.

"This is going to sting." He dabbed at her wound and she winced, gripping the edge of her desk. After the battleground of the Great Webster Station War for Decency had cleared, he'd marched Fancy into her office for triage and talk.

"Why are you always getting into these predicaments?" he asked, taping a bandage over the small cut Maybelle had inflicted.

"I always get out of them," she reminded him, tentatively exploring the rest of the lumps on her head.

"How would you have gotten out of this one if I hadn't put a stop to the nonsense?" Nonsense, yes, but some of it had been pretty nasty. Jeremiah knew the time had come to put a stop to it permanently. "I'd rather not see your skull get crushed over something as inconsequential as a window display, okay?"

Although she wasn't quite back to form, vehemence still fired Fancy's words. "Freedom of speech is inconsequential?"

"Of course not. I just don't think putting a loincloth on Tarzan will result in the trashing of the Bill of Rights." He bent down to kiss her bandaged temple. "All better?"

Fancy leaned her head against his chest, finding comfort in his crisp shirt and conservative tie. She hugged his waist. "Better," she murmured into his buttons. "At least it won't be long before this kind of thing is a nonissue."

"Why's that?" Jeremiah sent his hands down her narrow back, skimming over the smooth skin her polka-dot sundress exposed. She seemed so fragile to him; he hoped her feminist sensibilities would forgive him for wanting to protect her.

"My birthday's coming up in only eight days. I'll be thirty."

"Yes?"

"So I'll be an adult! A docile adult. Well-suited to a respectable businessman such as yourself. There will be no more embarrassing predicaments, you'll be happy to hear."

He set her back a little to see what the heck was going on in her face. Her eyes were unblinkingly serious. "What are you talking about?" he said with a short laugh of disbelief. "Whatever gave you the idea I wanted you to change, thirty years old or not?"

"W-well . . ." she stammered, clearly confused. He wondered just how hard a hit her head had taken.

"My God, Fancy." Hands on either cheek, he turned her face up to his. "For one thing, after what just happened out there it should be pretty obvious that age has nothing to do with maturity. But more importantly, you should know that your joie de vivre is one of the things I've loved about you from the beginning. I figured if I was lucky, I'd become more like you."

An expression of slightly bashful, definitely unburdened bliss transformed her face. "I can still be me?" she whispered, eyes shining, lips barely moving. "You love the *me* in me?"

Jeremiah smiled. "Even the part of you that dives into mermaid fountains," he promised. "Especially the part that dives into mermaid fountains."

"Maybe you'll even consider joining me?"

He laughed. "That might be asking too much."

Fancy threw her arms around his neck. They were kissing madly when Libby opened the office door without knocking. Fancy tried to alert Jeremiah, but he wouldn't release her mouth. All she managed were a few muffled grunts and squirms that he took as evidence of her passion.

Libby watched without expression for several seconds. Then she smiled and rolled her eyes. "Adults!" she said in exasperation. "Can't leave 'em alone for a minute."

Webster Station Chronicle
Talk of the Town by Mitzi Janeway

Brouhaha-Ha-Ha-Ha-Ha, Part II

Did any of you notice that the Great Webster Station War for Decency climaxed on the very last official day of spring—June 20th? All I can say is, *what a way to go!!*

For those of you who missed the war, Pringle's front-page photos just don't do it justice! One had to be there to fully appreciate the sight of an ice-cream cone smashed atop Margaret Burton's pointy head. To see Maybelle Clark's home-run swing (Fancy's head was the baseball!), the split in Eudora's pants (pink nylon, if you must know), Stella's tackling demonstration and Hester's lopsided wig. And what of *moi*, you wonder? How did your intrepid reporter fare? As I had the foresight to dress for a riot, my only casualties were the fingernails of my right hand (torn to smithereens when I ripped Fritzi's picket sign in half.) I don't mind sacrificing for the cause, but please 'scuse me while I make a quick call to Sue Swertlow for an emergency manicure!

Since the melee, I've done some investigating and confirming. You may find the following list of damages amusing: two cases of laryngitis, three smashed ice-cream cones, one torn-asunder picket sign, two broken heels, one pair of split pants, three head lumps, seven bruises (blue, yellow, red, purple and every combination thereof), eight ripped fingernails, and one steamed publisher (see editorial page!).

Other Undoings

There's no rest for the weary. Besides the announcement of Oliver's last-in-the-series (he promises!) Garden Club speech, "Kudzu: Declaring Chemical Warfare," there's also *Fiddler*'s revised rehearsal schedule (page 4) 'cause of Stella's strained throat.

I almost missed Libby Quick's relatively quiet departure from town. (Did her Loblolly push-up-bra-and-heavy-makeup escapade have anything to do with that?!) Don't worry, though, folks—young Miss Libby was heard to state that she's coming back real soon!!

It wouldn't be right to end a column without catching up on what's happening (besides brouhahas) in the life of the O'Briens. Fancy's big three-oh birthday bash (let's hope nobody takes the bash part literally) will be held at the Loblolly, 7:00 p.m. sharp, Friday night. This is the official invite to any and all who'd care to attend—and that includes, Fancy made it a point to say, the ladies from the LSD!! Should be interesting, no? You can be sure I'll be there with bells on!

I can't wait to see who Stella shows up with. Didja know she's been having clandestine meetings with Benjamin Phipps, who's quite the catch because of all those frequent-flyer miles he accumulates through Phipps Travel? Hmm. I wonder if this means Hester has lost the War for Decency but won the battle for Mitch?!!

"'THE RIGHT TO FREE speech carries with it the burden of responsibility,'" Stella read. "Is Jeremiah referring to you or Hester?"

"Both of us." Fancy looked up from her desk, where she was calmly going over party lists. "And all of us."

Stella popped another throat lozenge. "Don't I know it."

Fancy consulted the food list. Aubergine Rizzo was down for chili. "He wasn't just referring to our bumps and bruises. The entire episode was ridiculous even before it erupted into actual physical warfare."

Stella eyed her daughter over the edge of yesterday's *Chronicle.* "Are you the same bikini-ball player who flashed a V for victory as she was escorted off by campus security?" she asked, adding reproachfully, "Hester shouldn't have tried to chop off my head."

"That was an accident. And you did push her."

"She was blocking our door," Stella said hotly. "What? Are you going to join the LSD now? It's bad enough that you've gone and invited them to the party."

"Now, Mom," Fancy soothed. She'd been amazingly benevolent and unruffled lately. Nothing bothered her—not even the prospect of the thirtieth birthday she'd been dreading for months. It seemed merely a cause for celebration now that she knew it was going to be the start of a wonderful new life, instead of the end of the old. "Jeremiah is right about adults needing to work out a compromise before resorting to fighting," she said, paraphrasing his editorial. She'd taken his words, and him, to heart.

Brett barged into the office. "A loincloth! Fancy, how could you?"

"It's a compromise. What's wrong with that?"

Brett clutched her head. "This is just like the library art-book fiasco," she moaned. "The town was in an uproar and looking to stay that way when along comes Jeremiah, counseling Lucy and Hester into a half-baked compromise. And Webster Station reverted to its boring old self again."

"So we should continue the war for your amusement, Brett?" Fancy thought of the avidness with which the townspeople read Mitzi's column and the lightning speed of their grapevine. "Or for the amusement of the town at large?"

Brett grinned impishly. "You got it."

"Well, sorry. 'Y'all' will have to find something else to gossip about. Having done more than my share, I'm officially retired."

"No, you're twitterpated. This is all Jeremiah's fault." Brett looked disgusted.

Fancy smiled beatifically. "My feelings for him have nothing to do with the legitimacy of his argument. Besides, next time there could be serious bloodshed." She tapped her temple. "I don't want that on my conscience."

"Speaking of bloodshed—" Brett nodded toward the outer shop "—Hester's waiting for you."

Fancy jumped to her feet, scattering the lists. "And you left her out there alone?"

She hurried from the office, not entirely sure she could trust her opponent. Hester, nostrils quivering suspiciously, was standing beside the bottles of massage oil. "Mrs. High-tower?" Fancy said hesitantly.

Hester turned, lips clamped into a prim line. She pried them apart and said, "You may call me Hester."

Fancy rocked back on her heels. "Hester," she repeated awkwardly.

Hester cleared her throat for a pronouncement. "The Ladies' Society for Decency is a nonviolent group."

"That's also Haute Water's policy."

"I trust we all learned a lesson." Hester wrapped her hands around the strap of her canvas bag. "Your Mr. Quick made a few incisive points in his editorial." She trembled with the turmoil of her inner struggle. "I've decided that I shall practice forbearance and forgiveness. Come what may." Her mouth twisted as she added beneath her breath, "Even if it kills me."

Fancy's dimple surfaced. "It almost killed you *not* to."

"No, it almost killed your mother. I mailed her a card this morning in apology."

"I must apologize, too, Hester. I hope you find my Tarzan's loincloth an acceptable compromise?"

"It will do for a start."

Although Fancy's smile turned steely, she left it at that.

Hester was glancing furtively around the shop. "As long as I'm here, and since the society has voted to cancel the boycott—" she squared her shoulders, daring Fancy to laugh "—I'm interested in purchasing a custom blend of essential oils."

Fancy slipped behind the counter while Hester examined the sample bottles as if she'd found the Holy Grail. "Don't tell Stella," she whispered.

Fancy nodded her assent. "Or Mitzi."

"Or Mama."

"Or...Mitch?" Fancy added, thinking, *Poor Mitch. He hasn't got a chance.*

FANCY'S PARTY had grown beyond all proportion. When it was only going to be for her birthday—what she hadn't considered an especially joyous occasion—her mother had planned to host a small get-together at the cottage. After

Fancy had turned the party into a celebration of the Great War's armistice, the Loblolly became the natural choice.

Everyone had come, even the members of the LSD. "Another boycott gone by the wayside," Fancy commented as she accepted Aubergine's contribution to the buffet, a huge cauldron of Rizzorific Fireball Chili.

"Maybelle even closed the café for the night," Aubergine said cheerfully. She peeled a sheet of foil off a platter of gingersnaps and went to add it to the dessert table.

"Aunt Hester used to man the punch bowl at the annual Spring Fling, though Mom swears she's never seen her dance," said Jessica Dandy. She hugged Fancy. "Happy birthday. Don't worry, thirty isn't *that* old!"

"Gosh, thanks," Fancy said as Jessica rushed off to join the young crowd who'd staked out the jukebox. Doctor and Betty Jo were already ensconced in one of the booths, billing and cooing.

Brett arrived next, brandishing a gift-wrapped box. "Happy, happy, Fancy. I brought you a little something."

"But did you bring a date?" Brett was wearing a nearly see-through ecru lace dress over a tan body stocking.

"Not on your life," she scoffed. "I'm here to have fun!" Waving, she headed for the dance floor.

Fancy would've liked to dance herself, but she'd lost track of Jeremiah and no other partner looked appealing. She tapped her foot, enjoying the atmosphere even though she felt strangely alone among the many friends she'd accumulated since moving to Webster Station. She had everything a woman could ask for. Except her man. Where was he?

As predicted, Hester Hightower was passing out cups of punch. Each recipient also received a few words of advice: "Don't you think that getup should've stayed in the bedroom, Brett?" Or, "Melissa, do you have to dance in such a flagrant manner?" Needless to say, the level of the punch was receding very slowly. That is, until Hester's back was turned and Mitch slipped something from his pocket, making a furtive motion over the cut-crystal bowl. Fancy couldn't believe her eyes. Mitch had just spiked the punch!

Mitzi sailed out of the crowd. "Did not!"

"Did, too," Fritzi, right behind her, insisted.

Mitzi grabbed Fancy's arm. "Settle this for us. Have I ever, *ever* written that my sister is an alcoholic?" Her head bobbed, making her spangly earrings swing like chandeliers in an earthquake.

Fritzi shook her head, loose jowls flapping like a basset hound's. "Just as good as. Nobody will ever forget those schnapps bottles! And what was that about my skin?"

"I wrote that my skin looks younger than yours. Is it a crime to tell the truth?"

Fritzi's whippet-slim body quivered with outrage beneath a limp linen suit. "I may be wrinkled, but face it, Mitzi, you're fat!"

Mitzi gasped. "I am not! I'm pleasingly plump!"

"This is supposed to be a smoke-the-peace-pipe party, girls," Fancy interjected to no avail.

"Then I'll be booting your 'pleasingly plump' behind out of office come November," said Fritzi. "In fact, now's the perfect time to announce my candidacy." She hurried off toward the bandstand.

Mitzi flounced after her. "The day this town elects you over me is the day pigs fly!"

And that was when Fancy finally spotted Jeremiah on the far side of the dance floor. Warmth enveloped her from head to toe as she realized all over again how much he meant to her. It was because of him that she'd finally accepted herself for what she was, and because of him that she knew she could become even more. Thirty was looking like it would be the best year of her life!

Standing on the tips of her rose-colored slingbacks, she waved to get his attention. He didn't notice. Unwilling to wait any longer, she took a deep breath and plunged into the throng.

Beau grabbed her by the waist, muttered, "Dance me past Willa," and away they went. Frustrated, Fancy let Beau circle her toward the crowd of men who'd surrounded Willa Clark. The young woman was fever-flushed, giggling and batting her lashes faster than a hummingbird's wings, eyes abnormally bright. Fancy pushed Beau through the admirers.

"Put this boy out of his misery," she told Willa. "Dance with him, please." Without waiting to see what happened, she turned and plowed a very determined path to Jeremiah.

Finally there he was, tall and handsome in a tailored dark blue suit. He looked down at her with his gorgeous, welcoming golden brown eyes and said, "Have you heard about Pringle and Alice Ann?"

If she groaned, and she wasn't sure it was audible over the thumping music, anyway, Fancy figured she deserved to be forgiven. It could be that she'd made *too* many friends in Webster Station, she decided, nonetheless trying to look interested. "No, I haven't heard. Big news?"

Alice Ann stood between the two tall men. "We're engaged."

Fancy was flabbergasted. "You and *Pringle?*"

"Now that's flattering," the photographer said through a mouthful of nachos.

"I didn't mean it that way," Fancy sputtered. She looked to Alice Ann for help. "I thought you wanted to date Beau."

Alice Ann gazed up, way up, at Pringle with blind adoration. "Why would I be interested in Beau when there's a photographer like Pringle available?"

Pringle's skin took on a color. Red. "She only wants me for my darkroom skills."

Alice Ann chortled. "That's one way of putting it."

Fancy was discombobulated. "Am I the only one who had no idea?"

Alice Ann shook her head. "Probably the one and only time Pringle and I get a mention in 'Talk of the Town' and you miss it."

"I think I might have missed a column when we were at the beach," she recalled. Jeez, miss one Mitzi and you're completely out of the loop.

"We leave next month for Africa," Alice Ann announced.

"What's in Africa?" Fancy was getting an odd feeling about this.

"*National Geographic* loves Africa," Alice Ann explained. "We're going to be a free-lance writer/photographer team."

"And after Africa, Alice Ann says there's bound to be a war starting somewhere," Pringle added. "She wants to work the trenches."

Fancy narrowed her eyes at Alice Ann. "Isn't this sort of . . . reckless?" It was astounding. Alice Ann was reckless. Bobby was committed. Willa was irresistible. And Hester? Fancy wondered, just as Hester trotted past in Mitch's arms, her wig bobbing in time to the music. Yes, apparently Hester was feeling a mite uninhibited.

Fancy was reaching for the reassurance of Jeremiah's hand when the lights darkened and the crowd burst into "Happy Birthday to You." Aubergine, round and rosy in a lacy maternity top even though she was only four months pregnant, entered from the kitchen, wheeling a huge birthday cake, brilliantly aflame with thirty candles.

Eyes shiny with unshed tears, Fancy looked around the circle of smiling faces. She was one lucky thirty-year-old.

Jeremiah's hand squeezed hers, and she knew that at this moment there was only one thing wrong with the life she'd finally settled into.

She was going to have to eat a slice of a birthday cake baked by Aubergine Rizzo.

"FAN-CEEE?"

Fancy smiled into the darkness. "Over here, Mom."

Stella scuffled through the crowded gravel parking lot to where her daughter sat on the hood of a car. "Hester's doing the twist. She still hasn't realized the punch is spiked and must've drunk a gallon of it." She peered at Fancy. "Why are you out here all alone? It's not like you to miss a good party."

"I needed to catch my breath after opening all those presents," Fancy said dryly. Apparently she'd told a few too many folks about her apprehension about turning thirty. She'd received a prescription for bifocals, several packages of support hose, one of Mama's old canes and a gift certificate for a face-lift from Dr. Dandy. Other gifts had pertained to her window displays: a life preserver, scuba gear and, from the Janeways, a heavy woolen 1900s-style bathing suit, complete with moth-eaten bloomers and a ruffled cap.

"Pull up a hood, Mom. Are you okay about losing Mitch?"

Stella slapped the car. "Bosh! What would I want with such a mama's boy? I was only seeing him to get Hester all hot and bothered. I'd decided early on that she deserved it for all the trouble she caused Haute Water."

"The fight for Mitch was a ruse?"

"Of course. Even Mitzi was fooled." Stella sounded very pleased with herself. "Not that I misled Mitch. He knew we were just friends. He even got into it when he saw how it was affecting Hester."

Fancy looped her arm through Stella's. "Oh, Mom, when am I ever gonna marry you off? Is there any reason to hope that Ben Phipps . . . ?"

"I'm afraid not. Our clandestine meetings were for reasons of business, not romance." Stella paused, then plunged. "I'm booking an around-the-world cruise through his agency."

Limp with surprise, Fancy slid off the hood, heels hitting the gravel in a scattering of pebbles. "Around the world!"

Stella slid down beside her. "Fancy, dear, it's not that I haven't appreciated your efforts. Chester, Bolt and Rupert were amusing, but I've always yearned for adventure." She gestured wildly. "I want to scout Mayan ruins! See a bullfight! Spelunk! Sail the South Seas! Bungy jump!"

"Mother, I'm amazed. I never suspected."

"You see why I couldn't go through with any of those engagements."

"So why didn't you do this years ago, before you . . ."

"Got old?" Stella supplied. "Who's to say how a forty-nine-year-old should act if not the forty-nine-year-old herself?"

While Fancy was nodding in agreement—she'd certainly learned that lesson—she knew there was more to it. "Something held you back. Fess up, Mom."

"All right," Stella said, folding her arms. "I've been concerned about you, Fancy, in the same way you were concerned about me. I stayed around to see *you* settled and happy." At Fancy's stunned surprise, she smiled in gratification. "Now you've fit in so well here I can go off to my adventures with a clear conscience. I promise to drop in now and then with trinkets for the grandchildren."

"Do I look pregnant?" Fancy asked with a shaky, emotional laugh.

"Well, Jeremiah looks virile."

Fancy tilted back her head. Even through the darkness, Stella could see the happiness in her daughter's smile. "Jeremiah's already had his family."

"Don't be a dumb bunny, Fan. It's as plain as the grin on your face that there's not a thing in the world that man wouldn't do for you. Even change another thousand dirty diapers." Stella brushed off the seat of her dress. "Let's get back to the party. The cake should've been removed by now."

The double doors of the Loblolly opened as they neared, letting out a blast of light and noise and music. Fancy recognized Jeremiah's silhouette; she felt all syrupy and sentimental merely at the sight of him.

"Mm-hmm," Stella hummed appreciatively. "I must say, I picked you out a fine specimen for a husband."

"*You* picked . . ." Fancy started to say, but Jeremiah had taken her hand and was pulling her back into the Loblolly. The jukebox was playing Bonnie Raitt's "Something to Talk About."

"Hark," he said, "they're playing our song."

"You set that up." Fancy laughed as he pulled her close. Her heart was pounding against her ribs, even more loudly than the music, at least to her own heightened senses.

"Who could blame me?" Jeremiah let both his hands slide down to her swaying hips. "Have I told you how beautiful you are tonight?"

Suddenly Fancy couldn't wait for the party to end. Until then, they'd have to practice restraint, dammit. Dancing so close was not the way to do it. She twirled out to the limits of his reach and posed. "It's the Dorothy Lamour look," she said sweetly, referring to her outfit. She was wearing a sarong skirt of petal-pink silk with a matching bra top that bared her midriff. A big overblouse of sheer organza only slightly blurred the lines of her body.

Jeremiah spun her back into his arms. "You look like *l'amour*, all right," he said, the words vibrating sexily in his throat.

Although Fancy would've been happy to spend the rest of the party in his arms, Jeremiah soon swept her off to a booth for more privacy. The battered tabletop was lit with several votive candles, which also illuminated a gift-wrapped box. "From Libby and me," he explained. "She chose part of it."

"Oh." While Libby had warmed up before leaving for Atlanta, Fancy still thought it prudent to prepare herself for an especially gagging gag gift. A box of laxatives, perhaps, or a prepaid burial plot. She tore off the paper, opened the box, parted the tissue paper and found... "A seashell."

Jeremiah seemed a little anxious. "Libby swore you'd love it."

Fancy cupped the shell in her palms, running her finger-tips over the ridges, ribs and swirls. It was polished to a gleam, striped in brown, pink and cream. She chose to in-terpret Libby's message optimistically. "I do love it, Jere-miah. I truly do." It didn't make everything perfect; probably there were plenty of skirmishes ahead for her and Libby. But that was okay. Fancy knew she could handle them—as long as Jeremiah was there to handle them with her.

He put an arm around her shoulders and she leaned into his chest, feeling wonderfully happy and loved and—fi-nally—secure.

"There's another part to the gift—" he began when Willa interrupted by sliding into the seat opposite them. Her hair was tousled, only partly by design, her narrow face look-ing pale beneath a rainbow of makeup.

"You've got to help me, Fancy," she cried in a shaky voice. "'Irresistible' is too irresistible! I barely used a drop this morning and they still won't leave me alone." Before Fancy could reply, Willa looked past her and shrieked. "Here comes Boyd!" She slithered out of the booth, throwing Fancy a harried glance as she disappeared into the crowd. "Meet me in the ladies' room, pronto!"

THE PARTY ENDED with a splash—appropriately but not conveniently—when Hester, on her twentieth trip to the punch bowl, knocked it over. Since she'd already drunk all but the dregs, the mess was negligible. However, Mama Mitchell decreed that she'd never share the Mitchmobile with such a booze hound and Fancy ended up driving Hester home. Jeremiah took Willa—sneaking her out the back door while she frantically calculated how many tomato-juice baths would make her resistible again.

In the confusion Fancy and Jeremiah didn't get to make plans to extend the evening, and that was why Fancy found herself once again alone in her bedroom, the tinkling wind chimes frazzling her nerves. To distract herself, she lifted the seashell to her ear, expecting to hear the rushing sound of the sea.

The shell was silent. "That's not right," she murmured, poking one finger into the chamber and pulling out a folded handkerchief, monogrammed J.P.Q.

What had Jeremiah said? *Libby chose part of it.... There's another part to the gift....* Heart in her mouth, Fancy unfolded the handkerchief. A diamond ring winked up at her.

An engagement ring.

Jeremiah had been planning to ask her to marry him!

"Shoot," she said shortly. The travails of Willa, Mitzi, Fritzi, Hester and Mitch had foiled her once-in-a-lifetime proposal. Fancy scowled.

Then Fancy smiled. Perhaps the moment could be salvaged. In a very appropriate style.

She made a hasty decision. "A Quick decision," she chuckled, rushing around the house to gather up supplies.

She loaded everything into her car, made a short stop at Haute Water and arrived at the *Chronicle* parking lot only seventeen minutes after discovering the ring.

How fortunate that Jeremiah had given her a key to work on the bathroom, she thought as she used it to silently enter the loft. How fortunate the tilers had finished the grouting. And how fortunate, she determined with a glance at the empty couch, that Beau was such an alley cat.

She arranged things in the bathroom, then tiptoed to the kitchen after making a quick check on Jeremiah, who was sleeping sprawled across his bed fully clothed. He must've known to expect her, she decided, unwrapping a wheel of Camembert. She washed grapes, sliced an apple, arranged crackers on a plate. She uncorked a bottle of wine and found glasses in a cupboard, then carried everything into the bathroom.

Hoping the sound of the rushing water wouldn't wake Jeremiah before she was ready for him, she turned on the taps to fill the new whirlpool tub. From her tote bag, she took the bottle of essential oils she'd mixed at Haute Water—she hadn't taken the time to label it but in her mind its name was "Forevermore"—and added several drops to the steamy water. Then another for good measure. Just in case it really was a magic potion.

She stripped, shut off the water and went to look over Jeremiah's CDs. Selecting a stack of Mozart and Vivaldi, she adjusted the volume so the music would float softly through the apartment.

She crept up onto his bed, seeing that he was beginning to waken. She kissed his cheek. He murmured sleepily and automatically reached for her. She slipped away into the dark apartment, running silently back to the bathroom.

Jeremiah arrived only seconds later. "Is this a dream?" he asked, pausing in the doorway in amazement.

Candles illuminated the room with a flickering golden light, the shadows they cast shrouding modern details so the space appeared as soft-edged as a seductive dream. The air was scented with flowers and herbs and something he couldn't quite identify, although it made his body quicken in anticipation. The tall windows were draped in floaty lengths of sheer bronze fabric and a valance of tapestry-patterned velvet.

His gaze was drawn past a low table set with food and wine to the bathtub. Fancy's arm extended through the wafting steam, an empty wineglass in her hand. "Fill me up, will you?" she said.

He saw she was wearing the ring.

He walked over and filled her glass, setting the bottle on the floor of bronze-glazed tiles without taking his eyes off her. He drank in her lambent eyes, her soft moist skin, her lush pink lips, her dark hair all tousled around her smiling face. His body was charged with the intensity of a love greater than any he'd ever known.

Fancy swept her arm across the bubbling water in invitation. "Care to join me?"

She watched with gleaming eyes as he unselfconsciously shucked his rumpled clothes in a few swift motions. The glow of the candles gave his lean body a warm golden tan. He seemed all muscle and long bones and stunning masculine beauty to her. He looked like a regal warrior—the conqueror of her heart.

Jeremiah stepped into the water, settling himself opposite her. She slid forward to get as close as possible. His hands went around her waist, fitting her into the open V of his thighs. Their naked, wet bodies slid together, interlocking like the pieces of a puzzle. He kissed her for a long, long time—until she was light-headed.

He released her finally, snagging the bottle of wine around the neck and casually tossing back a greedy mouthful. "Now I know why you browbeat the plumber into finishing so fast."

Fancy set aside her glass; she would drink wine from his mouth, instead. She kissed him openmouthed, laving his tongue, sucking his lips until the rich tang of wine had blended with the taste of him into a potion more potent than magic.

Jeremiah laced his fingers across her derriere and leaned back against the sloping side of the tub, sliding lower in the water. Sighing with satisfaction, Fancy lifted her head off his chest to look him squarely in the eye. "Aren't you going to say anything about the ring?"

He slipped another inch; water licked his collarbone. "What's to say? I'd planned a proposal of a different sort. You're doing much better."

"Mmm." Fancy's eyelids lowered, her mouth curving with bliss.

"You are the master stage-setter, angel. This is your show."

She blinked, eyes suddenly alight with humor. "This is one scene that'll never make it to the Haute Water window."

He laughed. "I should've known from the very first that I'd end up in a bathtub with you."

"And if you have any hope of making it permanent, you'd better get on with it before I turn into a prune."

The porcelain sides of the whirlpool were proving to be very slick; the water was now bubbling at his chin. He *had* better get on with it. "Fancy, I know I'm not exactly the man you'd planned to marry..."

She shook her head vehemently. "Jeremiah Quick, you are exactly the man for me. Exactly."

At last she'd recognized what he'd known from the first. "And you, my sweet spring Fancy, are exactly the woman for me." They kissed. "So you'll marry me?"

"Yes, Froggie, I'll marry you." Her hand rose from the water, the diamond on her finger refracting the candlelight into starbursts. "Would I be wearing—" she started to say just as she realized that without the support of her left arm she was going to fall. She hit Jeremiah's chest with a huge splash and a slap of wet skin. The momentum plunged them into the bubbling water.

Jeremiah was smiling as he went under.

Webster Station Chronicle
Talk of the Town by Mitzi Janeway

Slap-Happy and Punch-Drunk

Wasn't that a wingding? Didn't that cake take the cake and that punch pack a punch? Wasn't that the party to end all parties?

For any poor souls who missed the gala, let me assure you Miss Fancy O'Brien's birthday/peace-pipe party was an outrageous success! Not only did the ladies of the LSD show up—they had F-U-N! Yes, that was Hester whizzing around the dance floor. I thought Mitch would have a heart attack—to say nothing of Mama! After the cake (my lips are sealed) and the gift-opening (Fancy plans to donate most of them to Emerald Square), the evening's high points were Oliver Sidley's impromptu, hiccuping recitation of "Learning to Love Kudzu," a frazzled Willa Clark slapping Boyd Dooley across the face, and Fancy and Jeremiah, dressed in a turn-of-the-century bathing costume and scuba gear respectively, doo-wopping to "Something to Talk About." Yup, Mr. Boss-Man let down his hair and boogied!

Fancy Quick? Fancy That!

I can't restrain myself anymore or I'll burst my bloomers! This is a rootin'-tootin' *Chronicle* exclusive, the

whiz-bang flashiest news flash of the decade! Fancy and
Jeremiah are officially *engaged!!* The li'l devils won't
tell me how or why or where it happened, but I was the
first to know 'cause I caught them sneaking from J.Q.'s
apartment at eight the morning after. Anyhoo, Fancy-
no-longer-free is sporting a gorgeous diamond, and
Jeremiah's talking about a Quick summer wedding.
Quite the fitting tribute to the spring to end all springs,
wouldn't you say?

I Pledge Allegiance to Fun and Games
And I haven't even touched on the scads of other gossip that's whipped this town into a frenzy. There's the
weird pink tinge to Willa's skin and her peculiar tomato smell, (I guess Beau likes a "hot tomatah" 'cause
he's still hanging around—even if Willa's other beaus
have cooled considerably!), Pringle and Alice Ann's
African safari, Stella Oh!'s ticket round the world (did
Hester pay her way?) and my own *dear* sister's announcement that she's running for mayor. Fritzi's
planning to run on an Immorality is Indecent plat-
form, with Hester as her campaign manager. I think my
own motto will be If You're Still Standing You Ain't
Having Enough Fun! I betcha Fancy and Jeremiah will
vote for me! Kissy-kissy till next time, lovebirds!!!

Temptation

Do You Have A
Secret Fantasy?

Everybody does.

Maybe it's to be rich and famous or to have a no-strings
affair with a sexy mysterious stranger. Or to have a sizzling
second chance with a former sweetheart...

You'll find these dreams—and much more—in Temptation's
exciting new yearlong series, Secret Fantasies!

Look out for **Memory Lapse** by **Kathleen O'Brien**
in January 1996.

Apartment for rent
One bedroom
Bachelor Arms
555-1234

Come live and love in L.A. with the tenants of Bachelor Arms. Enjoy a year's worth of wonderful love stories and meet colourful neighbours you'll bump into again and again.

First, we'll introduce you to Bachelor Arms residents Josh, Tru and Garrett—three to-die-for and determined bachelor friends—who do everything they can to avoid walking down the aisle. Bestselling author Kate Hoffmann brings us these romantic comedies in the new continuity series from Temptation:

THE STRONG SILENT TYPE (December 1995)

A HAPPILY UNMARRIED MAN (January 1996)

Soon to move into Bachelor Arms are the heroes and heroines in books by our most popular authors—JoAnn Ross, Candace Schuler and Judith Arnold. You'll read a new book every month.

Don't miss the goings-on at Bachelor Arms.

Temptation

This month's
irresistible novels from

Temptation

THE TWELVE GIFTS OF CHRISTMAS
by Rita Clay Estrada

Pete Cade might be the hunk every woman dreams of finding under her tree, but he wasn't ready to give the special gift at the top of Carly Michaels's Christmas list—a father for her daughter.

THE STRONG SILENT TYPE by Kate Hoffmann

Come live and love in L.A. with the tenants of Bachelors Arms. Second in a captivating mini-series.

Strong and silent Josh Banks had never been the subject of gossip before. But suddenly everyone was warning him about wild women—ever since he'd promised to keep party girl Taryn Wilde out of trouble. He could handle her...couldn't he?

FANCY-FREE by Carrie Alexander

Some residents don't approve of newcomer Fancy O'Brien taking a bath—in town—to publicize the opening of her bath boutique. But Jeremiah Quick is glad Fancy has arrived. He thinks Fancy's the right woman for him. Too bad *Fancy* thinks he's the right man for her mother...

BARGAIN BASEMENT BABY by Leandra Logan

Marriage had never appealed to Greg Baron. But since he was going to be a father, he didn't have much choice. If only the Baron family wasn't so thrilled to finally have an heir. If only his image of Jane Haley pregnant wasn't so delectable...

Spoil yourself next month
with these four novels from

Temptation

A HAPPILY UNMARRIED MAN by Kate Hoffmann

Third in the Bachelors Arms mini-series.

Garrett McCabe's two friends—Tru and Josh—warned him
that he was making a big mistake attacking Emily Taylor in his
newspaper column. He would have to apologize, but he sensed
Emily wasn't going to make it easy for him.

MEMORY LAPSE by Kathleen O'Brien

Do you have a Secret Fantasy?

Drew Townsend does. And in his secret fantasy Laura Nolan
returns. Three years ago, she ran away, but now she has come
back to find out what secrets lay buried in the past—a past she
can't really remember!

DREAMS (PART ONE) by Jayne Ann Krentz

The first of a stirring two-part epic tale

Diana Prentice found Colby Savagar disconcerting. The sheer
fierceness of his passion overwhelmed her and left her in a
turmoil. For she knew somehow there had been another place,
another time when he had taken by force what she now gave
willingly...

DREAMS (PART TWO) by Jayne Ann Krentz

The completion of this special two-part story

Pregnant! Diana Prentice knew she should be ecstatic—
carrying Colby Savagar's child. But the idea of motherhood
frightened her. Almost as much as her recurring dreams that
beckoned her back to Fulbrook Corners and its timeless legend.

A year's supply of Mills & Boon Romances—absolutely FREE!

Would you like to win a year's supply of heartwarming and passionate romances? Well, you can and they're FREE! Simply complete the wordsearch puzzle below and send it to us by 30th June 1996. The first 5 correct entries picked after the closing date will win a years supply of Mills & Boon Romances (six books every month—worth over £100). What could be easier?

READER SERVICE
ROMANCE
RESIST
HEART
MEMORIES
PAGES
KISS
SPINE
TEMPTATION
LOVE
COLLECTION
ROSES
PACK
PARCEL
TITLES
DREAMS
COUPLE
SPECIAL EDITION
EMOTION
DESIRE
SILHOUETTE
MOODS
PASSION

Please turn over for details of how to enter...

How to enter

Hidden in the grid are words which relate to our books and romance. You'll find the list overleaf and they can be read backwards, forwards, up, down or diagonally. As you find each word, circle it or put a line through it.

When you have found all the words, don't forget to fill in your name and address in the space provided below and pop this page into an envelope (you don't need a stamp) and post it today. Hurry—competition ends 30th June 1996.

Mills & Boon Wordsearch
FREEPOST
Croydon
Surrey
CR9 3WZ

Are you a Reader Service Subscriber?   Yes ☐   No ☐

Ms/Mrs/Miss/Mr _____

Address _____

_____

_____ Postcode _____

One application per household.

You may be mailed with other offers from other reputable companies as a result of this application. If you would prefer not to receive such offers, please tick box. ☐

COMP295
F